W9-ACD-992

Just Desserts

Tim Heald

Just Desserts

Charles Scribner's Sons / New York

Library of Congress Cataloging in Publication Data

Heald, Tim.
    Just desserts.

    I. Title.
PZ4.H4342Ju 1978   [PR6058.E167]   823'.9'14   78–10856
ISBN 0–684–16098–6

1 3 5 7 9 11 13 15 17 19 H/C 20 18 16 14 12 10 8 6 4 2

PRINTED IN THE UNITED STATES OF AMERICA

For Lucy

Acknowledgements

Though I would hate to suggest that there is the remotest similarity between anything that happens in this book and anything that could conceivably happen in her restaurant, I would like to record my thanks to Prue Leith of Leith's who very kindly tried to answer some of my ludicrous questions about the restaurant business. I should also like to thank Virginia Muir for some murderously original suggestions which were distinctly chilling – particularly from a medical student!

Prologue

Escoffier Savarin Smith, known to his friends as 'Scoff', made a neat incision in the nectarine's velvet skin and began to peel. Thirty seconds later the covering lay coiled on the plate in one single piece. He regarded it for a moment with a look of scarcely perceptible satisfaction and then took a slow sip from the long-stemmed, narrow-fluted glass. He swilled the liquid round, swallowed, and smiled.

Mr Smith was sitting at a table in the kitchen of his celebrated restaurant in the unfashionable London suburb of East Sheen. It was a regular habit of his to sit thus, white linen napkin tucked into his shirt front, and to have a little pick-me-up after everyone had gone. This morning it was half past one, which was a little later than usual, and in front of him were two full bottles of Krug, which was a great deal more than usual. There was also an envelope, just to the left of the second bottle, which was addressed in very thick, black, Gothic handwriting to 'Gabrielle'.

All around him was the formidable *batterie de cuisine* which, together with a dominating and gregarious personality, had made him one of the greatest restaurateurs Britain had ever known: copper mixing bowls and saucepans, garlic presses, hachoirs, mandolines, *bains-marie*, whisks, skewers, knives and forks and strange devices of his own design. Mr Smith surveyed it lazily and drank three glasses of champagne in quick succession. That accomplished, he walked to the range, crouched down to examine the blue cylinder at one side, and turned a switch before making a brief inspection of the doors and windows to ensure that the electrician's tape he had just applied was securely in place.

7

Afterwards he returned to his seat and began, thoughtfully, to consume the nectarine.

It was not until after breakfast that Gabrielle arrived at the Dour Dragoon to begin the day's work. When she entered the kitchen she found *le patron* sprawled forward across the table, head resting between the two bottles, now empty, and one hand against the plate on which the peel had been joined by the stone of the nectarine. Escoffier Savarin Smith's napkin had fallen, unaccountably, to the floor, and he was, of course, extremely dead.

Chapter One

Simon Bognor of the Special Investigations Department of the Board of Trade was a man ill-equipped by nature, upbringing and experience for the painstaking and sensitive job in which he found himself. His position was, indeed, one of recurring embarrassment both to himself and his superiors and stemmed from a simple, but apparently irretrievable, misunderstanding during his interview many years before with the Appointments Board at Oxford University. 'There is another branch of the Civil Service,' the man had said, and Bognor, absent-mindedly assuming that he was talking about the Treasury, had somehow become embroiled in a recruitment process which he was too lazy and incompetent to reverse.

Like others doomed to a job which was not only beyond him but which was also seen to be beyond him, he took some solace in food and drink. He and his girlfriend, Monica, frequently ate out, and when they did they ate well. When they ate in they tended to spend more time, effort and money on the preparation of their meals than would generally be thought quite decent. As a result Bognor was plump and florid, knew the difference between a Château Bel-Air and a Château Belair, could rescue a curdled aioli and make his own curry powder. His boss, Parkinson, knew all this and therefore summoned him on the morning of Escoffier Savarin Smith's death.

Bognor, as usual during these interviews which were invariably painful, stared fixedly at the portrait of Her Majesty Queen Elizabeth which dominated the wall behind Parkinson.

9

'Fancy yourself as a gastronome, isn't that so?' asked Parkinson.

'I enjoy my food, if that's what you mean,' said Bognor, recollecting his unhappy spell on attachment in Canberra. He had never eaten so badly in his life, and it would be typical of Parkinson to reassign him there or to some other gastronomic wilderness simply out of spite.

'Your modesty ill becomes you,' said Parkinson.

Bognor said nothing, but continued to stare at his monarch. After a moment's silence Parkinson continued, 'So you will know all about Escoffier Savarin Smith?'

'Yes. As a matter of fact Monica and I are going to his restaurant tonight. He does the most extraordinary chocolate omelette, and it's the only place in London where they know how to deal with guinea fowl.'

'I shouldn't bother,' said Parkinson. 'He's dead.'

'Good God.' Bognor was shocked. 'We were only there about a couple of months ago. He seemed fine then. What happened?'

'It looks like suicide. I gather there was a note. He appears to have sealed off the kitchen with Scotch tape or something and then turned on the gas.'

'I thought North Sea gas . . .'

'This wasn't North Sea gas. It was the emergency supply. They kept a spare cylinder for power cuts and emergencies. It was perfectly effective.'

'Do we have any idea why?'

'Not yet.' Parkinson smiled. 'I'm not even one hundred per cent certain it was suicide. Of course it may have been. I'm just not quite convinced.' He paused and frowned at his subordinate. 'You knew he was one of ours?'

'How do you mean?' Bognor was perplexed as always by the ramifications of the Board; and it occurred to him that any association between Parkinson and Smith was about as unlikely as his own involvement.

'I mean,' said Parkinson, 'that he helped us from time to time. Provided us with information, tip-offs, odds and ends. He was surprisingly well informed.'

'Really.'

Bognor now saw where this was leading. He just prayed that Parkinson was not going to ask him to masquerade as a waiter or a chef. Parkinson had a habit of asking him to go in as an undercover agent in the most unlikely and humiliating circumstances. He would never forget his futile attempts to pass himself off as a newspaper reporter after the murder of St John Derby of the *Daily Globe* – though that had not been as chillingly ghastly as Collingdale's last case. Collingdale had had to sign up as a novice friar at Beaubridge and had been found strangled in the potato patch. Bognor shuddered.

'Where did he get his information?' he asked. Whenever he had seen Smith at the restaurant he had seemed too jovial and disorganized to have gleaned much during working hours. If he had had to put money on anyone being involved in the sort of amateur espionage that Parkinson was suggesting, he would have plumped for Smith's partner, Gabrielle, the Eurasian. She was a Mata Hari figure, while Smith was a fat food buff with a fading reputation as a Lothario, hypochondriac tendencies, and a widely acknowledged drink problem.

'You know the place,' said Parkinson. 'You must have seen the sort of people who went there.'

Bognor laughed. 'I hardly think we'd have much use for the sort of things Lady Aubergine would have access to. Or Aubrey Pring. And Nuala O'Flaherty is only a sort of champagne provo. Not the real thing at all. Her name's actually Norah. Norah Wills. Did you know that?'

'I did not.' Parkinson's icy tone made it clear that he didn't care either. 'Do you recognize either of these two?' He passed a couple of photographs across the desk. One showed a dark, shaggily suave person around forty-five; the other a Madison Avenue type with a button-down shirt and spectacles, who looked a little like Elliott Richardson, the ex-American Ambassador.

'Yes, as a matter of fact,' said Bognor. 'They were both there one night for some sort of party. I'm not sure it wasn't Smith's birthday or something. I remember it being spectacularly boisterous.'

'And you remember them?'

Bognor flushed slightly. 'I have a good memory for faces, and it *was* a very noisy party. Not the sort of party you would forget.'

'But you don't know who they are?'

'No idea.'

Parkinson sighed. 'In that case,' he said, 'I shall have to enlighten you. The one with the hair and the Slavonic features is Dmitri Petrov, the so-called Managing Director of the Soviet Synthetics Consortium. The more presentable one is Anthony J. Ebertson III, a so-called cultural counsellor at the American Embassy. Are you beginning to see what I'm getting at?'

'They're so-called imposters,' said Bognor, heart sinking yet faster. 'Mr Ebertson knows nothing about culture and Mr Petrov knows nothing about synthetics, and they're engaged in some form of espionage at which I can only guess.'

'Which in the circumstances makes me suspicious.'

'I can see that, but *how* precisely?'

'I'm not able to be precise,' said Parkinson. 'That's what you're employed for – to give precision to my half-formed notions and incipient suspicions, which is what I would be obliged if you would do now.'

'You mean . . .' Bognor's perplexity was more apparent than real. He knew only too well what Parkinson meant, but the stammered refusal to admit it was a habitual defensive mechanism.

'I mean,' said Parkinson, 'that the verdict on your Mr Smith will be that he gassed himself while the balance of his mind was disturbed, and that there is no reason to suspect foul play. This will be perfectly acceptable to the great British public and the great British press but not, alas, to me. As I have indicated, we have reason to think otherwise. So there you are. *Bon appetit!*'

Parkinson smiled viciously, evidently amused at what he would doubtless have described as his *bon mot*, and began to sort through the papers on his desk. The interview was apparently over. Bognor rose, stretched and ambled out of the room but not before Parkinson had added, crisply and unnecessarily: 'A little exercise would do you no harm, Bognor. Don't make this job an excuse for too much gourmandizing, and if I were you I'd take up squash.'

Bognor, who'd been meaning to take up squash for years, did not reply.

'Oh, and Bognor . . .'

The door was not yet shut. Reluctantly Bognor took two paces back and turned round. 'Yes?'

'I don't want anyone to know precisely what you're doing.'

Bognor braced himself, certain now that Parkinson was going to ask him once more to participate in some dangerous and degrading charade. 'Since I don't know precisely what I'm doing myself,' he volunteered, 'that shouldn't present too much of a problem.'

Parkinson frowned. It was a rule of their relationship that such witticisms were left to him. Bognor was becoming insubordinate. 'You may say, Bognor,' he said, 'that you are working for us, but only that you are looking at . . . oh . . . at the possibilities of expansion in the top end of the food market, or something similarly anodyne. But don't let anyone think you suspect anything about our friend Mr Smith.'

'Right,' said Bognor. 'I'll keep in touch.' This time his exit was more effectively accomplished. He paced slowly along the subterranean passages, made more hideous still by peeling pea-green paint and miles of cylindrical metal ventilation shaft. At least Bognor supposed it was a ventilation shaft. He had never really considered it for long, except once when it had occurred to him that if it was a ventilation shaft, then a tightly knit group of politically motivated men could knock out the Special Investigations Department with a single suitable gas cylinder. Just like poor old Scoff Smith. A whiff of gas and pouf he was gone. The Gastronomer Royal extinguished in a suspicion of aroma. Bognor smiled sourly and stopped by the newly installed coffee and tea vending machine. There was nothing gastronomic about this. It had been installed purely for reasons of economy and to eliminate the tea trolley ladies who had long been considered an unacceptable security risk as well as being too expensive in these days of the new austerity. The machine, unlike the tea trolley ladies, claimed to dispense coffee as well as tea, but it didn't fool Bognor. Whatever the liquid was, it was certainly not tea or coffee. As usual he selected the drink purporting to be tea, on the grounds that it was the cheaper of the two, and took it back to his desk. The taste was just as he had expected, but it still had the power to make him wince.

He grimaced over it for a few moments while wondering what to do next. Dinner at the Dour Dragoon was, he supposed, off. *Le patron est mort ici,* he thought to himself grimly, but on the other hand it was just possible that the feast would go on and that Scoff Smith's staff would display a sort of showbiz stoicism.

In the event he discovered that their attitude was more epicurean than stoic. 'This is a recorded message,' said the telephone when he dialled the Dragoon's number. 'Owing to unforeseen circumstances the restaurant is closed until further notice. We apologize for any inconvenience.'

'Oh, shit,' said Bognor with a vehemence which surprised him. The news had put a spoke in his gastronomic as well as his professional wheel. He would now have to find another place for dinner and another way of getting down to work.

The Extravaganza was no substitute for the Dour Dragoon, and both he and Monica realized it the moment they arrived. It was brand new, yet had a musty odour of yesterday's cigarettes, spilt plonk and no daylight. It had been recommended by a friend of Monica's who compiled reports for the *Good Food Guide*. Monica was impressed by her friend's aggressive obsession with food and drink; Bognor had had his suspicions about her ever since dining at her house and spotting an empty magnum of Château Waitrose by the pedal bin in the kitchen. Not that there was anything wrong with Château Waitrose, it was just that she had been serving wine from interesting Italian bottles and claiming that she had found it just outside Siena, 'At the most divine little palazzo owned by this simply ravishing count.' Bognor had not actually accused her of passing off supermarket wine as chianti, but he had said as much to Monica in the car on the way home. There had been a row.

Now sitting alone in this fusty little bar toying with a weak Campari and contemplating a menu as long as his arm, he felt sufficiently aggrieved to bring the matter up again. Instead he said simply, 'Bloody woman.'

Monica picked up a peanut, examined it for dust, then ate it tentatively as if it might be booby-trapped and go off in her mouth. When she had destroyed and swallowed it, she said, 'You know that's not fair, Simon, Ailsa is very good at restaurants.'

Bognor looked round the bar theatrically. 'So I see,' he said.

'Oh, come on. Give them a chance, we haven't even ordered yet. Besides, she didn't exactly recommend it, she simply said she knew the man who owned it.'

'Now you tell me.'

'Well . . .' She selected another peanut, unable to think of anything suitably placatory. 'I still think she could help you start off this new assignment.'

'Assignment . . . assignment,' mimicked Bognor. 'Why must you use words like "assignment"? It's the sort of word Parkinson uses. Why on earth can't you say "job" like any normal person? And I am most certainly not having Ailsa bloody Larkin ruining my latest job, assignment, or whatever. She's already caused enough trouble for one evening.'

A waiter appeared, ballpoint poised. He had that peculiar look of combined servility and contempt which Bognor found particularly offensive. He also had dirty fingernails and a thumb yellow with nicotine. His swarthy looks and lank black hair suggested something Latin. He said nothing, merely hovered, one eyebrow raised in an attitude of half-hearted expectancy.

'Have you decided?' asked Bognor.

Monica gave him a look intended to wither but which was so anaemic that it merely had the effect of making him laugh. Luckily, after a moment's hesitation, she joined him. The waiter remained motionless, pen and eyebrow poised in mute readiness.

'I'd like the Fritto misto and then the Stiffado,' said Monica. 'Are the vegetables fresh?'

'Green beans, courgettes, spinach,' said the waiter expressionlessly.

'Yes, but are they fresh?'

He frowned. 'Yes, they are fresh.'

Bognor and Monica exchanged glances and shrugs, and she settled for the courgettes. Bognor chose Ravioli and a speciality of the house called Pollo Sophia Loren. He also ordered a carafe of red.

'I know,' he said, suddenly, when the nearly dumb waiter had shuffled off into some nether region. 'Aubrey Pring.'

'Aubrey Pring?'

'Yes, you know, Aubrey Pring – he was in the Dragoon once when we were there. He does the *Guide to Good Dining*.'

'And that frightful column in the *Chronicle*.'

'It's not frightful. It's rather good actually.'

Monica laughed without humour. 'The wine snob's guide to an early cirrhosis,' she said. 'If he eats and drinks half what he claims, then he ought to be dead by now.'

'Oh, rubbish,' said Bognor. 'He's only about a year older than me.'

'And what is that supposed to prove?' Monica swilled her drink round her mouth as if it was a gargle. 'Anyway, what about Aubrey Pring?'

'Just that I knew him at Oxford.'

'Well?'

'No, not particularly. In fact to be absolutely honest I think "only vaguely" would be the proper way to put it. He was at Wadham. Only I did know him. He was president of the Wine and Food Soc.'

'That follows,' said Monica as icily as a mouthful of lukewarm apéritif allowed. 'Have you seen him since?'

'Well, I've seen him at the Dour Dragoon, like I said, but I admit I haven't actually . . .'

Embarrassing confession was prevented by the re-appearance of the glum waiter who told them, gracelessly, that their table was ready, and then ushered them to it. It

16

was a perfectly respectable table as tables went. The table-cloth was pink and clean, the wax night-light affair in a sort of inverted goldfish bowl shimmered romantically, and there was a rose in a vase. It looked wan enough to be real. The meal, when it appeared, was by no means as disgusting as they had supposed while in the bar, and by the end of it they were feeling more or less content, if less than euphoric. Just as two brandies arrived they were both suddenly aware of noise. It was not that the restaurant had hitherto been silent, but there were no more than half a dozen other couples in the large, rather starkly Apicello-style room and, as is the way with apprehensive diners in half empty restaurants, they conversed, when they did, in virtual whispers. Whether this affected the staff or whether the uncharacter-istically dour mien of the staff was there in the first place Bognor could not conceive. At all events the noise from the bar was unexpected and out of place. Whoever had arrived was clearly in convivial mood. Moreover the pitch of their voices and the slightly braying quality of their laughter suggested that they expected convivial surroundings. It also suggested alcohol, freely imbibed.

'At least someone is happy,' said Monica.

'Aren't *you* happy?'

'Not unhappy, anyway.' She put her hand across the table and rested it momentarily on Bognor's. He smiled back at her intending to convey warmth but actually transmitting a mild embarrassment. Bognor was not by temperament what he called 'physical'. And certainly not in public. Besides he was too old to indulge in petting, however mild, in restaur-ants. Although he was only in his mid-thirties, he was, as everyone always told him, old for his age.

Offstage in the bar the sound of raucous conviviality increased.

'Oh, God,' said Monica, 'do you think there's going to be one of those scenes? Someone does sound terribly ob-streperous.'

They both listened, but it was impossible to distinguish exactly what was being said, nor indeed whether a complaint was being expressed, or if it was merely bonhomie. It was difficult, too, to determine whether the noise emanated from a single couple, or from a char-à-banc-load of revellers.

'Talk of the devil,' said Bognor suddenly. He drew on his cheroot and leant forward, frowning. 'It is, you know. There's only one person I've ever known who could make a noise like that.'

'Even though you only knew him vaguely.' Monica was not generally quick on the uptake, but she was where Bognor was concerned. The long years of their liaison had made them almost psychic together.

'I only knew *him* vaguely,' said Bognor, a shade archly, 'but everyone in the university was intimately acquainted with the noise he made. As you can hear, it's a very loud one, and utterly distinctive.'

As he said this, the noise erupted into the restaurant itself. Most of it came from a short stout person with a vivid scarlet face and loud check trousers. In one hand he grasped a bottle of champagne. His other fist contained a fat cigar, and the arm attached to it seemed to be on the point of strangling a large flushed blonde in a very little black dress.

'I thought,' said Monica, 'the rule was that you held bottles by the neck and birds by the bottom and never . . .'

'Round the waist, not the bottom,' said Bognor. 'No, not Aubrey. He's always made a point of making his own rules.'

'Which he then breaks.'

'No, never.'

They both watched, fascinated, as the couple lurched to a corner table, under the long-suffering guidance of the waiter.

'Well?' muttered Monica. 'He doesn't seem to have recognized you. Are you going to make yourself known?'

If Bognor had been standing he would have shuffled about with embarrassment. As it was he merely said, 'He hasn't looked over here, that's all. Besides, in his present state he wouldn't recognize anyone.'

'Oh, but surely he'd recognize *you*. Even if you only knew him vaguely you must have made a great impression on him.'

'All right,' said Bognor, stubbing out his cheroot with the air of one goaded beyond the bounds of reasonable be-haviour, and before Monica could restrain him, he was moving purposefully in the direction of the Pring table. Even as he did he could feel his resolve slacken. Pring and his friend were, on closer inspection, even more distressingly glassy eyed than he had previously assumed. He was also aware that his shoes squeaked, and that the restaurant had grown even more silent. There were not many eyes available, but he sensed, unhappily, that they were on him. All, that is, except those of Aubrey Pring and the blonde, who were engrossed now in mute contemplation of each other, inebriation clearly compounding their mutual lust.

'Ahem,' coughed Bognor, arriving at Mr Pring's elbow.

'Aha,' echoed Mr Pring menacingly, swivelling to meet Bognor's averted gaze. 'I take it that you are in what, for want of a better word, I shall call "charge".'

Bognor blinked. 'I'm sorry,' he said, 'No, not in the least.' He put out a hand. 'Bognor,' he said, 'Balliol. The Wine and Food Soc. You probably won't remember but . . .'

For a second Aubrey Pring's face was contorted in a dreadful effort of concentration, and then just as Bognor feared that this must result in, at worst, coronary thrombosis and, at best, failure, the diminutive gastronome staggered to his feet, took Bognor's hand in his own and exclaimed: 'Good God! Bognors-and-Mash! Long time no see! Sit down. Take a pew. What'll you have?'

'Well, actually . . .' Bognor, like others who undertake daring missions on sudden impulses, had not planned his campaign beyond the first skirmish. This unexpected initial success stymied him. Around him he was aware that their fellow guests had lost interest in what they had clearly expected to be a confrontation. Lost in confused thought, Bognor was dimly aware that Pring was still speaking.

'I'm sorry,' said Bognor, 'I didn't quite, I mean.' Then he realized that he was being introduced. Pring was saying, 'Aubergine Bristol . . . Ginny, this is a very old friend of mine indeed, known to all of us in the Wine and Food Soc. as "Bognors-and-Mash" on account of his extraordinary interest in the sausage which, in the days when we first knew one another was, even for the fastidious, a staple form of diet. Bognor, old fruit, do sit down and have a glass of something. We're in the middle of drowning our sorrows "For" ' and here Pring assumed a declamatory stance:

> *'Death has illumined the Land of Sleep,*
> *And his lifeless body lay*
> *A worn-out fetter, that the soul*
> *Had broken and thrown away!'*

Bognor dimly remembered Pring's rather embarrassing addiction to Longfellow and, very much to his surprise, found himself saying:

> *'He is dead, the sweet musician!*
> *He the sweetest of all singers!*
> *He has gone from us for ever,*
> *He has moved a little nearer*
> *To the Master of all music,*
> *To the Master of all singing!*
> *O my brother, Chibiabos!'*

'You've heard then?' asked Pring, after a moment's hesitation.

'Heard?'

'About Scoff?'

'Yes. Appalling. Look, I say,' Bognor sensed Monica growing restless behind him. 'I'd love to join you for a sec, but I am actually with someone. Do you think – ?'

Pring gestured expansively. 'My dear chap,' he said, 'of course. Why didn't you say?'

Bognor returned to his table where Monica remained, stony faced. 'He's asked us to join them,' he said.

'You must be joking.'

'No, really. Are you coming?'

'Must we?'

'We don't have to, but it could be useful. I'd prefer it.'

She pulled a face but rose, albeit with bad grace. As she did he reflected that though Aubergine Bristol was faintly absurd, Monica was undoubtedly on the dowdy side. He dismissed the thought instantly as unworthy, but it bothered him and recurred as he made the introductions.

'You knew Scoff then?' asked Pring when they were all seated and drinking champagne.

'Not really.'

'I think Simon means "only vaguely",' said Monica, flicking his shin under the table. If she looked dowdy alongside Aubergine Bristol she also seemed a lot sharper. Aubergine was wearing an expression of almost total vacuity.

'We were there last night,' said Pring. 'Had a drink with him and Gabrielle. Most extraordinary thing. Simply don't understand it. He seemed perfectly all right to me. Not even pissed.'

'I thought he seemed peculiar,' said Aubergine. 'In fact I think he's been peculiar for ages. Peculiarer and,' she hesitated before continuing, '. . . and peculiarer.'

'In what way?' asked Bognor.

She thought for a few seconds and then said, 'Oh, I don't know. Just sort of peculiar.'

'He drank too much,' said Pring. 'Occupational hazard. Let's have the other half.' He ordered another bottle and some food. 'Is the nosh here as bloody as the service?' he asked when the waiter had slunk off. 'Because if it is I'm not paying.'

'Ours was all right, actually,' said Monica, loyally. 'In fact the Stiffado was really quite good.'

'Oh,' said Pring without interest. 'We were told about it by that bloody woman, Ailsa Larkin.'

'So were we,' said Bognor.

'Friend of yours?' asked Pring.

'Friend of Monica's,' said Bognor.

'Oh.' He seemed to lose interest again and stared morosely at the tablecloth. This was infectious. They all stared morosely at the tablecloth until Pring jerked himself back to the present.

'So,' he said with a jollity which seemed forced and unnatural, 'As I said "long time no see". What happened to you? Someone told me you'd gone into the post office. You don't look as if you went into the post office.'

'No. Board of Trade actually,' said Bognor.

'Oh, well,' Pring looked patronizing. 'Not far out. What exactly do you do in the Board of Trade?'

Bognor took a deep breath, another slug of champagne,

and tried desperately to remember what Parkinson had suggested as a cover story. 'Well, as a matter of fact, it's funny you should mention that because I'm working on something to do with food at the moment,' he said. 'I do special investigations, you see.'

'Can't imagine it's the sort of food we're interested in,' said Pring. 'Investigating the precise digital component of the standard fish finger preparatory to a white paper produced under the auspices of the White Fish Authority, I suppose. Or how much soya you can legally put in a sausage. Or whether toast has to be made with bread.'

'No, actually,' said Bognor, stung by this all too accurate description of what habitually went on around him, 'we're looking at the top end of the market, trying to find how the government might help out there.'

'Perhaps you'll get the Queen's Award for Industry, Aubrey,' said Aubergine Bristol. 'I'm awfully peckish, I wish they'd bring our food.'

'And how,' asked Aubrey, perceptibly sobering, 'do you imagine the government might help? Nationalize the restaurant trade, I suppose? Or introduce a caviar subsidy? If there's one thing calculated to destroy what little decent eating's to be had in this country, it's government interference. They've practically ruined the wine trade as it is.'

'Oh that's not entirely fair,' said Bognor. 'The Prime Minister's very keen on his wine.'

'Only if it's British. He's not a wino – he's a reconstituted grape juice addict.'

'That's not really quite fair,' said Bognor, loath to be caught defending a prime minister and a government of whom he strongly disapproved but nevertheless feeling that his position demanded it.

'It is, and you know it,' said Pring heatedly. At that moment, before genuine misunderstanding could interfere with Bognor's intentions, the waiter arrived with pasta. It appeared hot and sufficient. 'About bloody time,' said Pring, 'and get us a couple of bottles of the Santa Cristina.' Both Bognor and Monica expostulated, but Pring flapped his hands about in limp gestures of dismissal. 'Tell you what,' he said, forking a great skein of noodles into his mouth. 'Why don't you join us on this jolly to Petheram tomorrow? You might pick up a few tips, and you'll meet some people.'

'What happens at Petheram?' asked Bognor.

'Pendennis Brothers,' said Pring. 'They do mainly Alsatian stuff, very good too. It's their annual tasting for the trade. Well, I say the trade, but it's not really the trade – it's for one or two of the better known wine and food writers and some top restaurateurs. I should come along. It will give you some valuable insights.'

'But I haven't been invited,' said Bognor, lamely.

'Well, I'm inviting you now,' said Pring, 'Freddie Pendennis is an old mucker of mine. He'll be delighted to see you. I say, Ginny, this pasta's perfectly passable.'

Little gobs of ragu now spattered his chin, and he seemed incapable of getting any noodles inside him intact. Every time he closed his mouth, a few pathetic white strands were left dangling outside only to disappear slowly from view with a wet sucking noise. They looked alive, and Bognor, against his will, was reminded of the way older dog breeders docked puppies' tails – by biting them off at birth. Both he and Monica were relieved when a decent interval had elapsed (during which an indecent quantity of chianti was consumed).

'We really must be going,' they said, and Pring at last seemed content to let them depart. '*À demain*,' he said, waving. 'The ten o'clock from Charing Cross. Platform six. We meet at the barrier. Don't buy a ticket.'

Chapter Two

Bognor arrived early at the barrier. He had a nervousness about missing any form of scheduled transport which amounted almost to a neurosis and meant that he invariably arrived at termini with time and a half to spare. On this occasion he was also keen to observe his fellow travellers before being formally introduced. He felt, without much justification, that it gave him an advantage. Bearing this in mind, he made quite certain that he was the first of the party to arrive and then retreated to the station bookstall, where he bought a *Daily Telegraph* and stood, occasionally glancing over the top of it in a manner which he believed, erroneously, to be anonymous and unsuspicious. It was fifteen minutes before he saw anybody who could conceivably have been a Pendennis-bound gastronome, and when he did he was far from being absolutely sure. The first person to hover expectantly at the entrance to platform six was a rather attractive blonde in green trousers and a cardigan. She clutched a sheaf of papers and a clipboard and appeared, as yet, unmarked by the ravages of food and drink which he associated with the profession. Bognor, not unappreciative, retreated behind the paper. A few minutes later, he glanced out from his camouflage and saw that the young woman was now engrossed in animated conversation with an elderly lobster-like gentleman who was crouched heavily over a serviceable walking stick. Bognor recognized him immediately. It was Erskine Blight-Purley, war hero, Francophile, bibliophile, oenomaniac and lecher of long-standing and renown. Despite the fact that he must now be over seventy, his elongated crustacean figure was dangerously close to the young woman, and from where he stood Bognor fancied that the unsteadily leery smile was one of concupiscence. The girl was laughing, slightly nervously. Blight-Purley had a reputation as an after-dinner speaker too. He was probably telling blue jokes.

Just as Bognor decided that it was time for him to announce himself, he saw a half-familiar figure walk briskly up to the girl in the green trousers and kiss her, equally purposefully, on the cheek. It was the man from the American Embassy, Anthony J. Ebertson III, and he appeared to be wearing a golfing suit in a loud check material composed exclusively of Oxford and Cambridge blues. The girl introduced him to Blight-Purley who nodded sourly but did not remove his hands from his stick. A second later another figure of identical familiarity joined them. It was Petrov, the man from Soviet Synthetics, wearing a Soviet equivalent of Ebertson's suit, an ill-cut affair in Lovat green. He too kissed the girl, though with an enthusiasm which had been missing from Ebertson's more perfunctory effort. Bognor experienced a frisson of excitement. As he folded his paper and walked over to join them the group suddenly exploded into something which almost resembled a party. Everyone, which is to say Aubrey Pring, Aubergine Bristol and some dozen or so bonhomous colleagues, converged at once. There was an enthusiastic rhubarb of greeting; the green girl distributed tickets and pieces of paper, people kissed each other, shook hands, clapped each other on the back – all except for Blight-Purley who stood slightly apart, hands still clasping the stick, and nodded shortly at anyone who had the temerity to look in his direction.

'Bognor, old Sausage!' exclaimed Pring. 'Glad you could make it. Mandy, have you got some bumf and a ticket for my old mucker Simon Bognor? Simon, this is Mandy Bullingdon of F and D Associates – they're doing the P R.'

'F and D?' asked Bognor, smiling hello.

'Food and Drink,' said Miss Bullingdon, displaying slightly irregular teeth and half a dimple. Bognor observed that one of her eyes was slightly larger than the other. 'Haven't we met somewhere before?' she was saying.

'I don't think so,' said Bognor. 'I'm afraid it's just one of those faces.'

'I'm sure I've met you somewhere. Gstaad in seventy-four? Or last year in Cannes? Aren't you a friend of Andrew Stevenson's?'

'No,' said Bognor, 'I'm awfully sorry, but I haven't ever been to Gstaad or Cannes, and I don't know anyone called Andrew Stevenson.' Then, not wishing to seem gratuitously dismissive, he said, 'We can't possibly have met anyway. I'd be sure to remember.'

'Simon,' interposed Pring, who was bustling, 'come and meet Erskine Blight-Purley. He'll tell you about the top end of the market; the top end of anything you care to ask about actually. You'll have to shout though. He's very deaf these days. If you're having real problems go for the left ear – it seems to be his best.'

'Bognor,' said Blight-Purley, after they'd been introduced and Pring had shot off to spread a little more goodwill, 'there was a chap called Bognor in the Dieppe show. No relation, I suppose?'

'No,' said Bognor, 'at least I don't think so.'

'Oh,' said Blight-Purley, not seeming to care one way or the other, 'and you're an intelligence chappie from the Board of Trade. I wouldn't have thought this was exactly your line of country.'

Bognor explained about the top end of the market as Pring and the woman from F and D marshalled them and drove them, like garrulous sheep, along the platform to the reserved compartments. In the train Blight-Purley managed to sit next to Amanda Bullingdon in a window seat facing the engine. How he accomplished this Bognor wasn't sure, but it was done with an easy effortlessness which he was forced to admire. Bognor sat with his back to the engine and immediately opposite him. Aubrey Pring was on his left and the remaining two seats were taken by the Russian and the American. This, clearly, was the compartment to be in. It was an elderly British Rail effort, faded blue and cream upholstery fusty with the dust of ages. Above the heads of the passengers were were pale pastels of South Coast watering places and mirrors chipped at the corners. It smelt of years of cigarette tobacco and armpits.

Clattering over the Thames it was the American, Ebertson, who broke the silence which had surprisingly descended.

'Anything more on Scoff?' He spoke in the cultured almost-English accents which Bognor had associated with the American Rhodes scholars he had known in Oxford. The question was addressed principally at Pring but was also for more general consideration.

'Funeral at Golders Green,' said Pring. 'Memorial service later some time.'

'Oh.' Ebertson shifted uneasily in his seat. It was obviously not the sort of response he had wanted. 'Does one attend the funeral?'

'I think not,' said Pring, slipping easily into the role of social secretary and arbiter of etiquette. 'Family and intimates only I should say. I shouldn't have said you were an intimate of Scoff, Anthony.'

'I should say not.' He spoke nervously as if his relationship while not apparently intimate, had not been without significance.

'Killed himself though? No question of what we used to call foul play?'

This was from Blight-Purley and was accompanied by a piercingly forensic stare which belied his geriatric appearance and suggested the intelligence which, coupled with more than ordinary courage, had made him such a formidable wartime reputation.

Pring looked owlish. 'That will be for the coroner to decide,' he said.

'Oh, come,' said Blight-Purley, leaning forward and pressing on the stick which still rested between his legs. 'We're all friends. I hardly think our private speculation is going to prejudice the due process of law.'

The train was passing through suburbia now. Neat rectangular lawns; small wooden sheds; blossom; vegetable patches tucked into corners.

Bognor stared out at it and, before he could catch himself, said:

27

'Your friend, Miss Bristol, seemed to think he'd been peculiar.'

Pring shot him a cool look. 'Ginny's imagination is nothing if not fanciful,' he said.

'I wouldn't say that,' said Blight-Purley, smiling. He was not going to let it drop. 'Ginny's always seemed rather level-headed in her assessments, even if she does express them more colourfully than most. I thought Smith had been a bit strange recently.'

'He was always strange,' said Petrov. He had a slow, sulky, brown voice, but he spoke with virtually no accent. 'He was a strange person. Perhaps he was a great person. I think many great men are also strange. Would you not agree?' He cocked an eyebrow at Bognor, who grunted affirmatively. Petrov leant across the compartment, hand outstretched. 'We have not been introduced. Petrov. Soviet Synthetics.' They shook hands formally, Bognor gave his name and profession. They exchanged cards.

Blight-Purley returned to worry the subject. 'I agree with Comrade Petrov. He *was* strange. He *had* been getting stranger. But it takes more than increasing strangeness to explain suicide. And to what can we ascribe the increase in strangeness? I take it we can agree on the original strange state, the initial eccentricity, if you like, but how to explain its increase?'

Pring was looking very uncomfortable. 'I'm not sure I like this sort of talk,' he said, '*de mortuis nil nisi bonum* and all that.'

'I've never understood that particular tag,' said Blight-Purley, 'but even if I did it doesn't apply here, surely. All we're doing is discussing the cause of his untimely end. I think that's reasonable. What do you think, Miss Bullingdon? You've been very silent.'

Miss Bullingdon had been looking out at London which was getting greener by the minute, giving way to the neat quasi-countryside of the Home Counties. 'I'm sorry,' she said. 'I was miles away. What did you say?'

'We were talking about Scoff Smith,' he said, 'wondering what could have happened. Whether it was suicide, and, if so, why. Aubrey is inclined to rule us out of court and accuse us of bad taste. What do you think my dear?'

Amanda Bullingdon blushed a little. 'I'm afraid I didn't know him very well. And ethics aren't my strong point. I'd hardly be in public relations if they were.' She turned back to the view. There was no sound except for that of elderly rolling stock on elderly rails. Bognor wondered whether she had known Scoff; her denial had seemed unnecessarily swift.

Conversation, when it resumed, turned to vintages and continued on that subject for forty minutes. Bognor, well aware of his amateur status, listened in silence to the distillation of drinking men's experience. It was quite beyond him, and he was relieved when the train drew into Petheram and no one had asked him a direct question.

Their group trooped out on to the platform blinking blearily in the bright sunlight. They were the only ones alighting at the station which was ramshackle and overgrown with bramble and dandelion. It seemed an obvious candidate for British Rail's next economy drive. As he stood awaiting direction, Bognor felt a hand on his elbow. It was Aubrey Pring, who propelled him firmly but gently out of earshot.

'I may have seemed unduly sensitive earlier,' he said, 'but Blight-Purley can go crashing in. I just think I ought to warn you off saying anything about Scoff when Amanda Bullingdon's around. You see she and Scoff, well. . . . I've probably said enough, but I thought I'd better warn you.'

'You mean . . .'

Pring nodded and winked. 'Exactly. Not that she was the only one, by any manner of means, but, well, there it is.'

'Does Blight-Purley realize?'

'I should imagine so. He knows most things.'

'Ah.' The information was interesting but not necessarily relevant. Smith's reputation as a ladies' man was almost, though not quite, in the same league as Blight-Purley's. Amanda Bullingdon was youngish, presentable, unattached and, as the idiom had it, 'into food and drink'.

'Come and meet Freddie Pendennis,' said Pring, setting off towards the exit where their friends and colleagues were grouped around a short man in pepper-and-salt plus fours.

'Aubrey!' he called out, arms akimbo, as Pring and Bognor approached. 'How jolly! This *is* a pleasure. I've got some Krug, specially for Ginny and to cheer us all up, and a Framboise which I *know* you're going to enjoy.' Pring managed to introduce Bognor in mid-sentence. 'How nice,' said Pendennis, barely pausing, 'so nice to see someone from the B of T. It's usually those absolute fiends from the Inland Revenue or, worse still, the dreaded VAT men. Customs and Excise does seem to produce a quite amazingly tiresome sort of person, haven't you found, Aubrey? I give them beer. And when they're *really* grim I give them brown ale. They seem to enjoy it what's more! Oh, well, there's no accounting for taste. But come along. Time for a little soupcon of something from Wolxheim and Molsheim.' He led the way out of the station and into a Volkswagen minibus standing in the forecourt. There were enough seats for all except Pendennis, who stood at the front with his back to the windscreen.

'Ladies and gentlemen,' he said, 'I'd just like to say, before we get down to the serious business of the day, what a joy it is to welcome you all to our annual summer tasting. Most of you have been before so you know more or less what to expect, and I hope those expectations are going to be fulfilled. For those few who are on their first visit, I should only like to say that this is an occasion on which you're expected to enjoy yourselves. We're not going to make you work. Obviously we'd like you to go away and tell everyone what superlative wine you've had, but apart from that nothing at all. So *bon appetit*!'

There was a round of discreet, subdued applause as the little bus turned down a lane white with hawthorn and cow-parsley. Bognor was next to Amanda Bullingdon.

'I'm sorry about that gaffe,' she said.

'What gaffe?' he asked, thinking of her liaison with Scoff Smith and of Blight-Purley's probing.

'My saying we'd met before. It sounds so like one of those remarks. But it wasn't. I really did think we'd met before.'

'That's OK,' said Bognor, 'it happens all the time. What exactly do you do at F and D?'

She pulled a face. 'Things like this mostly. Organizing jollies for the trade.'

'How long have you been with them?'

'Too long really. Five years.'

'Oh,' Bognor smiled politely. 'And before that?'

'I worked in a restaurant. At the Dour Dragoon actually.'

'Oh.' He felt nonplussed. 'I'm sorry.'

'That's all right.' It obviously wasn't all right, he thought. The girl must be suffering. On the other hand her suffering was far from obvious. Indeed she seemed remarkably cheerful in the circumstances despite her abrupt dismissal of Blight-Purley's earlier question.

'*Did* you know him well?' he asked, chancing his arm.

She looked hard at him, then smiled. 'Let's just say that if I *did* know him well the last person on earth I'd tell would be a gossipy old lecher like Erskine Blight-Purley.'

'Fair enough.' The bus had turned through a pair of heavy wrought-iron gates and was climbing a steep gravel drive. On either side were rows of gnarled knee-high plants trained to wire trellising.

'Vines?' asked Bognor.

'Looks like it,' said Amanda Bullingdon, shading her eyes with a well manicured hand. 'I didn't know they were producing their own. It's become a bit of a trend recently.'

'*Appellation Sussex Contrôlée*,' he said.

'That sort of thing.'

The bus rumbled over a cattle grid and came to a halt. The house was substantial, heavy, Victorian, its air of red-brick barracks softened with ivy and wistaria and complicated by some recent appendages in plate glass and reinforced concrete. 'Welcome to Château Petheram,' said Pendennis as they disgorged on to the gravel. 'Actually,' he confided to Bognor, giving him an unnecessary helping hand down from the vehicle, 'it's really called "The New House, Petheram", but I rather like the sound of Château Petheram.'

When they were all out Pendennis led the way into a high-ceilinged hall and straight down a winding stone stairway to the cellar where the serious business of the day was to take place. It had, indeed, a serious look to it. A series of trestle tables had been set up along the centre of the room and covered with plain white cloth and row upon row of bottles. Spaced around on the flagged floor were small tubs full of sawdust. Bognor knew enough about wine to realize that they were for spitting into.

'Now,' said Pendennis, clapping his hands for attention. 'Once more, old hands will recognize the formula, but for the benefit of our newcomers, we always make this a blind tasting. No labels on any bottles, as you can see. Just numbers. Everyone has a card and a pencil, so make your notes as you go round, and then we'll tell you what you've been drinking after lunch. Don't worry though, we won't embarrass anyone by asking them to read out their guesses – it's purely for amusement, though naturally we're interested in your comments. So. Off we go!'

Bognor had gone very white at the announcement of the blind tasting. Party games were a particular phobia of his, and he had absolutely no confidence in his ability to make intelligent remarks about the wines, let alone identify them. He sincerely hoped Pendennis would keep his word about embarrassment.

'You any good at this sort of thing?' It was Lady Aubergine. He had quite forgotten her, though she was not, he conceded, an obviously forgettable person. As last night, she was threatening to spill out of her outfit which today was white – an expensive brushed denim trouser suit with a dangerously low neckline.

'Not much,' he said.

'That makes two of us,' she said, flashing long, horsy teeth. 'And with a hangover like mine I haven't an earthly of identifying a thing. Why don't we go round the course together? Blind leading the blind.'

'Why not?' The others had already fallen on the drink as if it was a Saharan oasis. 'That is if there's any left.'

'I've never known Pendennis to run out of hooch,' said her ladyship putting her hand to her head. 'You haven't got any Alka-Seltzer have you?' she asked. 'I've got an ache like a monkey's whatsit.'

'Oh,' Bognor picked up the last two cards and pencils, 'no, I'm afraid not.'

'Pity,' she said, 'hair of the dog it will have to be. I had a Fernet Branca at home but it doesn't seem to have done the trick. Never mind.'

The first wine had, he thought, a slightly fruity flavour. He sucked his pencil and wondered whether 'Slightly fruity' was an adequate comment.

'Not spitting?' asked Lady Aubergine, who had been going through an impressive ritual of gargling and hawking into the sawdust.

'I'm not very good at it I'm afraid,' said Bognor. 'I'm always petrified in case I miss.'

'I know what you mean. I think I'll join you.' She poured another generous slug of the first wine and swallowed in one go, a performance which made her eyes water. 'Slightly fruity, I should say,' she said, beaming.

'Rather what I thought,' said Bognor.

'Moselle?'

'Well, yes, I suppose. . . .'

Lady Aubergine scribbled. Bognor, not afraid to cheat, looked over her shoulder. 'Slightly fruity', she wrote. 'Moselle?'

He sucked on his pencil again and after some hesitation wrote. 'Definitely fruityish flavour. Arguably Moselle'.

They went on to the second group of bottles.

'Tell me,' demanded Bognor as he watched Lady Aubergine gargle. Her eyes squinted at the glass, her nostrils dilated and her throat twitched. The noise suggested drains – or more precisely bathwater being forced fast through a well rifled plug-hole. 'Tell me,' said Bognor again, as she swallowed, 'what exactly is your connection with food and drink?'

She seemed to consider for a moment. 'I like them,' she said, finally. 'But I don't have any commercial connection. I'm what you might call a gastronomic groupie.' She brayed lightly. 'I can't afford to work for a living on account of what's called a private income. What do you think of this?' she asked, indicating the second wine.

'Too sweet for me.'

'It's meant to be sweet. That's a Château de Fargues, or I'm a virgin.' The words were Blight-Purley's. 'Sixty-seven I should say or . . .' he held the glass to his nose and moved his nostrils in a suggestive manner which reminded Bognor of a belly dancer he had once seen in Beirut, 'or possibly, just possibly, a sixty-six.'

'It couldn't be Yquem?' enquired Lady Aubergine. She was nibbling a water biscuit, thoughtfully provided by their hosts as a palate cleanser.

'Absolutely not,' he said. 'Much as they love us I don't see Pendennis doling out Château d'Yquem for a blind tasting. Even *their* generosity has its limits. That's a de Fargues. Not cheap either.'

They moved on down the table tasting as they went. Before long Bognor had become quite confused. The wine was wine all right but beyond that he was unable to decide. How fruity was fruity? How dry dry? No sooner had he noted 'Very dry indeed' of a wine which took the skin off his palate than he found another with even greater acidity. It was the same with the sweet ones. Just as he discovered a liquid as sugary as honey, it would be capped with one as cloying as treacle. Too late he realized he should have started with a points system or a sweet-metre.

'I should just drink the stuff,' said Lady Aubergine observing his difficulty with amusement. 'After a couple of glasses it all tastes exactly the same. If I were blindfolded I couldn't tell the difference between hock and claret.'

At the end of the trestles the white stopped and red began. Ahead of them the procession showed signs of inebriation. There was less spitting and more imbibing. Voices, which had never been subdued, were becoming raised, even raucous. One or two had returned to the whites 'just to make absolutely sure of that really rather remarkable bouquet'.

'I think I may be drunk again,' said Lady Aubergine. She was looking pinkish. 'How funny running into you at that ghastly dump last night. Did you know Aubrey well at Oxford?'

'Not very. He was one of those people everyone knew by sight and reputation. I don't think he really knew me.'

'Oh, I don't know. He seemed awfully pleased to see you.'

'Yes.'

'Of course, he hasn't really been happy since he came down, so he's always pleased to meet some old mucker to remind him of his misspent youth.'

Bognor felt suitably put down.

'Try some of this.' She poured him a glass of purplish red and misjudged it so that it overflowed on to Bognor's grey worsted. 'Oops,' she said. 'Sorry.'

'Doesn't matter,' said Bognor. 'It's very old.' It was, in fact, just back from the cleaners.

'Did you say you knew poor old Scoff? I don't remember.'

'It's a bit like Aubrey. I went to his restaurant and he'd come round and ask if everything was all right and we'd chat for about fifteen seconds. But I wouldn't say I knew him. Did you?'

'You could say so,' she said. 'I told you I was a gastronomic groupie, and you must know Scoff's reputation.'

'Not really,' said Bognor.

'Oh, come on. Anything in skirts. And anything under about forty and twelve stone in trousers. Though they say he'd lost his touch recently – occupational hazard – what the lower orders rather crudely refer to as "brewer's wilt". Not that I speak from personal experience you understand. My relationship with *le grand chef* was fleeting and many years ago. We thought of each other as collector's items. He liked to notch up titles and I'm rather penchant for the better sort of restaurateurs and hoteliers – not, to be absolutely honest, that they're much good at it. Wine scribes are definitely better. Ugh!' She wrinkled her nose at her glass of number twenty-three. 'Don't touch that. It's disgusting. Bolivian. Or Czech. Or, I know, bad Californian. That's it. Beverly Hills Burgundy.' She went over to the nearest tub and poured it away, making no effort to conceal the operation.

'Did Scoff have much success with titled ladies?'

'He scored once or twice but most of us seem to prefer pop stars or genuine artisans – plumbers or gardeners – that sort of person.' She lowered her voice and mentioned a duchess, a marchioness, a brace of baronesses and half a dozen sprigs of the nobility like herself – women whose names were properly prefixed with 'Hon' or 'Lady'. 'Mind you,' she continued, 'most of them were just curious, and I'm more or less certain some of them slept with him for his recipes. The only ones who lasted more than a few nights were people like Gabrielle or poor little Miss Bullingdon.'

'I see.' He chewed thoughtfully on a biscuit and inadvertently poured a glass of number twenty-three. It was every bit as disgusting as Lady Aubergine had suggested. 'But he'd lost his touch recently?'

'So they say.' She saw him grimace at the number twenty-three, removed his glass deftly and poured it into the sawdust.

'Try some of the twenty-seven. Aubrey will have written "nectar" on his card. I think it's a burgundy. By the way, what *exactly* are you doing about *le monde gastronomique* for your people?'

'Um,' said Bognor, 'well, more or less what I was trying to explain last night.'

Lady Aubergine, despite the drink, managed to look distinctly ho-hummish. Nevertheless she said: 'Aubrey will be very helpful in showing you round, but he doesn't know everyone and there are a number of pitfalls he's simply not aware of. If there's anything I can do . . . or, put it another way, I'll give you a hand.'

Further conspiracy was prevented by Pendennis banging a bottle on the table for silence. It was time for lunch.

No very serious attempt had been made to seat members of the opposite sex next to each other. This seemed sensible since there were not enough women to go round and several of the men would not have been interested even if there had. Moreover, none of the men would have been interested, surely, in the sagging, red-veined lady from *Wines and Winebibbers* who sat, barely sensible, between Petrov and a dapper hotelier from the Cotswolds.

Bognor, between Ebertson and Amanda Bullingdon,

studied the menu. Wine was listed on the left, food on the right. The first entry on the left was Bitschwiller N V.

'Bitschwiller?' said Bognor to Ebertson. 'I thought something was said about Krug?'

'We get Krug for tea,' said Ebertson. 'A charming Petheram perversion of your English ritual.'

'Krug and crumpets?' said Bognor feeling witty with wine.

'Something like that.'

'And the Bitschwiller?'

'Compliments of the widow herself. Another Petheram tradition.'

'Oh.' Bognor was again nonplussed. 'How so?'

'Pendennises are the people who really put Bitschwiller on the map. La Veuve was a friend of old man Pendennis way back before the war.'

'La Veuve Bitschwiller?'

'The old bitch herself.' Ebertson grinned. 'She's extraordinary, a real relic. You should try to meet her, you'd enjoy it.'

He leant across the table towards Erskine Blight-Purley who was absent-mindedly baring his teeth in the general direction of Amanda Bullingdon. 'Is it true that Gabrielle is going to take Scoff's place in Acapulco?'

'I hadn't heard,' said Blight-Purley, not removing his gaze.

'Like hell,' said Ebertson *sotto voce*. He returned to Bognor. 'That old buzzard hears everything. Doesn't miss a trick.'

'What's happening in Acapulco?'

'The Feast of the Five Continents. You know, you must have read about it. Real top end of the market stuff. Sort of twenty-course dinner cooked by the top chefs from every country on earth which has any pretensions to a cuisine more sophisticated than mealies and beans. Even, I might say, my own beloved United States whose contribution to the culinary arts, you have to admit, is dubious.'

'Clam chowder's nice,' said Bognor politely.

Ebertson leant back so that a waiter in sommelier's kit could pour him a glass of Bitschwiller. Bognor watched the pale golden liquid froth to the top of the glass and then subside gently. He leant back to allow the sommelier to do the same for him. He was fond of champagne and in his present state, which was one of mild befuddlement rather than real intoxication, he felt euphoric.

'Ever had hominy grits?' asked Ebertson.

'Never had hominy grits.'

'I don't advise it, but if you want to experience all that's worst in American cooking, try hominy grits.'

'What do they taste of?'

'They don't. That's the whole point of them. Bland is the name of the game. The argument is that you eliminate anything which might give offence. That way everybody likes it. What actually happens is that it's so outrageously bland that nobody *dis*likes it. That's not the same thing at all. Matter of fact, it's not a bad way to make people end up hating you.'

'Some people would argue that that's a criticism of the American character as much as American cooking.'

'They'd be entitled to. Hey, this looks good.' He bent low over the steaming terrine newly arrived on his plate and inhaled. 'Mmmm,' he said.

Bognor picked up the gherkin from the side of his helping and bit through it. 'Who's organizing this jamboree?' he asked.

'*Guide Bitschwiller*, the Mexicans, Association Hôtels de luxe du Monde, the Pasta Producers Federation . . . the usual gang. Rothschilds will be involved somewhere along the line.'

'Are *Guide Bitschwiller* and Maison Bitschwiller one and the . . . ?'

'Oh sure. You ought to swing an invite. I'm sure they'd be glad to have a guest from the British Board of Trade.'

'Are you going?'

'I'm working on it, but I'm not certain I can see any way to justify it. I can just about maintain that *haute cuisine* comes within my brief in cultural affairs here in England, but I'm not sure I can persuade Washington that my parish extends very far outside the UK. Western Europe, maybe, but I have an idea they'll baulk at Mexico. Still, we'll see.'

They ate their terrine in appreciative silence. When they

had finished Bognor said, 'And the buzz is that Gabrielle is going to be allowed to stand in for Scoff?'

'That's right.'

'Can she cook?'

'Well enough. Scoff was down for the chocolate omelette. You've had their chocolate omelette?' He leant back again as the sommelier poured a '71 Alsatian Riesling.

'Yes. Fantastic.'

'Agreed, but it's the conception and the ingredients that are inspired. Putting them together isn't that difficult. I've done it at home myself, and the result's a passable imitation of a Scoff special.'

'Really?'

'Really.'

'Tell me,' they were drinking a clear soup now, redolent of goose and cabbage, 'were most of you friends of Scoff? I mean most of the people here.'

Ebertson made a slurping noise as he funnelled soup off the spoon and looked round. 'Let's see,' he said. 'We most of us seem to have known Scoff all right. Petrov, yes. Aubrey certainly. Erskine – '

'What's that?' Blight-Purley had appeared rapt in soupy concentration, yet the mention of his name occasioned an immediate response.

'Scoff,' said Ebertson. 'Our friend from the Board of Trade wanted to know if we knew him, whether we were friends of his.'

Blight-Purley produced an oddly metallic grunt. 'Almost everyone who ever met him thought they were a friend of Scoff's,' he said, 'but I always used to wonder if *he* regarded himself as anyone's friend.'

It was one of those remarks which unfortunately came in a universal conversational gap. It was heard by everyone at the table save the roseate lady from *Wine and Winebibbers* who saved the day by suddenly staggering to her feet, napkin held to her mouth. She lurched towards the door evidently on the point of being dramatically, spectacularly unwell. Pendennis managed to combine extreme solicitude and intense disapproval in his expression as he hurried her out.

39

'La Veuve Bitschwiller strikes again,' muttered Ebertson.

'More likely the twenty-three,' said Bognor.

Ebertson looked at him appreciatively. 'You didn't like it either?' he said.

'No. Aubergine Bristol and I agreed it must have been Californian.'

'I can't say I'm a great admirer of Aubergine Bristol's gastronomic *savoire faire,* but on this occasion I'm inclined to agree.'

Pendennis returned, mopping his brow with a red and white spotted kerchief. 'Oh dear,' he said sitting down heavily, 'it happens every year. I really shall have to think about inviting her next time. On the other hand it wouldn't be the same without her premature departure. But enough, let us return to our *moutons.*'

The suggestion was more than usually apposite since they were now being issued with large helpings of Saddle of mutton, accompanied by Clos Vougeot. Conversation settled down to things gastronomical. Bognor alternated politely and enjoyably between Ebertson and Amanda Bullingdon, savouring his food and drink in the intervals between sentences and pausing occasionally to reflect that there must be worse ways of making a living than from some professional association with eating and drinking. It was all too easy to forget that he was only being spared the execrable civil service canteen lunch because he was attempting to establish the cause of Scoff Smith's death. Somehow, through the confusion which always occurred at the beginning of his investigations (and which sometimes continued until their conclusion), he was beginning to think that his objective was more than usually complicated. It was not so much the cause of death which had to be established as the cause of the cause. Suicide by gas poisoning was the certain coroner's verdict. What he had to find out, he feared, was not whether it really was suicide, but why the man should have killed himself at all. Was it an entirely natural reaction to some sad spontaneous depression or was the depression deliberately induced? Bognor wondered.

They had just finished a peculiarly high Münster cheese and were sipping at their Framboise when Freddie Pendennis once again stood and called for order. There were a number of toasts to propose, he said, the first of which, sadly, was the memory of their friend and mentor, Escoffier Savarin Smith. He had, he continued, nothing to add to what had already been said in *The Times* and elsewhere but he would like simply to propose that we all stand and drink to the memory of Scoff and to express a hope that he was even now in the kitchen of the gods preparing food which could scarcely be more heavenly than that which he had produced for us on earth. This flowery tribute concluded, the company shuffled to its collective feet and drank Framboise with the muffled muttering which is characteristic of English middle-class toast drinking. This done, Pendennis asked his guests to remain standing for the two traditional toasts. First of all he asked everyone to drink to la Veuve Bitschwiller. Once more glasses were raised and there was a chorus of mumbled salutation. 'La Veuve ... la Veuve.' And finally, 'The Queen,' he said, slowly and reverently but, it seemed to Bognor, with markedly less reverence than he had reserved for la Veuve Bitschwiller. For a third time glasses were raised and the words reverberated around the table. Blight-Purley, Bognor noticed, was the only one to add the traditional subordinate sentence: 'God bless her.'

Framboise was replenished. An assortment of strangely shaped bottles materialized. So did cigars: five-inch Havana Petit Coronas from Upmann. Heavy blue smoke began to clog the atmosphere. Bognor felt his own sense of well being on the verge of turning to biliousness. Through the rising fog he saw that Blight-Purley was attempting to attract his attention. He was saying something about lunch.

'Very much,' said Bognor, assuming he was passing judgement on the meal just eaten.

'One o'clock then,' he said, his voice suddenly audible as surrounding sound subsided. It was an invitation, Bognor realized; nothing to do with food already consumed but a portent of food to come. He was stretching a veiny hand across the table and Bognor accepted the contents. 'My card,' said Blight-Purley, 'in case you can't make it. The club at twelve-thirty.'

'Sorry,' said Bognor as conversation once again became impeded by that of others. 'What club?'

'The Mess,' he said, 'Thursday.' Bognor had a distinct impression of a yellow gleam in the rheumy eyes. There was indeed a universal yellow about the man – a jaundiced sallowness which stemmed from debauchery of a sort Bognor found oddly sinister. Why did he want to have lunch? It would hardly be for the pleasure of his company. From what he had seen of him so far Bognor was uncomfortably sure that Blight-Purley smelt a rat.

'Did you guess any of the wines do you think?' asked Amanda Bullingdon.

'Not really,' he said, 'I'm afraid I didn't try terribly hard after the first few.'

She smiled. 'The secret is simply to keep quiet. Freddie's very kind. He enjoys catching out the know-alls but he's perfectly happy to leave the novices alone.

'In that case I shall keep absolutely silent.'

'I should,' she said. 'Most people in this business talk *far* too much.'

Bognor made a mental note of the fact, though it was an impression he had already gained for himself.

A few seconds later the discussion of the wines began. It was informal and relaxed but deceptively so. Pendennis obviously enjoyed the role of genial questionmaster but behind the bland facade he was clearly getting a lot of fun from the barely veiled hostility of the more prominent oenophiles among his guests. Most of the company were as taciturn as Bognor, but a small group seemed concerned to maintain their reputation. Aubrey Pring, naturally, had to be seen to be knowledgeable. So in a less bumptious way did Blight-Purley, whose sardonic, throw-away style of delivery did little to hide the seriousness with which he was taking it. Both Petrov and Ebertson competed, with frequent unconvincing disclaimers about their amateur status. A young bespectacled Master of Wine from one of the great London auction houses appeared more knowledgeable than any of them, answering questions in the clipped, flat tones that Bognor associated with lesser accountants and solicitors' clerks. Aubergine Bristol eschewed silence, which did not come easily to her, but was shrewd enough to keep her comments to opinions rather than facts. These, happily, were entirely favourable until Pendennis arrived at the dread number twenty-three.

'Twenty-three,' he exclaimed. 'The joker in the pack. I don't somehow think you're going to get this one.' He beamed around the table.

'I don't think any of us would *want* to get it,' said Lady Aubergine loudly. 'Absolute stinko stuff, Freddie. Even Mr Bognor couldn't drink his, could you?' She glared down the table seeking Bognor's support. He could cheerfully have drowned her in number twenty-three. Everyone was looking at him. Pendennis did not look un-angry.

'I . . . er . . . well,' Bognor felt purple, 'that is . . . '

'Simon guessed Californian Cabernet, but he's probably too modest to admit it. I guess he's probably right, though I rather think it could be a Zinfandel. With respect, Freddie, I felt it lacked a little of the rotundity of a good Cabernet, but give it three or four years and I dare say . . .'

Pendennis seemed mollified by this. The crisis was past. Bognor mopped his forehead and half turned to grin gratitude at his neighbour, Ebertson.

'I like the idea of Zinfandel,' said Pendennis, 'but it's not a grape you'll find outside the United States, I think, Anthony, and this isn't an American wine. Mr Bognor's right about the Cabernet though.' Bognor blushed again. He certainly couldn't tell Cabernet from Pinot Noir. He wished, for the first time that day, that he was in the canteen.

'So it's a European wine?' This was Aubrey.

'Yes, European.'

'But not French.'

'No, Erskine, you're absolutely right. It's not French.'

'Is it Saperavi?' asked Petrov, 'I thought it had something of the flavour of Georgia. Like blood.' He laughed.

'There speaks a loyal Muscovite,' said Ebertson. 'That

wine's too thin-blooded for Georgian. Georgian's thick as treacle. My guess is it's from Switzerland.'

'Warmer,' said Pendennis, 'or rather, not. It's a cold climate wine but not Swiss.'

There was a general scratching of heads. 'German,' volunteered the Master of Wine without enthusiasm.

'No.' Pendennis beamed round. 'Fourteen fifty-three might give a clue to any historians among us.'

'We lost Bordeaux,' said Aubrey Pring quickly, 'but I hardly think . . . '

'And,' continued Pendennis, 'had we then possessed an imaginative minister for trade and industry what would his proper, flexible response have been? Self-sufficiency would have cut our import bills – just as desirable then as now, I'm sure.'

'You're surely not suggesting that this is a product of our own inclement shores,' said Blight-Purley, eyes screwed small in disbelief.

> ' "*Frosts are slain and flowers begotten,*
> *And in green underwood and cover*
> *Blossom by blossom the spring begins.*" '

'I hardly think that's what Swinburne had in mind,' said Pring, much miffed. 'Are you seriously asking us to believe, Freddie, that number twenty-three is an English wine?'

'Indeed I am.'

'But no one's producing red in England,' said Pring. 'It's a non-starter. White, yes I know, but an English red is out of the question and for good reason. I know all the English wine producers, and not one of them is even contemplating a red.'

'Perhaps you don't know your English wine producers as well as you think,' said Pendennis with a suggestion of truculence. 'Or rather, perhaps they're better at keeping secrets than you realize. Anyway, I think it's time to put you out of your misery. Number twenty-three is the first of the Château Petheram. I agree it will improve in bottle, but we were impatient to give it an airing.'

There was a silence which Bognor mentally recorded as

'stunned'. Then to his surprise he found himself standing and saying, 'In the circumstances, ladies and gentlemen I think a further toast is in order. I give you Château Petheram!' They drank to Château Petheram, looking suitably shamefaced about it.

Then Pendennis continued: 'We've already tried it out on la Veuve and her son, Philippe, and I believe you will be impressed by her response.' Theatrically he drew a piece of paper from his pocket, put on a pair of half-moon spectacles and read: ' "My dear Freddie, Philippe and I are agreed that your first English red is a remarkable achievement. In the circumstances we would count it a privilege if you would attend the dinner in Acapulco and bring with you a case or two of Ch. Petheram." ' He put the letter away slowly. 'So you see my friends, la Veuve displays rather more faith than you have done. Let's hope she's right.'

There was a chorus of 'hear, hears' and conversation became general once more. It was clear that those who were out of Pendennis' earshot were all saying the same, summed up by Anthony Ebertson, who remarked to Bognor, 'Something "fishy", as you British would say, about this. That rotgut stuff is piss awful and everyone knows it. You can keep it in bottle till the Second Coming, and it'll still be piss awful. What in hell are they playing at?'

'They're probably acting on the assumption that a certain sort of wine snob will buy anything,' said Bognor.

'*Touché*, Mr Bognor, but I still don't see why. There must be easier ways of making money.'

Bognor shrugged. It was all very mysterious. On the other hand it increasingly seemed that a trip to Acapulco was in order. He wondered what Parkinson would say to that.

They broke up soon after to wander around the estate. Bognor spent the next hour or so staring blankly at vines and presses and barrels while the others asked respectful and knowledgeable questions. Afterwards they adjourned for the much-vaunted Krug before departing for the five-thirty from Petheram to London, Charing Cross. At the station there was a final exchanging of cards and promises. In Bognor's case the only firm commitment was his Thursday lunch with Blight-Purley. Otherwise it had merely been initiation. He had made some useful contacts, penetrated the Scoff circle, and enjoyed an excellent meal. He had found no solutions but, on the other hand, there were now some new and interesting questions to be asked.

Chapter Three

'Acapulco!'

Parkinson had the ability to render normally neutral or even attractive words positively indecent by the merest inflexion. 'Acapulco!' he said again, investing the word, of which Bognor had hitherto been rather fond, with a whole range of nefarious and undesirable qualities, of which Bognor had not previously been aware.

'Yes,' he said, fixing Her Majesty's portrait with his usual unblinking stare and trying to ignore the rebuke, implied in Parkinson's utterance of the well-known Mexican resort. 'Yes,' he said, 'Acapulco.'

It is odd how very quiet a basement under central London can seem at times. Normally Bognor thought of the office as a bustling, noisy place full of talk and hurry. At this moment it was unnaturally, almost hurtfully silent, yet it would have been difficult for a casual third party to recognize the extent of Parkinson's anger. He sat, quite impassive, behind his desk. His usual pinko-grey complexion seemed a little pinker and a little greyer than usual, but it was not until you noticed the pencil held tightly in his hands that you would have realized that something was not quite right. Just as Bognor's gaze shifted downwards from the portrait to the top of his boss's desk, the pencil broke. Bognor looked away and said: 'I think it would be free. And if I can't get it for nothing, then, of course, I shan't go.'

'Ah.' Parkinson smiled, or more accurately, grimaced. 'Very good of you, Bognor. And what exactly are you going to be able to discover in, ah, Acapulco, that you can't discover a little nearer home?'

'Well,' said Bognor, 'it's just that the international Scoff set will be there and, well, one might pick up a thing or two.' He was aware that this sounded lame. 'I got a distinct feeling that Acapulco is going to be significant,' he added.

'I am quite simply lost for words,' said Parkinson, staring despairingly at the two halves of the pencil. 'I seem to remember asking you merely to investigate the suggested suicide of a restaurateur in a London suburb. Within twenty-four hours this investigation leads you to Acapulco. Yet, as far as I can see, you have not even visited the suburban restaurant owned and run by the deceased. I am unhappily aware of the curious deductive processes which inform your work, Bognor, but even by your own bizarre standards this is amazing. In other words, Bognor, for Christ's sake pull yourself together, be your age, and stop fantasizing. This isn't bloody *Vogue*, you know, it's the Board of bloody Trade!'

'I'm sorry,' Bognor adopted his most mulish expression. 'I just happen to think it would be useful. And for the record I've no particular wish to go to Acapulco anyway. All my friends tell me it's not a particularly exciting place. It just *sounds* exciting. Besides this junket isn't for several weeks yet and naturally I'm going down to the Dour Dragoon. The only reason I haven't been already is that I had the offer of this day in Petheram, and it turned out better than I could possibly have hoped. You wanted me to take a close look at Ebertson and Petrov and I did.'

'And you also struck up a relationship with Colonel Blight-Purley.'

'Well, hardly a relationship. Anyway, so what? He's one of us, isn't he?'

'There is no need at all for further flippancy.' Parkinson was deploring the whole exercise and particularly this conversation. '*Colonel* Blight-Purley,' continued Parkinson, laying such stress on the rank as to suggest that Blight-Purley was not properly entitled to it, 'is a menace. As he has no doubt told you already, several times, he had a spectacularly successful career in wartime military intelligence.'

'I've read about it. I've read his book. But to be fair to him he never once mentioned it yesterday.'

'That's as may be. The point is that it is one thing to parachute gallantly in and out of France and the Balkans chatting up partisans, and quite another to engage in the extremely sophisticated business of espionage in a nuclear society. Wouldn't you agree?'

'I suppose so.'

'Hmm. Perhaps you'd have been better suited to a role in Blight-Purley's "show" as he would doubtless describe it.' Bognor thought of the Colonel's question about Dieppe, and began to feel quite well disposed towards him. Parkinson was continuing. 'Ever since the war ended and men like Blight-Purley were thanked for doing a good job and sent back to some appropriate work outside, he and people like him have made themselves a perfect nuisance to the professionals like . . . ' he hesitated and then said bleakly, 'ourselves. There's none worse than Blight-Purley. He still believes he has what he calls "a part to play", and he interferes constantly. There are those, not a million miles from the Foreign Office, who are impressed by his old school tie and his name dropping and who encourage him in this nonsense. But he has no encouragement in this office, Bognor, and I'll thank you to remember it. We have enough problems without Blight-Purley's particular brand of cowboys and Indians. So would you confine your contact with him to the purely social?'

'But,' protested Bognor, 'in this particular case he is distinctly relevant. I mean he knew Scoff Smith well, and he's tied up with the whole wine and food business, *and* he's got something he wants to tell me.'

'I'm just warning you, that's all.'

'Thank you very much.'

'So what is your programme from now on?'

'I thought I'd nip down to the Dour Dragoon and see what's going on.'

'Inquest? Funeral?'

'I thought not. I'm not supposed to be investigating Scoff himself am I? I don't want to attract undue attention.'

'So how will you explain your visit to the late Mr Smith's restaurant?'

'As we agreed. I shall say that I'm investigating various possibilities to do with the top end of the market and say that since the restaurant is still going to be represented in Acapulco...'

Parkinson slammed a palm down on the desk in an inefficient and anglicized version of a karate chop. 'I do not wish to hear that word again,' he began and then the phone rang. 'Who?' he said, and then became obsequious – so obsequious that the effect was to be insulting. 'Ah, Colonel Blight-Purley.... Yes, young Bognor ... oh, quite, yes. One of our bright young men.... Very kind of you.... Oh good, thanks for letting me know. ... Indeed, yes. Next time we want anything on Cracow I'll most definitely be in touch. Of course. Good-bye.'

He turned fiercely on Bognor. 'Your new friend and mentor. He just rang to tell me he'd be taking you under his wing, making sure you were all right.'

'I thought,' said Bognor, 'that he received no encouragement in this office?'

Parkinson said nothing but it was clear from his expression that Bognor's departure for East Sheen was long overdue. Bognor, who was not as insensitive to his superior's moods and opinions as his speech and behaviour would sometimes suggest, duly departed.

He made his journey to south-west London on a number nine bus, a form of transport dear to the soul of the Board of Trade since it gave an impression of economy. The top of the bus was virtually empty and Bognor sat in the front enjoying the view of the Thames at Hammersmith and Barnes and of other people's gardens and bedrooms. By the time he arrived, pulling half-heartedly on a thin Dutch cheroot, he was in a happier frame of mind, far from thoughts of dead chefs and Mexico. He got out at Mortlake garage, the end of the line, just south of the finish of the Oxford and Cambridge boat race, and was musing on boat races he had seen when he was suddenly aware of a familiar sober-suited figure who had been sitting on the bottom of the bus.

'Goodness,' he exclaimed at once. 'Mr Petrov. How do

you do? We met yesterday you remember, Bognor, Board of Trade.' His outstretched hand was received with something less than enthusiasm, and he realized, once he had made the greeting, that Mr Petrov was not in the least pleased to see him. He was reacting like a vicar surprised on his way to the brothel. There were two ways of responding to this. One was to do as the man wished and leave him alone. The other was to make a pest of oneself. Bognor decided on the latter.

'What brings you to Mortlake then?' he asked jovially.

'Mortlake?' The Russian responded as if he had never heard of the place. They were walking towards the railway line. A narrow footbridge crossed it a few yards further on, and as they reached it the Russian turned left to walk over it. '*Au revoir*,' he said, waving as jauntily as he could, 'good to see you so soon.'

Bognor did not hesitate. 'I'm going this way too,' he said, 'you don't mind if I join you?' The Russian began to scowl but merely said, 'Of course not.'

'Do you make synthetics in Sheen?' he asked pleasantly, 'or is there a good market for them here?' The railway line marked the boundary between Mortlake and Sheen, and they were now passing small Victorian cottages recently renovated to make *bijou* residences of the style favoured by actors, journalists and television personalities.

'No,' said Petrov, evading a colourful, flower-filled basket which hung out over the pavement from a wrought iron bracket. 'I am not here for synthetics.'

'Aha,' said Bognor. 'The only other reason I can think of for coming here is to patronize the Dour Dragoon. Except that they don't open for lunch. Anyway, that's my destination. May I take it that it's yours too?'

The Russian looked at him sharply. 'I am going to express my condolences,' he said. 'But you were not a friend of Escoffier's? And, as you say, lunch is not available.'

'*Touché*,' said Bognor, 'but I'm trying to compile a report about what we call "the top end of the market", and you can't get nearer the top end than the Dour Dragoon.'

'The timing is a little inappropriate.' Petrov was obviously put out. 'The restaurant has been closed. They will not be in the mood for chit-chat.'

'It's hardly chit-chat,' said Bognor, piqued, despite himself. 'The Dragoon has three stars in *Michelin* and *Bitschwiller*. No other restaurant in Britain can match that. Gabrielle will be the only British representative in Acapulco. It is very important for me to talk to her.'

'You are forgetting Freddie Pendennis and his grape juice,' said Petrov. 'Besides Gabrielle is not British. She is from the Isle Maurice.'

'Mauritius is part of the Commonwealth,' said Bognor. 'Besides, you know what I mean. And I've already spoken to Pendennis.'

They continued in silence, their lack of words made less embarrassing by the roar of south-west London's traffic and the thunder of Heathrow-bound jets above. The *chi-chi* houses had given way to shops – a mixture of long established small greengrocers and butchers, the occasional mini-supermarket, and new 'antique' shops specializing in the stripping of pine. It was an odd place to find Britain's best restaurant. Five minutes later they turned down a leafy alleyway of converted cottages, the first of which had a painted sign swinging limply in the zephyr. There were no words on it, only a mournful visage surmounting a tunic of plum and gold braid and topped by a bedraggled shako, with a drooping plume.

'I've never seen it in daylight,' said Bognor. 'Moonlight certainly adds a necessary touch of glamour.'

Petrov made no reply but rang the doorbell, stabbing it impatiently and forcefully with a fat, hairy thumb. Releasing his pressure he allowed a bare ten seconds before pressing again, longer this time and still less patiently. This time the door was opened, albeit reluctantly and not very far. 'Ah, Signor Petrov.' The voice was male, subdued and southern European. The door opened sufficiently to admit one. Once Petrov was inside it had closed before Bognor had followed him. 'Oh shit!' he said, pressing the bell push himself. It opened again immediately, but not far enough for Bognor to insinuate his less than sylph-like form. 'Sorry,' said the voice, 'restaurant is closed for lunch – *chiuso* – finished – *kaput*.' Again the door was shut. Again Bognor pressed the button, and was answered with another still more immediate opening. 'No,' said the voice, 'sorry. Is finished.'

'I don't want anything to eat,' said Bognor, peevishly, 'I just want to talk to Mademoiselle Gabrielle.'

The door nudged back another grudging inch.

'Mademoiselle Gabrielle?'

'Yes . . . *oui* . . . *si* . . . *prego*.' Bognor was monosyllabic in any number of European languages, '*per favore*!' he went on desperately.

'You have an appointment?'

'No. Well, yes, in a manner of speaking. Tell her Bognor, Board of Trade. Here. . . . ' he rummaged in his pocket for a visiting card and thrust it through the aperture. 'Take her that. Say I'm very sorry, but it is rather important.'

'Moment,' the hand took the card and closed the door, leaving Bognor to mutter on the pavement, cursing life and restaurateurs in general, and Russian agents masquerading under ludicrous 'covers' in particular. Surely Petrov could have pleaded for him. It was not only bad manners, it was rotten espionage. Surely there was honour among agents?

Eventually the door opened again and this time a woman's voice, beguilingly accented, said 'Mr Bognor?'

'Yes.'

'You wanted to talk to me?'

'If you wouldn't mind.'

He recognized Gabrielle, even through the small opening she had left. Better still she recognized him. 'Ah,' she said, 'but you have been here before. Several times. Why didn't you say so?' She opened the door fully to admit him. 'Forgive me,' she said, 'I did not recognize your name. You know how it is. We have a great many clients, but it is not always possible to match the name to the face.'

'But I haven't been *that* often,' said Bognor, 'and I'm afraid this is by way of business.'

'*Au contraire*. You have been often enough to be recognized. I'm sorry, please come in.' Mourning, he decided, rather suited her. She was wearing a long black gown which concealed legs that occasionally in shorter garments or trousers seemed unbecomingly plump. The décolletage showed off her ample breasts, and the jet black choker around her neck and the similar Alice band which held her raven hair gave her a sophistication which had not always been apparent.

'Thank you.'

'I hope you don't mind the kitchen,' she said, leading the way through the dining area. 'We re-open this evening and, as you can imagine, it is not easy. However, I am sure it is what he would have wished. Would you care for an apéritif? There is a bottle of Bitschwiller in the fridge.'

Unreasonably the mention of that name again so soon gave him a frisson of alarm. 'That would be very agreeable,' he said. 'I do hope I'm not interrupting anything.'

'*Au contraire*,' she said. 'It's a pleasure to have some company. The work is routine at the moment and delegation is all.' So, on entering the kitchen, it seemed. Two large copper pots were simmering gently on the stove. Two small Chinese youths were seated at a table chopping onions and green peppers.

'I didn't really mean cooking,' said Bognor, as she took an open bottle of Bitschwiller from the vast refrigerator which occupied most of the larder adjoining the kitchen proper. I got the impression that you and Mr Petrov had something important to discuss.'

'Mr Petrov?'

'Yes. Dmitri Petrov. Soviet Synthetics. I was with him. We travelled down together on a number nine.'

'How strange. I haven't seen Dmitri since . . . since before Scoff died.' She smiled sadly and Bognor was duly devastated. Her looks were just beginning to coarsen, but he had always had a penchant for creole ladies. Pulling himself together he said. 'That's odd. I mean your chap just let him in.'

'Really?' she smiled again. 'Then I wonder where he can have got to. Which "chap" let him in?' She indicated the two Chinese.

'I don't think it was either of these. Italian or Spanish person.'

54

She frowned. 'That must be Massimo. I hadn't realized he was here. Just one minute. I'll see if he's in the office. He may be doing some accounts.' She left the room only to return in almost exactly sixty seconds, shrugging expressively. 'Not here,' she said. She looked at him as if to suggest, in the nicest possible way, that he was hallucinating.

'How odd,' he said, half convinced that he had been seeing things. 'We had quite a long conversation.'

'Never mind,' she said. 'There must be some explanation. Cheers!' she raised her glass. They drank. If there was an explanation she was not going to offer it. 'Now, what can I do for you?'

'Well, it was partly about Acapulco.'

'Ah, Acapulco.' She smiled. 'Lee!' she shouted suddenly. 'Not like that. Skins must be off. How many times did le patron tell you? Boiling water. *Vite*.' The wretched Lee bit his lip. He had progressed to tomatoes and was slicing them unpeeled. 'I'm sorry.' She returned to Bognor. 'You have to watch them all the time. Otherwise, *merde alors*, there is a catastrophe! Imagine. Tomatoes with skin, oh my God! You were saying, "Acapulco".' She made it sound much more exciting and desirable than Parkinson had done ealier that morning. The consonants were softer, the vowels longer.

'Yes, you see.' Bognor launched once more into his dissertation on the top end of the market. She listened apparently attentively and finally said, 'I am not sure how I can help you. It is true we try to maintain standards of excellence, something special. But as you know we are very small. There is no way we can be commercial enough to interest a government.'

'In yourselves perhaps not,' said Bognor, 'but perhaps if yours was an example which was followed more assiduously.'

'We don't like to divulge too many secrets, Mr Bognor,' she said, half humorously. 'We are a competitive business even though we are a small one.'

'I wouldn't dream of asking you to give anything away,' he said. 'It's just that you are the only three-star restaurant in England, and you are going to Acapulco as a sort of ambassador for *la cuisine anglaise*, and, well, if we are to make something out of gastronomy we have to learn from your example. Not so much in matters of detail as in more general matters of style.'

'I see,' she said. 'So what would you like me to tell you?'

At that moment Bognor only wanted to know what she had done with Dmitri Petrov, but instead he proceeded to ask questions about cost efficiency and buying and staff and, in short, how to run a restaurant which was better than good. At the end of half an hour he had learnt only that such excellence was a matter of flair and individuality and that all that could be taught was a technique which would ensure a mention in *Michelin* and *Bitschwiller* but would win no distinctions. By that time the bottle of Bitschwiller was finished and had gone to his bladder.

'Could I use your loo, do you think?' he asked.

'Oh,' the question seemed to surprise her more than when he had asked what sort of rum went into the chocolate omelette ('four different varieties,' she had replied). 'The public toilets are locked at the moment. You had better use the staff one. Through there.' She pointed to a door next to the washing-up machine. 'Go along the corridor, and it is the third on the right.'

He followed her directions and found a large lavatory decked out in Victorian tiles, original newspaper cartoons by Jak and Osbert Lancaster and a document certifying that Escoffier Savarin Smith was a member of the Grand Order of Water Rats. Beside the pedestal was a collected Ogden Nash and a copy of *Playboy*. The champagne had brought an unhealthy pink to his cheeks and, while washing his hands, Bognor peered at his reflection in the mirror of the medicine cupboard above the basin. The sight was not unexpected but, as usual, it brought him less satisfaction every time he looked at it. He grimaced, then on an inexplicable whim, opened the medicine cupboard. There was Alka-Seltzer, aspirin, paracetamol, Ambre solaire – all the assorted rubbish that one expects to find in a medicine cupboard, including one small bottle with a chemist's handwritten label on the side. 'Mr E. S. Smith', it said. 'Tablets. One to be taken nightly before retiring.' Bognor picked it off the shelf and unscrewed the top. It was empty. One or two grains were stuck to the sides and bottom but that was all. He replaced the cap and returned it, shutting the door. Then something in his reflection made him open the door again, take out the bottle and put it in his jacket pocket. 'You never know,' he said to himself. 'There might be something in it.'

Back in the kitchen, he thanked Gabrielle effusively, promised to be in touch, promised to see her in Acapulco, promised not to tell a soul the secret of the chocolate omelette, promised to bring Monica to dinner shortly, and finally left. On his way home he went into Mortlake garage, and pushed through a door marked 'staff only'. A group of drivers and conductors were sitting at a table drinking tea.

'Can't you read, mate?' admonished one. ' "Private". If you want the gents' it's outside. Next bus goes in quarter of an hour.'

'It's not that. I wonder if one of you was the conductor on the number nine which brought me here an hour or so ago.' He looked round the table trying to pick out a memorable face. Sullen suspicion looked back at him.

'You'll have to go around to lost property direct,' said one of them, surlily.

'It's not that,' he said, then recognized a conductor. 'Wasn't it you?' he said, pointing.

'Might have been,' said the man in the accent, he guessed, of County Cork. He remembered them now that the man had spoken. 'It's just,' continued Bognor, 'that I wondered if you had noticed the man who got off at the same time as me. Short, dark, wearing a rather square suit.'

'Foreign bloke?' enquired the man.

'That's right.' Bognor took a five pound note from his pocket, screwed it into his hand and said, 'Would you recognize him do you think?'

'I . . . ' He still seemed doubtful but Bognor made as if to put the money back in his pocket and the clippie responded in the way Bognor had hoped. 'I reckon I might if you were to point him out.'

'Good,' said Bognor, handing over the fiver. 'How can I find you if I want to know?'

'You're not police?' asked the man, nervous again, once he'd got the money. 'Not police,' said Bognor. 'No need to worry, and if I do need you, I'll see you're all right. Okay?'

The man was grudging, but the thought of money bettered his worries. The name was Seamus O'Rourke, and he could be found at the garage. He always worked the number nine. Bognor thanked him and took the next one back to the office.

Normally he would have told Parkinson of the strange vanishing trick perpetrated by Petrov, but in view of the frosty terms on which they had parted he decided against it. Instead he sent the bottle over to the lab for analysis and spent the afternoon going through files. There was not much in them that he hadn't already established. Blight-Purley's was full of wartime heroics but tailed off afterwards to become a dribble of alleged meddlesomeness. Nothing in it, however, to suggest dishonesty or anything but unswerving loyalty to Her Majesty and her government. The list of his sexual conquests, though, like his heroics dwindling with the years, was still impressive – not least because of its discretion. Although some *affaires* were spectacular, those which were not with starlets, Resistance heroines or one of his four wives were, to Bognor, previously unknown. They were with women whose moral righteousness was universally accepted and unquestioned. Ebertson's dossier was primarily innuendo. He just happened to have been around in some unlikely places when some odd events were taking place, notably Chile at the time of Allende's demise. Most of his postings had been in Central or Latin America and Eastern Europe. On a personal level he looked absolutely right for the job: impeccably cultivated in an upper middlebrow Ivy League way with a Bostonian wife and four good-looking polyglot children. No known vice, just an unblackmailable liking for life's little luxuries. Petrov had spent much longer in Britain. Before that he had been in Prague, leaving in the winter of 1968 – a significant departure date since it coincided with the removal of the unfortunate Mr Dubček and the

Russian invasion. His was a very thin file. No family. No wife. A suggestion, unsubstantiated, of homosexuality. Vaunted food and drink fetishism considered bogus. Lady Aubergine rated a passing reference but neither Aubrey Pring nor Amanda Bullingdon had an entry. The late Escoffier Savarin Smith, on the other hand, had pages. The principal item was the opening essay by Parkinson's predecessor, Tristram de Lesseps. De Lesseps had known Bruce Lockhart in Russia. He was one of the old school.

This person,

he had written in scratchy, tiny blue-inked hand,

was recruited personally by myself on 12 July 1952. He has recently returned from a spell in the kitchens of the Gritti Palace in Venice where I myself first met him, and it appears that his considerable capacities as a chef will enable him to travel widely in those countries which prize such attributes. In consequence he should be able to advise us informally of developments in the catering industry which could be of benefit to this department. We have always tried to maintain some representation in international hotels at all levels, but since the war the development of electronic listening devices and suchlike has led to a running down of our paid retainers. In my view there can be no substitute for such personal contact since an intelligent and observant hotel servant will not only see what a machine cannot but will also be able to make deductions from those observations. I am therefore hopeful that Mr Smith will be able to advise on the recruitment of such personnel. Finally I trust that he will himself be able to supply us with information on prominent and relevant personalities where required. He is presently to be employed at the Savoy Hotel where, naturally, he will have access to just such information as we will at times require.

De Lesseps went on to list Smith's background (Central European), parentage (small but ambitious hoteliers), and qualities which seemed in essence to be those of the inveterate gossip and anecdotalist. Unfortunately de Lesseps had been prematurely retired soon afterwards and Bognor suspected the army of peeping tom waiters had remained largely unrecruited. A pity.

He dutifully annotated the files, then signed them back in and decided to go home. On the way he stopped at an off licence in Soho where he bought four bottles of rum. Then he went next door to a grocer's where he bought a dozen large brown free-range eggs and a pound of dark Bournville chocolate. Back at the flat he found Monica sprawled on the sofa reading *Country Life*. Her shoes were on the floor and a gin and tonic was on the table beside her. She did not look up.

'Good day?' she asked. Bognor regarded her with tolerant disapproval. Frequently nowadays he wondered why they had never bothered to get married. This surely must be what marriage was like. 'So so.' He went to the fridge and got a tonic, mixed it with a generous gin, and sat down in the armchair with the William Morris pattern. It was beginning to go at the corners. A wife would notice and do something about it but, as Monica reminded him when he drew her attention to such things, she was only a mistress and, as such, free to come and go as she wished. He wished she was a little more inspired in those areas in which a mistress was supposed to excel. She was undoubtedly putting on weight, and she was becoming sloppy. If she were a wife he would tell her to pack in her ludicrous job at the art gallery, which now seemed to have become full time. It was originally supposed to have been mornings only, but she appeared to have drifted into a more time-consuming arrangement. There were occasions when, feeling ruthless, he felt like trading her in for a newer model. On the other hand he had to admit, as he had done when confronted with his reflection at the Dour Dragoon earlier, that he was not an appealing proposition. Like Monica he was not getting any prettier with time. Age had wearied him and the years condemned. In fact he was a bit of a failure. Even the flat and its fading, wearing fittings reflected it. Only the view reflected something of his earlier aspirations. The tops of the trees had that almost luminous lime green of early summer. He went over to the window and peered out at them. 'What's for supper?' he asked, taking a slug of gin.

'Chops,' she said, 'unless you want to go out.'

'Can't afford it.'

'Surely you get expenses on this job. Parkinson must realize you have to go out and try some pretty smart food.'

'Parkinson won't even let me go to Acapulco.'

'What do you mean *even*. I'm not surprised. All I'm suggesting is that he might allow you a decent meal out. Acapulco is another thing altogether.'

'I might be able to get to Acapulco for nothing.' He gazed back at the window. Sometimes life seemed to be against him. Increasingly the two most important people in it, namely Monica and Parkinson, seemed to be ganging up on him 'I've got a surprise pudding.'

'Oh.' She was back in the property pages of the *Country Life*. 'Look at this,' she said, 'Only £120000. Georgian manor house near Bath. It's got an orangery. I've always wanted an orangery.'

'I do wish you'd allow me to surprise you sometimes.'

'How do you mean? Perhaps you should be more surprising. Work at it, I mean.'

'I am. I just said, pudding.'

'Oh. Pudding. Well, go on then. Surprise me.'

'We're going to have one of the amazing Scoff Chocolate Omelettes à la Dour Dragoon.'

'Oh.' For the first time that evening she did seem mildly surprised. 'I didn't realize they were open again. You didn't say we were going out. I've got nothing to wear.'

'We're not going out. I'm making it here. I went round to the Dragoon this morning and Gabrielle gave me the ingredients. More or less. Four different sorts of rum, would you believe?'

'But you don't know what to do with it all.'

'I do more or less. Anyway Anthony Ebertson says it's quite easy to assemble. It's the ingredients which are the problem. We have got oranges haven't we?'

'Yes. But Ebertson can probably cook.'

'There's no need to be rude. You know perfectly well I'm a jolly good cook.'

'Hardly in the Scoff class. What else did you find out from Gabrielle?'

'It's not so much what I found as what I didn't find. She made Dmitri Petrov vanish.'

'She what?' She sat up on the sofa, really interested for the first time. 'What do you mean made him vanish?'

Bognor told her. 'So you see,' he said when he'd finished, 'a genuine piece of old black magic. Something she probably picked up from her old Mauritian mum. Here one minute, gone the next. Pouf! Up in a puff of smoke.'

Monica looked concerned. 'But Simon,' she said, 'shouldn't you have told someone? The police? Parkinson? Someone?'

He shrugged with exasperation. 'It was quite clear he didn't want me to be in on whatever it was he was doing there, and nor did she. He was being extremely furtive. I should think he and Massimo did a bunk out of the back and waited for me to go away. It's not that important.'

'Well, if you say it isn't,' she said. 'What else happened?'

He told her about the bottle from the medicine cupboard.

'Those analysts are going to be fed up with you,' she said. 'The last time wasn't exactly a success.'

'The last time?'

'When you gave them a biscuit tin which you expected to contain the cremated remains of that poodle, and it turned out to be the sweepings from a grate or something. It was probably just aspirin.'

'You don't need a prescription for aspirin,' he said coldly.

'Oh well, anti-hystamine for hay fever. Or librium. Something perfectly ordinary.'

'Nevertheless,' he said and then stopped. 'I'm going to battle with this omelette,' he grumbled. 'You're no bloody fun any more.'

She stuck her tongue out at him, and he stalked off to the kitchen to do battle with his expensive ingredients.

It took him a great deal longer than it took Monica to grill the chops and boil new potatoes and frozen peas. Once the mixture curdled, another time he left the whipped egg whites so that they started to subside again. When he lit some of the rum it flared up and singed his eyebrows but, fully half an hour after the chops had been eaten he marched to the table bearing a chocolate object on a dish, which looked at least passably like the pride of the Dour Dragoon.

'You know,' said Monica as she moved the first mouthful suspiciously round her mouth rather in the manner of the wine tasters at Petheram, 'it's actually not bad. It's not *quite* right, but it's almost there. I take it back. It really is almost a success.'

Bognor tasted his with the same exploratory diffidence. 'More than almost,' he said ruminatively. 'It *is* a success. Maybe *I* should go to Acapulco instead of Gabrielle.'

Their appreciation was shortlived. Second spoonfuls were poised just short of the lips when the telephone rang. 'Oh God!' said Bognor, putting his spoon down. 'Just listen. It's him.' And certainly to the trained ear the phone had the unmistakable, hectoring urgency of an office taskmaster. When he picked up the receiver it was just as obvious that the tidings were bad.

'What?' he exclaimed, going a greyish white. And then, 'Where?' Followed by, 'Are you sure?' And 'Already?' And finally, 'Okay, first thing.' When he replaced the receiver he went straight to the drinks cupboard and poured out two large cognacs. Returning to the table, he pushed his omelette to one side and conceded shakily. 'You were perfectly right. I shouldn't have just accepted it. They've found him. River police fished him out of the water an hour ago just east of Kew Bridge. And we're never going to know what happened because his people want it hushed up. They've claimed the body. It's being flown home tonight. Oh God!'

'Dead?' whispered Monica. 'Not . . . '

Bognor rinsed his palate with the cognac. 'Yes,' he said bitterly. 'Dead. Petrov.'

Chapter Four

He woke next morning with that familiar experience of shifting, in a matter of seconds, from joy at being alive to suspicion that all was not well to, finally, certainty that something was very badly wrong indeed.

'Is today Thursday?' he asked, sitting up and rubbing his eyes.

For answer she threw him the morning's *Times*. It was Thursday. Lunch with Blight-Purley.

'You have a dead Russian to explain,' said Monica, smiling with a touch of waspishness. 'Are you going to tell Parkinson you were with him yesterday?'

'Oh. Petrov.' That, he remembered, was the really bad news. 'I shall have the last of those free-range eggs, lightly boiled, with a couple of slices of toast and some proper coffee. Do we have proper coffee?'

'You know perfectly well we don't have proper coffee. We have Nescafé. All this moving in high gastronomic society is going to your head.'

Bognor made do with the Nescafé and pondered. In the circumstances it would be wiser to say nothing about his encounter with Petrov. It would only complicate matters, and it was hardly his fault that the wretched man had ended up in the river. If he hadn't been so standoffish and anti-social, he would have allowed Bognor to come into the Dour Dragoon at the same time, and he would have remained quite safe. On the other hand it was possible, if that had happened, that there might have been two corpses in the Thames. Bognor frowned. He hadn't thought of that. Indeed

it hadn't occurred to him that this was going to be a dangerous job. All the more reason for not getting over-involved.
He would keep the Petrov meeting under his proverbial hat,
at least until it became necessary to mention it.

He had meant to do some checking on Petrov's fate at the
office as soon as he arrived, but he was forestalled by a
visitor. It was one of the analysts. He seemed cross.

'Look here, Bognor,' he said, pouncing on him the second
he came through the door, 'just what are you playing at? I
would have thought you'd have learnt your lesson with that
bloody poodle!'

Bognor sat down wearily at his desk, extracted a definitely
dirty handkerchief and blew his nose. 'I'm not *playing* at
anything,' he said. 'I sent you a bottle with some grains of
stuff in that I wanted analysed. That's all. I don't want a lot
of heavy backchat. What's in it?'

'You mean you really don't know?'

'I haven't the foggiest. If I had I wouldn't be asking you
would I?'

The analyst sniffed. 'In that case I can only assume
someone is playing a practical joke on you, too.'

'Look,' said Bognor, 'will you stop beating about the bush?
This is turning into a rotten day. I'm very busy, and I sent
that bottle to you in good faith. Now will you kindly tell me
what the hell was in it?'

'Contraceptive pills.'

Bognor buried his face in his hands and counted to ten.
Then he removed it and said: '*Now* who's playing practical
jokes?'

'Certainly not me. They're contraceptive pills – or were.
Rather old-fashioned ones come to that. Much more
oestrogen than's fashionable today.'

'Oh. What does that mean?'

'High oestrogen basically meant more chance of˜blood-
clotting, thrombosis, all that.'

'Is there any reason why anyone should prescribe them
for a man?'

'Is that a serious question?'

'I'm afraid so, yes.'

'No.'

'But if a man were to take contraceptive pills – particularly ones like these, your high oestrogen things?'

The analyst looked both bemused, incredulous and thoughtful. 'He'd feminize,' he said, 'probably become impotent. If he were a drinker it might be worse. Oral contraceptives are detoxified in the liver. It could cause something unpleasant and hepatic.'

'I see,' said Bognor, thinking that perhaps he did indeed see something. 'So if a randy, hard-drinking man were to be fed with a daily dose of high oestrogen contraceptives, the chances are that he'd lose his sexual appetite and ability and develop some nasty liver complication into the bargain?'

'More or less.'

'Super.'

'I'm glad you think so.' The analyst shuffled out, not greatly mollified, leaving Bognor to draw some conclusions. It seemed that the pills were not what had been prescribed. He had better find out what *had* been prescribed. That way he could confirm his theory that there had been some substitution. Would impotence, he wondered, be enough to induce suicide? In the case of a man like Smith, with an outsize and publicly acclaimed libido, the answer was probably yes. So. Smith was prescribed relatively harmless, run-of-the-mill pills and someone removed them and put oral contraceptives in their place.

Who? That downstairs lavatory was obviously used by all the staff, so that Gabrielle, the two Chinese boys, the sinister Massimo and others as yet unknown could have done it. Opportunity was not a serious problem. Motive had to be established. Also the design, if design it was, was sophisticated. It had feminine suggestions. Bognor scribbled on his blotter. 'Scoff murdered by woman.' As he did the buzzer went. 'Come through at once, please,' said Parkinson's voice, gritty with irritation.

'Well?' he enquired abrasively before Bognor was able to sit down.

'Well, what?'

Parkinson ignored the rejoinder. Instead he consulted his

files. 'The police doctor didn't have a chance of more than a quick look. Contusions. Bruising. Enough to knock him out but not to kill him. He drowned. He could have done it on his way into the river depending where he jumped from.'

'Or was pushed from.'

'Quite. Unfortunately it doesn't look as if we'll ever know. I hesitate to ask . . . ' he hesitated, 'but do you have any bright ideas? Or even, God help us, any ideas of any kind at all?'

'Not about Petrov, but I think I have have a lead on Scoff Smith.' Bognor told him about the bottle and the analysis. To his surprise Parkinson took it in his stride. 'Check with his doctor. See what he was giving him. It must have been trivial or the coroner would start asking awkward questions. It might just be a start.' He leant back in his chair and fixed Bognor with one of his looks.

'If someone was feeding him contraceptive pills, then who – ?'

'My guess is Gabrielle,' said Bognor, 'but I admit I have no particular reason for saying that except that she could presumably get her hands on contraceptives and also feed them into Scoff's bottle easily.'

'Two good arguments against that,' said Parkinson. 'The first is that if they were her own pills she'd be pregnant by now. Or at least she'd be taking a risk on it. The second is that she was supposed to be the principal recipient of Scoff's much vaunted sexual favours. She'd hardly kill the goose that, as it were, laid the golden whatsit.'

'I suppose not. Maybe she was bored with Scoff's sexual demands and thought this was a good way out.'

'Do we know if there was a will?'

'No.'

'What I need to know is whether Petrov's death is connected with Scoff's.' Parkinson seemed almost to be talking to himself. Indeed, Bognor reckoned, it was the only explanation for his relatively pleasant mood. He looked up at Bognor. 'I hope it's nothing to do with you,' he said, his voice regaining its aggression. 'You haven't been rumbled, have you? The minute people realize you suspect Scoff's wasn't a straightforward suicide then you might as well give up because you won't discover anything.'

'I don't see how I can have been,' said Bognor. Then, changing the subject, he said, 'What about Petrov? How's it going to be explained?'

'No explanations. No investigations. Nothing. As far as anyone is concerned Mr Petrov has simply gone home to Russia.'

'But why? And how?'

'Nothing to do with me, as you can imagine. Unfortunately other branches of government have rather greater influence than ourselves, and it seems that in these days of détente no one on either side of the iron curtain wants a messy bout of publicity over someone who was so very obviously a Russian agent.'

'Iron curtain,' said Bognor. 'That's a curiously archaic expression.'

'I'm a curiously archaic person,' said Parkinson allowing himself a flicker of a smile. 'But, alas, we're going to have to forget Petrov. The secrets of the dead don't necessarily go to the grave with them, but in this case they've gone to Moscow, courtesy of Aeroflot.'

'Still. One can but probe.'

'Well, just probe gently. We are in what is known as a sensitive area.'

'You don't think the Russians did it themselves?'

'Hardly. There's no immediately apparent reason, and in any case they would presumably have preferred to get him home alive and ask him a few of your probing questions before throwing him in the Moskva.'

'I suppose so.' Bognor stared gloomily. 'So where do we go from here?'

'Where do *you* go from here, you mean. That's your problem. Check out the contraceptives and follow from there. Don't lose sight of the Petrov business. And don't say anything unduly untowards to our friend le Colonel, when you have lunch later on.'

Bognor flinched. 'No.' He got up to go.

'Oh, and Bognor.'

He paused at the door.

'I don't recommend the Mess pâté. Not enough garlic.'

'Oh.' Bognor smiled glacially. 'Is that an order?'

'Merely a suggestion,' said Parkinson. 'Yours is not the only palate in the Board of Trade.'

'I don't recommend the Mess pâté. Not enough garlic.' Blight-Purley glowered over the top of the menu at his guest. 'On the other hand the snails have too much, even for snails. The smoked trout is perfectly adequate.' He broke a roll with his left, blue-veined arthritic hand, but discarded it before transporting it to his mouth.

The Mess, alias the Anglo-French Naval and Military, was on a smaller scale than the more famous London Service clubs like the Rag and the In and Out. As its name suggested, members were men who had served in either the French or British armed forces, but in practice this tended to mean Britons who had fought with the Resistance or, less commonly, veterans of de Gaulle's Free French. At all events British members were clearly Francophiles, and French, Anglophiles. Provided this was so the military qualifications could sometimes be allowed to lapse or at least stretched to accommodate the occasional professor of French. The food was marginally more sophisticated than in other clubs, the décor identical, and the heirlooms incomparably less distinguished – a direct result of the club's recent, post-war foundation.

'More of a meat loaf?' said Bognor, eating a little of his roll.

'I'm sorry.' Blight-Purley was at a loss.

'The pâté. More of a meat loaf than a pâté.' Bognor was anxious not to appear gastronomically illiterate.

'You could say so. Sherry all right?'

'Yes, thank you.'

'After the trout I recommend the Gigot. I know it's what we had at Petheram, but it's even better here. First rate.'

'Okay.'

The waitress was St James's club standard issue, which is to say that she was demure beyond her years, stout, and encased in a black jumper and skirt with a white pinafore and cap. After she'd gone, Blight-Purley said, 'You'll be glad to hear I've had a word with la Veuve, and she'd be delighted to invite you to Acapulco.'

'What?' Bognor coughed on his roll. 'How do you mean?'

'I mean Bitschwiller have invited you to go to the fiesta in Acapulco as their guest.'

'You mean – ?'

'All expenses paid. There'll be a party of us going and la Veuve was most interested when I told her what you were up to. Between you and me she's more than disappointed at the downward turn in champagne sales. She's a wonderful old girl and devoted to us. She's the only woman I've ever known who can recite the *Tale of Peter Rabbit* word for word. She had an English nanny. Remarkable what English nannies have done for champagne sales to the UK over the years.'

The wine list appeared before Bognor could comment on this cryptic observation. Blight-Purley pursed his lips. 'Claret?' he enquired of his guest. Bognor nodded. 'In that case,' said the Colonel, 'we'll have a bottle of the thirty-nine.' He waited for the discreet nod and *sotto voce*, 'Very good sir,' which sounds like a cliché but is nevertheless the trademark of wine waiters throughout clubland, and then, when that worthy was out of earshot said, 'Cantemerle. You know it?'

'Er . . . ' Bognor was not certain whether a pretence at knowledge would be discovered, or whether ignorance would make him seem ridiculous.

'No,' he ventured, tentatively.

Blight-Purley registered nothing whatever. 'Petrov,' he said suddenly. 'Strange that it should happen so soon after Scoff. What do you make of it?'

'Petrov? What about Petrov?'

'Oh, come on,' he said, left hand screwing into the roll again. 'A certain naïveté, even ignorance, over the best fifth-growth claret in existence I might understand. But I don't accept the same over Petrov.'

'All right,' said Bognor, 'but how do *you* know?'

Blight-Purley chuckled. 'Would you believe a little bird?

Probably not. Nevertheless, you must accept that I *do* know, and I'm rather disturbed. I'd also like to help you unravel this particular skein.'

'But,' protested Bognor, as the trout arrived, 'I'm not unravelling any skeins, I'm merely looking at the top end of the market.'

'Quite,' said Blight-Purley helping himself to horseradish. They both began to eat in silence. Bognor gazed around the room speculating half-heartedly on the identities of the other lunchers. They were, of course, all male and all had at least a tinge of that air of spry dereliction which so character-ized his host.

'I gather,' said Blight-Purley, deftly pulling a trout bone from between front teeth, 'that the body's been flown home already.'

Bognor went on eating, mindful of Parkinson's warning. 'I'm sorry,' he said, when he'd finished his mouthful, 'but I'm afraid I'm a much less glamorous investigator than you seem to think.'

The wine waiter returned with a bottle of Château Cantemerle and there followed a ritual showing, uncorking, pouring, swilling around and sniffing and swallowing, until in the end Blight-Purley nodded very slightly and murmured, 'Yes.'

'Look,' he said, leaning across the table, eyes aglint, 'I'm trying to assist after my fashion.'

'I'm very grateful,' said Bognor.

'Don't be so bloody priggish. How much do you know about Scoff?'

'Not a great deal.'

'Did Parkinson tell you about his network?'

'No . . . that is . . . well, no, actually.'

'Chances are, of course, that Parkinson never knew. My impression of Parkinson is that he's not as interested in that sort of thing as he should be.'

Bognor watched the older man with interest. Perhaps he really was trying to help. Perhaps, moreover, he was really in a position to do so. The face was debauched, bordering on senility, and yet there was a considerable residual intelligence lurking under the battered exterior. However, search though he might, he was quite unable to find in it any suggestion of generosity or kindness. It seemed to him to be a face which spoke of malice and self-interest. If so, then what, Bognor wondered, was his motive?

The black and white waitress brought the lamb, together with gratin dauphinois and mange-touts. It was not what Bognor would have expected in the average London club, where the cuisine pandered to the nostalgia of its members by reproducing as nearly as possible the food of the nursery and the boarding school: puddings steamed and cabbage likewise, both to the point of exhaustion. The lamb was pink. When Blight-Purley prodded at it with his fork it oozed blood. He gave a little smirk of pleasure.

'Excellent,' he said, watching the thin trickle of red against the white china. 'Welsh?' he asked, looking up at the waitress.

'I'm sorry, sir?'

'Welsh lamb?'

'I'm sorry, sir, I don't know.'

The old man shrugged and began to eat. 'You'll forgive me if I say that Parkinson's methods and more especially his enthusiasms are not quite what I am used to.'

Bognor chewed reflectively as Blight-Purley swallowed and went on. 'Nothing against him personally, but I'm not at all sure he quite understood the extent of the service that Scoff was able to offer. In consequence I'm inclined to think that perhaps, at times, Scoff was induced to offer those services, how shall we put it . . . elsewhere. Do you follow me?'

'I think so.' Bognor was only half-plussed.

'You see, Scoff had a great many friends in the business. Now let us suppose . . . ' he sawed enthusiastically at his meat. 'Let us suppose that you are a prominent and blame-lessly married politician who is, unknown to the world at large, conducting an illicit liaison with – such men have deplorably little taste for more exotic inamorata – his secretary. It has been known to happen.'

'Quite.' The lamb was indubitably succulent.

72

'Let us further suppose that this paragon wishes to accompany his paramour in what the vernacular describes as "a dirty weekend".'

'Yes.'

'Well. . . .' Blight-Purley carefully laid his knife and fork on his plate and leant across them in the manner of an oral examiner about to pounce. 'Where would you take her? Bearing in mind that the adulterer is a man of comparatively limited imagination.'

'Um.' It was not a problem with which Bognor, blamelessly unmarried, had yet been faced. The time, he reflected, visualizing his inevitable nuptials with Monica, was still to come. 'How about Brighton?' he offered.

'More than likely, but where in Brighton?'

He thought. 'The Excelsior.'

'Very good.' Blight-Purley's reaction was one of a schoolmaster whose recalcitrant pupil has at last satisfied him that he is not quite an imbecile. 'Exactly the reputation for raffish discretion he would want. Illicit passion concealed from prying eyes by the waving fronds of the palm court. And yet,' and here Blight-Purley seemed to assume a more than usually luminous yellow glow, 'he would have reckoned without Fritz Finkelman.'

Bognor's eyes questioned the revelation but he did not speak.

'Finkelman,' continued the Colonel, taking a long draught of the Cantemerle, 'is general manager of the Excelsior and has been for fifteen years. He is an excellent manager. He misses nothing. Every guest is known to him and so is their every movement. *Natürlich*. It is part of his job. He is also, of course, or was, a good friend of *our* late friend Escoffier Savarin Smith. Do you begin to see what I'm driving at?'

'I think so. There was something to that effect in Smith's file at the BOT.'

'I've seen the entry. That was de Lesseps. One of the old school.' A thin nostalgic smile played briefly round Blight-Purley's lips. 'Scoff had a thousand Finkelmans all over Britain. And some in Europe, too, come to that.'

'But Parkinson never took advantage of them?'

'I rather think not. Not enough. Little pieces of information, odds and ends, but not enough to provide Scoff with the stimulus or the lucre that he needed.'

'And so?'

'That's rather for you to find out. I don't *know* anything else for sure but my feelings are that Scoff was playing an extremely dangerous game. The Cantemerle slips down easily, don't you think?'

'Yes. But what sort of game?' Bognor hated riddles. It was deplorable that he had to spend his life dealing in them.

'He believed everyone had his price. Fair enough. That's always been my assumption in life.' Bognor winced inwardly. 'So he decided to operate on that basis. He had more information than Parkinson had any use for, so he decided to flog off the surplus to the highest bidder.'

'Newspapers?'

Blight-Purley regarded his guest with friendly superciliousness. 'Scoff's stories were infinitely more problematical than the average newspaper would stomach. Conceivably your particular acidulous or foolhardy gossip columnist, your Nigel Dempster for instance, might be tempted, but I hardly think his editor would thank him for it. No, seriously, there were two sorts of story Scoff was dealing in. One concerned the back room chaps. Whitehall coves of no interest to the press. The other were the peccadilloes of cabinet ministers and the like. Difficult to substantiate by journalists, and Scoff's contacts liked to appear discreet. If the stories had appeared in the press they could have been traced back. Rather different if they were picked up by our people – or, of course, by, er . . . other people's people.' He wiped his mouth on a napkin and pushed his plate back.

'And what do you think happened then?'

'Once again I think that's for you to discover. My own impression was that Scoff was out of his depth: Ebertson and Petrov, for instance. They may have seemed very affable and agreeable on the surface, but we all know our Brecht.' He sang very softly, '*Und der Haifisch. . . .*'

Bognor, too, finished his lamb. The waitress reappeared. They agreed on Stilton.

'Which brings us to Petrov,' said Blight-Purley.

Bognor still refused to be drawn.

'I still don't know why you're telling me all this. It just doesn't fall within my province. In any case it's all hypothetical.'

'Even if Petrov didn't connive in Scoff's death,' said Blight-Purley, 'I would guess that he was trying to grab some of the pickings.'

'You mean that the network would have survived Scoff's death?'

Blight-Purley raised an eyebrow barely perceptibly. 'I seem to have gained your attention at last,' he muttered. 'Empires tend to outlive their emperors, at least until the heir proves himself inadequate. If there is any suggestion that the new emperor – or empress – is going to be a weak ruler then the vultures approach the corpse with less caution than otherwise.'

'And you think Ebertson would be trying to pick up the pieces as well?'

'That would seem to follow.'

'And you think Ebertson had something to do with killing Petrov?'

Blight-Purley shook his head and waited until he had finished a mouthful of cheese before continuing. 'I didn't say that, and even if I had you rightly point out that this is all conjecture. All I am saying is that Scoff Smith had a certain amount of information which could have been of use or value to a number of people. He led them on while he was alive. He may even have tried playing them off against each other. If you're looking for motives, then I suggest you think of the network as providing one.'

'Thank you.'

Bognor wondered again what Blight-Purley's own motive was. Was he just meddlesome? Or was he working for someone? If so, who?

'How did you manage to engineer an invitation to Acapulco for me?'

'Delphine and I have known each other a long time.'

'Since the war?'

75

'Before the war, but the war cemented our friendship. Mutual antipathy towards the Bosch.'

'I see.'

Blight-Purley shoved back his chair, picked up his stick and began to limp towards the exit. 'I doubt whether you do,' he said. 'But it doesn't terribly matter. You keen on cricket?'

'Quite. Why?'

'Just a thought. There's a match every year. Wine writers and other parasites versus the trade. In a couple of weeks. Might be worth a visit.'

They passed through into the smoking room; worn red leather; signed photographs of De Gaulle, Churchill, Eisenhower and other lesser lights, many in the stiff kepis of the French armed forces. Coffee was on a sideboard. They helped themselves to black and Blight-Purley ordered a brace of club Madeiras while Bognor lit one of his cheap cheroots.

'I hope I've been of some help.'

'Very much, sir.' Bognor judged the 'sir' to be judicious. 'Acapulco should be very instructive. The cricket sounds fun, too. Perhaps you could let me know more about it when the time comes?'

'I was thinking of Smith's network.'

Bognor drew on the cheroot. 'I don't want to seem ungracious,' he said, 'but quite honestly I'm not all that interested in Scoff's network, and I'm perfectly happy to accept the idea of suicide if the coroner's jury has done the same.'

The madeira came and was sipped.

'Then why,' Blight-Purley was at his most patronizing, 'did you call on Gabrielle yesterday morning?'

Bognor suddenly felt a hot flush creeping over him. It had nothing to do with the Madeira.

'Me? At Scoff's? Yesterday morning? No, not me. Definitely not me.'

'Ah. Perhaps there's some mistake.'

They looked at each other. It was quite clear to both of them that there was no mistake.

'Well,' said Blight-Purley eventually, 'we'll leave it like

76

that then. You should be hearing from la Veuve *au sujet d'Acapulco*. Meanwhile I'm always here if I'm needed.'

Madeira and coffee was finished. Blight-Purley escorted him to the front door. 'Don't be under any illusions,' he said, as he made his farewell. 'Scoff Smith laboured under an illusion and look where it got him. It's meat and drink to us, but it isn't to everyone; it may be another man's poison. And it wouldn't do you any harm to raise your profile a little.'

'Thanks,' said Bognor, waving in an unconcerned manner he was far from feeling.

Blight-Purley raised his stick in acknowledgement and stood on the steps of the Mess for a moment, a lobstery, slightly sinister figure with his arthritic limbs and yellowish eyes. Bognor wondered if he was any nicer than he looked.

Instead of returning directly to the office he once more took a bus, this time a thirty-three, though its destination was, again, East Sheen. Discreet enquiries on the phone that morning had elicited the name of Scoff's doctor. The coroner had been difficult at first but had succumbed quickly enough when Bognor had started listing credentials and talking about the national interest. He had thought of risking the doctor by phone as well but decided against it, which was why at three-thirty he was once more walking along the leafy suburban streets of south-west London.

The receptionist in the surgery was adamant. 'You wouldn't even get in if it was an emergency,' she said, blue rinse abristle. 'Dr Burgess is fully booked.'

'This is an emergency.'

She looked Bognor up and down. 'It doesn't look like an emergency, but as I said, it wouldn't make the slightest difference. He still wouldn't see you.'

'Even if I were dying?'

'You're not dying.'

'How do you know?' Bognor recognized that the conversation was ludicrous. He produced his identity card and watched the grudging conversion from scourge of the malingering public to lackey of the all-powerful establishment. 'I'll slip you in after the next patient,' she said, 'but try not to keep him too long. He really is very busy.' Bognor grunted and sat down to read the frayed two-year-old colour magazines which constituted the waiting room's principal reading matter. He was still negotiating the elusive humour of a very old *Punch* when the buzzer buzzed and the blue-haired lady, now almost ingratiating, said, 'Mr Bognor. Doctor will see you now. It's the first door on the left.'

The doctor was middle-aged, crinkle-haired, impatient. He was sitting at his desk scribbling on a medical record, presumably the previous patient's. 'Yes,' he said, not looking up.

Bognor again produced his card. 'I wanted to ask one or two questions about one of your late patients.'

He looked up now, irritated. 'Who are you?'

'Bognor. Board of Trade.' He jabbed at the card with his finger.

'Who let you in?'

'Does that matter?' Bognor was suddenly off-guard. On the wall behind the desk was a framed scroll, illuminated in many colours. It proclaimed that at some ceremony or other in Epernay 'Gilbert Burgess' had been *'élève à la dignité de chevalier de l'ordre des coteaux de Champagne'*. That was an odd coincidence, but as he was considering it he realized that the doctor was continuing to protest, indeed was asking him to leave. He had risen now and was going on about business and patients and interlopers and bureaucracy.

'It's about Scoff Smith,' said Bognor. 'I understand he was a patient of yours.'

'A private patient, yes. But I don't see what business it is of yours.'

Bognor was not greatly interested in the status of Scoff's professional relationship with Dr Burgess. 'Are you going to help me or not?' he asked.

'Mr Smith was a personal friend of mine,' said the doctor 'as well as being a patient. I'm really not at liberty to discuss him. You ought to know that.'

'Even if it helped to establish the cause of death?'

78

'We know the cause of death,' said Burgess. 'He gassed himself, poor fellow.'

'Even if we accept that, we don't know precisely why he did so. That's why I want your help. Were you treating him for depression?'

'I can't answer that.'

'Were you treating him for anything else? Had you prescribed anything?'

'I'm sorry,' said the doctor, 'but if this sort of thing has to be discussed, it will have to be discussed at the inquest, not with any tuppenny-ha'penny Tom, Dick or Harry who comes barging in here from some lickspittle government department.'

Bognor was used to abuse. He merely frowned. 'You see,' he said, 'we know you had prescribed something because we found the bottle. We just want to know what it was.'

'If you found the bottle why do you come round pestering me? It only has to be analysed.'

Bognor was not to be drawn. 'Naturally,' he said. 'I can arrange for an independent analysis to be done. It just seemed simpler to come and ask.' He watched carefully as he made the suggestion. Was it imagination or was there a flicker of apprehension in the doctor's expression?

'Oh, all right,' he said, caving in abruptly. 'I don't understand what all the fuss is about. He had migraine. Nothing new. He'd had it for years. I prescribed codeine. Nothing new in that either.'

'I see,' said Bognor. 'And that's it. You'd never prescribed anything else for him?'

'No.'

'Had he been to see you about depression?'

'I'm sorry, I'd rather not say.'

'But you'll say it in the coroner's court?'

'If necessary, I suppose I might. But it probably won't arise. It's what they call an open and shut case.'

'Perhaps.' Bognor enjoyed the opportunity of appearing mysterious. 'Would you say that it's possible to induce depression by artificial means?'

'Of course. The market is saturated with depressants and

stimulants. Half my colleagues spend their time damping down what they themselves have stoked up or vice versa.'

'But you don't approve.'

'No, frankly, I don't.'

'So even if Scoff had come to you suffering from depression you'd have given him a pep talk rather than pep pills.'

'If you put it like that, yes.'

'But, going back to my earlier question, would you say you can induce depression artificially? A bad enough depression to make you suicidal?'

'Most depression is artificially induced in the sense that it's caused by other people being nasty to you,' said Burgess. 'If you beat your dog the dog will cringe. That's the object of the exercise.'

'And you think something like that was happening to Scoff?'

'That I can't say.'

'Can't or won't?' Bognor tried to stare him down but failed.

'I must ask you to leave now,' said the doctor. 'I've already said far more than I should. Next time would you please phone for an appointment?'

'If I did I wouldn't get one.'

'No.' Burgess pressed the button on his desk. 'Good-bye,' he said.

Bognor left, wondering who had been responsible for making the good doctor a chevalier of the *'ordre des coteaux de Champagne'*. Scoff? It seemed most likely. Was it important? Arguably not, and yet the recurrence of champagne in general and Bitschwiller in particular was beginning to worry him. In such circles perhaps it was inevitable. He bought an evening paper at the news-stand on the corner of the main road but was unable to concentrate properly on the headline, which told of the country's continuing economic woe. Instead he assessed the day's meetings. The doctor had been treating Scoff for migraine but claimed to have pre-scribed nothing else. He had more or less admitted that Scoff had been to him for depression. Yet he had still not prescribed anything. It finally was out of the question that he might have prescribed contraceptive pills. There must have been a substitution by someone else, someone else who bargained on the contraceptives inducing impotence. Also, by depriving Scoff of his migraine tablets, the migraines would have gone untreated. They would have been insupportable. Nasty.

Blight-Purley's allegations about the Scoff network were intriguing, too. If true, they opened up a tantalizing variety of potential motives. Scoff's double-dealing, his auctioning of damaging secrets, could certainly have provoked retaliation. Alternatively, he might have been 'murdered' by someone whose secret he had discovered. He might even have been indulging in a little blackmail on the side. Blackmail, as Bognor had discovered on previous assignments, was sometimes practised by the most outwardly respectable, and Scoff was clearly involved in enough disreputable practices already not to have baulked at blackmail. Or perhaps someone wanted Scoff out of the way so that they could take over the network. It could be an avaricious individual, or it could be one of the international intelligence agencies as exemplified by Ebertson and Petrov. The possibilities were dazzling and mind-boggling. It seemed increasingly likely that Bognor had stumbled on a sort of espionage gang-warfare. That went on, God knew, but he had never previously supposed that it went on in food and drink.

'Food and drink,' he muttered. Perhaps Amanda Bullingdon knew something. She seemed to be a markedly more peripheral figure than any of the others he had encountered, her involvement more detached and commercial, her attachment to comestibles and potables less personal and passionate. He had better have another word with her; perhaps even reveal a little more of his hand. As the bus bumped uncomfortably over the half-repaired bridge at Hammersmith he fell to contemplating Miss Bullingdon. She seemed completely innocent, and yet the most innocent-seeming were frequently the most dangerous – a fictional adage which Bognor had found true in real life, too.

Back at the office, there was a message for him. Bognor always lived in hope that on his return there would be a message which would transform his life completely: a telegram from Littlewoods, announcing a massive football win; a call from the Premium Bond people; even a new posting or transfer. Usually there was nothing, but this time there was a pencilled note saying 'Mr Ebertson rang from the American Embassy. Please call back before six.'

It was five to. He dialled 499 9000 and was soon greeted with a breezy, 'Hi, Simon.'

'Hello,' said Bognor, britishly.

'Simon, I have some good news for you. I called Delphine Bitschwiller this morning, and it turns out she's taking a party of Europeans over to Acapulco for the Feast of the Five Continents. She wants me to come along, and when I told her about you she fairly jumped at the idea. I told her to contact you at the Board of Trade, London. Was that right?'

Bognor's mind raced or came as near to it as that essentially pedestrian organ was able to. The process unfortunately interfered with speech. Two proxy invitations to Acapulco in the space of a few hours seemed a little silly. Who had got in first? Blight-Purley or Ebertson? And why were they and the Veuve so keen for him to go to Mexico? 'Simon, are you there?'

'Yes, I'm here. Tell me did you get the impression that la Veuve knew anything about me?'

'Not a thing till I told her. Oh, except for one thing, she seemed to think she knew some relation of yours. Someone called Bognor who was killed in the raid at Dieppe. That make sense?'

'Yes,' said Bognor, drily, 'that makes sense.'

Chapter Five

The invitation was simple in that deceptive way which only the very grand can achieve: an enormous white card with 'M. Simon Bognor' written on it in copperplate plus the information in black type, heavily embossed, that Madame Bitschwiller requested the company of the said Bognor at dinner at Las Brisas, Acapulco, Mexico on 2nd June. The reply was to be directed to Champagne Bitschwiller, Reims, France. That was all. In a separate envelope came the nuts and bolts: a ticket to Charles de Gaulle airport, Roissy, where the Bitschwiller chartered Boeing would be waiting for the English party to join it; an itinerary; brochures, postcards; a history of Bitschwiller; and so on. Bognor sucked his teeth and flicked at the corner of the invitation with his fingertips. Why should la Veuve ask him to dine in Acapulco? Was the British Board of Trade really so prestigious an organization that Maison Bitschwiller should give him an expenses-paid holiday in Acapulco? It was most mysterious. And if the prospect had not been so mouth-watering, it would have seemed more than a little sinister. Parkinson, when confronted with the invitation, was as angry as before but finally succumbed.

'One proviso,' he had said. 'If there are no results I dock your holiday double.'

'How do you mean?'

'You're to spend five days in this ghetto of the international jet set?'

'Yes.'

'If it's a success, then well and good. If it's a failure you lose ten days' holiday.'

'Ten?'

'That's what I said. And now before you go larking off there, for Christ's sake get off your arse and get down to some logical thinking. I want to know why Scoff Smith was killed, but . . . '

'I know,' said Bognor wearily. 'You want me to keep a lower profile than ever because no one must suspect that we suspect.'

'Something like that,' he said. 'Don't let them think you're any cleverer than you look.'

For a day he made lists and diagrams, his usual substitute for logic. What he wrote down and what he drew was no more logical than what he thought, but it looked more logical and it made him feel better.

Scoff Smith was a small-time spymaster with a network of restaurateurs and hoteliers who reported on their clients and guests.

he wrote. That was supposition, first suggested by the report in the files and amplified by Blight-Purley. He could not prove it. When he'd asked Parkinson what sort of information Scoff supplied, he had said that it was fairly small beans, and that most of it was gleaned from Scoff's own restaurant or from his travels and attendance at international meals like that in Acapulco. He was dismissive about the idea of any network and told Bognor not to be melodramatic. Nevertheless the idea made a certain sense, and he could think of no more plausible starting point. He continued to write.

Scoff gave/sold information to Parkinson and, possibly to other British government agencies. He also gave/sold it to Ebertson and Petrov as well as others as yet unknown.

So far so good. He threw the pencil on to his blotter and paced.

'Scoff committed suicide, but was pressured into it artificially with high oestrogen contraceptives. He wasn't a natural depressive but he got migraines. The contraceptives didn't do the migraines any good and they destroyed his

84

sex-drive as well as messing up his liver. Hardly surprising he knocked himself off.'

He was talking to himself now, walking slowly up and down the room, frowning, hands sunk deep in the pockets of his tweed jacket, the brown one with the leather patches on the elbows. 'Anyone who worked at the Dragoon could have done it but obviously only the women would have had the pills. On the other hand if this was a high-powered international espionage job the pills could have come from anywhere. They would have been tools of the trade; part of the kit. Okay. So anyone working for a half competent organization could have got hold of them.' He had wanted Gabrielle to become the principal suspect, but he was beginning to realize that there was no reason why she should be. She might be the only person at the Dragoon who would know that the network existed, which meant that she was the only person who could have done it on her own initiative. That didn't rule out the chance of any one of the other people on the staff being cogs in some enemy wheel. 'Oh, shit,' he said, returning to his desk and picking up the pencil once more. Someone had once said that his deductive processes were slightly slower than Dr Watson's while another critic had opined, in a semi-official complaint, that he was 'an amiable twit' whose 'efforts at sleuthing are always good for a laugh'. At times like this he was compelled to acknowledge the germs of truth in these assessments. All the same he could not, for the life of him, see what Holmes or Bond would have done in similar circumstances. His life was not characterized by the cast-iron simplicities which so marked theirs. His was full of confusion and bafflement. Recognizing this he turned to his usual remedy. He made a list.

'Opportunity,' he wrote. 'Entire staff of Dour Dragoon.' That took care of that. Or did it? Regular guests and friends who wandered backstage to congratulate the chef or inspect the kitchen might contrive an opportunity. If so that would widen it to include, say, Aubrey, Blight-Purley, Ebertson, probably not Petrov who was not on terms of intimacy, Aubergine Bristol, perhaps Amanda Bullingdon, though he had the impression that whereas Lady Aubergine's fleeting affair had passed into friendship, Amanda Bullingdon's had ended in a certain coldness. 'Oh, shit!' he said again, recognizing the futility of his listmaking. The more he thought about murder the longer the list became until he convinced himself that both motive and opportunity were universally available. But then there was Petrov. 'Petrov,' he wrote firmly in block capitals, stabbing at the paper in frustration and fury.

He had been with Petrov that morning. He had seemed shifty. He had gained admittance to the Dragoon, as far as he could see on the authority of Massimo, the head waiter. Bognor had himself managed to get in, what, five minutes afterwards? By which time the Russian had disappeared and no one would admit to having seen him. Then the wretched man turns up in the Thames and is spirited back to his country of origin with scarcely as much as a 'by-your-leave'. Bognor sighed. Under normal circumstances the matter might have been easily solved by asking the question direct, if necessary in court or at least in a police station. Political sophistries made this impossible. Even the indirect question was difficult. He was hamstrung. First he was asked to discover the 'murderer' of a man who was universally accepted as a suicide. Second he was charged with finding the assassin of a person the existence of whose very corpse was now a matter of conjecture. 'Habeas Corpus,' muttered Bognor. 'What bloody Corpus?'

His frustration continued for several days. It would be untrue to say that during that time the Smith–Petrov affair was relegated to the pending file, but it would be quite as false to suggest there there was anything approaching a development. Bognor returned to the Dragoon but learnt little more from Gabrielle than how to make a mayonnaise with thirty-two egg yolks. He attended a number of wine tastings and visited Smithfield and Billingsgate where the sight of so much meat and fish in the raw provoked a sudden and uncharacteristic attack of vegetarianism. He discovered that waiters and managers were generally contemptuous of their public (far more so than most entertainers), and that fifty per cent of a chef's wage came in a variety of cleverly contrived percentages designed to maximize profits. He assessed the export potential of Mendip snails, the plausibility of reintroducing the lamprey to the waters of the Severn, and the chances of marketing some essentially British comestible to rival the hamburger, now that the Icelanders had interfered with the price and availability of cod while the weather had interfered with the price and availability of the potato. As a disguise of his real intentions his behaviour was masterly, but it had the disadvantage of masking those intentions even from himself. He became, in a word, immersed. His weight increased; his complexion worsened; but he had no further inkling of what had caused the deaths of Scoff Smith and Dmitri Petrov until one morning when fate intervened once more in the person of Colonel Erskine Blight-Purley.

'Got your flannels creased for tomorrow?' enquired the Colonel grimacing at him over a glass of Eitelsbacher Karthäuserhofberg Kronenberg Kabinett in a cellar somewhere off Pall Mall.

'I'm sorry,' Bognor sniffed and swirled in what had now become a passable imitation of genuine winemanship.

'Cricket,' said Blight-Purley. 'I've marked you down as number seven. You never said whether you bowled.'

'I don't play cricket,' said Bognor. 'At least I haven't played since school.'

'Oh well, never mind. Number seven doesn't have to produce anything unduly remarkable.'

'I'm still not quite with you.'

'I told you.' Blight-Purley quaffed, well satisfied with the contents of his glass. 'Wine buffs and bibbers against winegrowers, shippers and so on. Pendennis and I are non-playing captains. We play alternately in town and country. Honourable Artillery Company ground in London and Petheram village pitch in the country. Petheram again this year, and I just hope Freddie Pendennis doesn't try to inflict his Petheram Rouge on us at lunch. He's got more chance of taking wickets with that than the ball, but still. I can give you a lift if you'd like. My flat. About nine.'

Bognor was beyond speech. At that moment Aubrey Pring joined them. 'This Graacher Himmelreich is most interesting,' he said. 'Just that balance of mellow fruitfulness and flint which you get from really decent Krautwein. Don't you agree, Purley?'

Blight-Purley's eyes yellowed. He was, Bognor sensed, a man who was unduly sensitive about the double barrel to his name. 'I was just briefing young Bognor about tomorrow,' he said. 'We rely on your inimitable leg tweakers, as usual, Pring.'

'Of course,' said Aubrey. 'I'm delighted you can play, Simon. I don't remember you playing at Oxford.'

'No.'

'Did you perform for the Erratics?'

'Actually, no.'

'Oh. You bat? Or bowl?'

'Neither.'

'I've put him down at seven,' said Blight-Purley, 'and I've no doubt he'll turn an arm over in extremis.'

'That shouldn't be necessary.' Aubrey reached across and picked up the bottle of Moselle to replenish their glasses. 'We've got Basil Luton playing for us this year remember. He's distinctly quick. Played a couple of games for Dorset last year. He has that extraordinary ability to make the ball fizz in the air. It sounds like a doodle bug. Petrifying.'

'Especially after lunch.'

'Quite.'

Conversation turned away from cricket and Bognor turned away from them. He found himself staring into the faintly lopsided eyes of Amanda Bullingdon.

'You look rather green,' she said. 'Is all this food and drink getting you down?'

'It's not that. That bastard Blight-Purley's trying to get me into cricket gear tomorrow.'

'Better than trying to get you into bed.'

'Has he been giving you trouble?'

She shrugged. 'Nothing I can't manage, but he has been trying. Ghastly old goat. His breath is disastrous. I hope you *are* playing.'

'I don't seem to have been given much choice.'

'You can always say "no". That's what I do.'

'It's hardly the same.'

'Maybe not. By the way. . . .'

'Yes.' The girl was suddenly conspiratorial.

She led him away from the throng of drinkers: 'What's happened to Petrov? I rang his office to get him to this "do", and they said he'd gone home. Has he? It was very sudden. Nobody seems to know anything, or if they do they're not saying.'

Bognor was not going to take any additional risks. 'I hadn't heard, but if they say he's gone home suddenly then home, I imagine, he has gone.'

The girl seemed concerned. 'He was an awfully vulnerable sort of person,' she said. 'I always felt sorry for him. He didn't quite fit, and he seemed to be under pressure. Much more recently, too. I remember when I was with Scoff he was always trying to curry favour with him but in a way which was . . . oh, I don't know . . . odd. And the last time I saw him he said something very peculiar.'

Bognor was still concentrating on the awful ordeal ahead of him on the cricket field at Petheram. 'Said something peculiar?'

'Yes. He said: "I think if the devil doesn't exist, but man has created him, he has created him in his own image and likeness." '

'That sounds like a quote,' said Bognor.

'That's what I thought,' she said, nodding eagerly, 'so I asked him. He said it was from Dostoevsky – the *Brothers Karamazov*. He'd been reading it. He said Dostoevsky could afford to be optimistic because he'd never had to endure life under a communist dictatorship.'

'I thought Dostoevsky was a pessimist.'

'I think he was being ironic.' She grinned teasingly.

'Very Russian,' said Bognor, put out. 'But what does it mean?'

'I'm not really sure,' she said, 'except that someone was getting him down.'

'Some*one* or some*thing*?'

'I think some*one*,' she said. 'But that's an impression more than anything else.' Bognor filed the impression at the back of his mind. Someone had been getting at Petrov. He guessed it was his masters in Moscow, exerting pressure.

'I wish Blight-Purley hadn't put me down for his bloody cricket,' he said, fingering his ever expanding paunch.

She frowned at him. 'You haven't been listening to a word I've said,' she complained. 'I shall enjoy watching your attempts.'

'Are you going to be there?'

She looked superior. 'Every year,' she said, 'I help Gabrielle with the catering, which I admit can be a little fraught. Scoff used to keep wicket. He was surprisingly good.'

The cricket provoked a grumbling row that evening at the flat. Monica was compelled to sort through cupboards, ring a couple of ex-boyfriends and generally put herself out in an attempt to provide her lover with appropriate kit for the match. Not until eleven was this accumulated: a very tight pair of cream trousers with grass-stained knees, very off-white pads which barely covered the grass-stains, a very old Viyella shirt; a similarly antique padded protector for his genitals (liable to be struck unexpectedly by the ridiculously hard leather ball), and a lurid, purple and green striped cap which Bognor feared signified some distinction he did not, in fact enjoy.

'Happy now?' asked Monica, surveying the clothing, laid out on the bed.

'Not in the least,' he said. 'I am going to be humiliated. I know it.'

She began to pack the clothing into a canvas Gladstone bag-style suitcase which had belonged to her father and had old P and O labels to prove it. 'I've half a mind to come,' she said. 'The idea of witnessing your ritual humiliation is rather appealing.'

He swore at her, half humorously, but in the end – which was nine o'clock the following morning – he arrived at Blight-Purley's flat alone. He found Aubrey Pring and Aubergine Bristol already ensconced in the drawing room drinking black coffee and Fernet Branca. Both had long canvas cases not unlike Bognor's.

'*You're* not playing surely?' he asked Aubergine when they had all exchanged bleary greetings.

'She's a very useful middle-order bat,' said Pring, stiffly, 'and a considerable first-change bowler.'

'Not to mention her ability as a slip fielder,' added Blight-Purley, who was wearing flannel trousers with a blazer of many colours. It was too early in the morning for such a jacket but Bognor forbore to say so. Instead he exclaimed, 'Goodness. I remember a girlfriend of mine who once bowled the Master of Balliol for nothing, but I thought she was an exception.'

'I'm not much good really,' said Miss Bristol with the typical mock modesty of her class, 'but I do rather enjoy it, and men get frightfully cross playing against a bird.'

'I can imagine,' said Bognor, declining the offer of coffee and Fernet Branca.

'Drink up,' said the Colonel to the others, 'we must be on the road. Play begins at eleven.'

The drive was deplorable. Blight-Purley's car was an old grey Jaguar, and he drove it in a remarkably eccentric way, appearing to dawdle whenever the road was fast and open, and speed up at corners. He would sit for hours behind such slow-moving vehicles as tractors and milk-floats when it was clear that overtaking was quite safe, and then just as his visibility was obscured by a hill or a bend he would pull out, jerking the car into a higher gear and career past, pulling in sometimes with only a coat of paint to spare.

In these circumstances Bognor failed to properly appreciate the glories of an early English summer and conversation faltered. When they finally arrived at the ground all three passengers needed calming down, though Blight-Purley, presumably accustomed to the dangers of his own driving, was quite relaxed.

The Petheram ground was all that a village cricket ground should be – or almost all. True it was not actually on the green, being situated just outside the village away from any

91

houses. Nor was there an adjacent public house with ale-quaffing yokels seated on benches outside. On the other hand, it was bordered on two sides by fine oaks and elms and on a third by a low hedge which prevented a herd of Ayrshires from encroaching on to the playing area. The fourth boundary was formed by a gentle slope surmounted by a plateau on which stood two practice nets and a white pavilion with thatched roof and a balcony. On the other side today was a marquee adorned with bunting. At either end of the ground were white sightscreens on wheels and in the middle two men were pushing a heavy roller up and down the narrow closely mown strip of green which was the wicket. The stumps, shiny light yellow-brown, were already in place at either end. Bognor experienced a feeling he had not had since school – an extreme form of nervousness which made him feel physically sick. Already there was a small crowd gathered between the tent and the pavilion. The majority had glasses in their hands and whereas under normal village cricket circumstances those glasses would have contained lukewarm mud brown beer with scarcely any fizz, today's were full of clear light golden sparkling wine which Bognor adduced, correctly as it turned out, to be non-vintage Bitschwiller.

The four of them advanced on the drink which was inside the tent. They drank silently and thirstily with none of that pretence of tasting and savouring and assessing which usually characterized their drinking. Bognor noticed that some of the men were already changed into their whites. One or two looked distressingly lithe and young, and the blazers, multi-striped like Blight-Purley's, suggested a level of achievement way above Bognor's. Freddie Pendennis hailed Blight-Purley from across the tent.

'Didn't see you arrive,' he shouted. 'Hadn't we better toss?'

Blight-Purley delved in his trouser pocket and produced a shiny silver coin. 'Lucky Churchill crown,' he muttered, walking slowly to the exit with Aubrey Pring.

'You look jolly apprehensive,' said Aubergine, accepting a second glass with alacrity. 'I'm glad that you're entering into the spirit of the thing.'

'The thing?' Bognor was wondering where they would put him to field. You could get killed fielding. Once, many years ago, he had been standing at square leg when a batsman had swept the ball towards his head, and raising his arm in self defence rather than any attempt to make the catch, he had been struck on the elbow. The ball had bounced off him and over the boundary for six. His housemaster had counted it a dropped catch. He winced at the memory.

'Well,' Aubergine Bristol was saying, 'the food and drink business. I call playing cricket with us very much beyond the call of duty.'

'I suppose so. Goodness, isn't that Ebertson?' He pointed in the direction of a willowy figure in beautifully starched and creased whites. The effect was marginally spoilt by the cap he was wearing which was more appropriate to baseball than cricket.

'Yes,' she said. 'He played last year. He was rather fun. Terrible cross-bat shots all the time and a tendency to shout whenever he hit anything. Also he went shooting off into the covers after the first ball but we soon cured him of that. Otherwise he was fine.'

They had a third glass, and then Pring came bustling in looking officious. 'You chaps had better get your togs on,' he said to them. 'Blight-Purley's lucky crown let him down as usual and Pendennis is batting first. We start in ten minutes.'

'Blast,' said Aubergine, 'I have to go and change in the car. I can't think why in this day and age, but the changing rooms are a bit primitive. No privacy.' She gulped down her drink and went off.

Bognor, too, shuffled off to the pavilion.

'Anywhere you want to field in particular?'

'No.'

'Mid-on suit you?'

'I suppose so.'

'Then you can drop back to third man at the other end.'

'Right you are.' Bognor felt sick again. He controlled the urge.

'They're playing ffrench-Thomas again, I'm afraid.'

'Not Hugh ffrench-Thomas?'

'Alas, yes,' Pring frowned. 'We had him leg before for five last year. One of the benefits of Blight-Purley's umpiring. But the year before he made ninety.'

ffrench-Thomas had been at Oxford the same year and gone on to play for Surrey. He had had an England trial, but his attitude was thought too dilettante and that was as far as he had got.

'What does he do now?' asked Bognor, hovering nervously at the pavilion door.

'I thought you'd know. He's the Bitschwiller rep.'

'*Guide Bitschwiller* or the champagne?'

'The champagne. The *Guide*'s man is one of those absurd closely guarded secrets. No one knows who he is.'

Even in his nervous and slightly intoxicated state the information seemed important. However, time was pressing. He hurried inside the building, becoming aware as he did of a strong odour of stale sweat and blanco. All around was cricketing detritus – discarded pads and boxes, old bails and underpants, bats and balls. On the walls there were fading sepia photographs of cricketers in boaters and heavy curling moustaches, some of them solo action shots, others posed team photos with, in the approved Edwardian manner, at least one player sprawled full length on the ground. Two men clad only in jock-straps were arguing about the rival merits of the Australian and West Indian fast bowlers. They nodded to him perfunctorily and continued their discussion while he changed. The trousers were so tight that he couldn't do them up round the waist. Despairing, he threaded his tie through the loops and knotted it in a hamfisted granny at the front, then tucked the shirt in at the back and hoped, forlornly, that he did not look as ludicrous as he felt.

On the grass outside, he found the other ten members of his side grouped in a semi-circle round Aubrey Pring who was wielding a cricket bat. 'Come along, Simon,' he called. 'Quick spot of fielding practice just to limber up. Here, catch!' and so saying he lofted the ball gently in Bognor's direction. Mercifully, he caught it, though clumsily, and threw it back underarm. His hands stung.

The game got off to a quiet start, so quiet that it was easy for him to forget that he was a participant. He had always enjoyed cricket as a spectacle. It looked pretty, and the languid unfussy movements of the players, the polite unvocal applause, the regular and inimitable sound of willow bat on leather ball, always had the effect of making him sleepy in an oddly patriotic way. The 'Enigma Variations' had the same effect. The champagne helped, so that after the first few overs he abandoned the half-remembered habit of walking a few steps towards the batsman as the bowler ran in, and sank further back on his heels. Basil Luton was bowling from one end and a fair-haired youth from one of the consumer organizations at the other. Runs accumulated. Twice the ball was prodded in Bognor's direction, and on both occasions it was moving so slowly that he had no problem in stopping it. Suddenly one of the batsmen had an uncharacteristically violent heave at a straight ball from Luton and was struck on the foot. Immediately half a dozen men appealed for leg before wicket – Bognor joining in rather tardily when he realized what had happened. Blight-Purley was umpiring at the right end (umpiring by honorary captains was a quirk peculiar to this fixture) and his finger was raised immediately and unequivocally to signify the batsman's dismissal. Twenty-two for one.

The next man in turned out to be ffrench-Thomas. He seemed much as Bognor remembered him except that his complexion was a touch higher, and there was more of his forehead. To Bognor's horror he advanced down the wicket to the first ball he received and crashed it two yards to Bognor's right. Even if he had been wide awake he would hardly have seen it, much less stopped it, but even so Bognor's complete lack of reaction was indicative of his somnolence. The bad impression was not helped by his flatfooted run to the hedge, where he had to crawl on all fours before retrieving it, and then by his throwing it ineffectually and underarm so that the wicket-keeper had to run halfway to him to pick it up. By the time he had jogged back to his position he was red faced, and only partly due to

95

his exertions. ffrench-Thomas' next stroke was still more dramatic. Charging the bowler once again he thrashed the ball straight back down the pitch. It was an immaculate drive, perfectly timed, and the ball rocketed through the air at a little below head height. It easily missed the bowler whose follow through took him slightly to the left, but Blight-Purley, standing in his umpiring position immediately behind the far stumps, was forced to take evasive action. It was not dignified nor conventional but it was swift and effective. He simply collapsed in a heap, knocking over the wicket as he did. The ball continued on its way for four runs and Pendennis, umpiring at square leg, together with two or three other players and a noisily solicitous ffrench-Thomas, converged on the fallen Colonel. Bognor watched. There was no harm done. The stricken man was raised to his feet and dusted down. He was asked if he would like to leave the field. He preferred not. The game continued; the remaining balls of the over were bowled and everyone changed over for Aubrey Pring to begin with his 'leg-tweakers'.

The incident had unsettled Bognor. Had the ball hit Blight-Purley it would have, at the very least, knocked him cold. He wondered if he himself could have ducked quite so nimbly, and rather feared not. He also wondered whether ffrench-Thomas had known what he was doing. A batsman so skilled and experienced would have no difficulty in placing the ball where he wanted. It was reasonable to infer that he had *aimed* his blow in the general direction of Blight-Purley's head. Reasonable, though no more. Certainly he had given every impression of concern and remorse. And yet. . . .

Bognor settled down to watch Pring's leg-tweakers. They were not very good. Whether or not the ball actually tweaked he was unable to see from his fielding position, but it was plain that the genial parabola described by the ball before it hit the ground could under no circumstances be called menacing. The batsman had ample opportunity to think about how to deal with each one. Nevertheless ffrench-Thomas treated the first three deliveries with quite exaggerated respect smothering each one with his bat, so that it rolled only a few yards away, yielding no score. It was precisely the sort of play which gave cricket its bad name, especially with foreigners. By the fourth, though, the batsman had plainly had enough. He took two casual paces down the wicket, dropped gently on one knee and hit the ball with deceptive pace towards square leg. In the previous over Blight-Purley had been at the far end of the wicket. Now, of course, he had become square leg umpire, and, improbable though it may seem, the ball was once more travelling straight at him. Again, the evasive action was extraordinarily prompt for one so apparently aged and infirm. The ball screamed several feet over the prostrated Colonel and crossed the boundary at the second bounce while, for a second time, players converged on the victim. This time Blight-Purley's anger was plain. He was not in the least frightened, but he was purple with rage. Replacing his panama hat with its gaudy orange and scarlet ribbon, he repudiated ffrench-Thomas' attempts at apology with a terse 'Typical Teddy Hall behaviour!' (A reference to the Bitschwiller man's former college.) Then, resuming his umpiring stance, he waved well-wishers away with his stick and settled down to adjudicate. The players and Pendennis were slow to get back to their places, but eventually did so, and play resumed. ffrench-Thomas dealt perfunctorily with Pring's two remaining leg-tweakers and the game settled back into its lethargic pattern. So it continued until ten minutes later when one of Pring's tweakers failed to tweak. Instead, it continued in an absolutely undeviating line several feet wide of the leg stump. ffrench-Thomas, mildly surprised by the extra innocuousness, flailed in vain and was hit just above the knee. Pring optimistically pivoted on his heel and shouted, both arms high above his head, 'How was that?' The Colonel did not hesitate. It was perfectly clear to all those present that, under the rules of cricket, ffrench-Thomas was still very much in. Yet Blight-Purley's finger was once more raised to the skies in the unmistakable gesture of dismissal. For an instant the batsman and his opponents stared disbelievingly at the judicial finger and then, with manifest irritation and cynicism, ffrench-Thomas put his bat under

97

his arm, began to undo his gloves and marched back to the pavilion, head in air, mouth set in petulant stiff-lippishness.

'That was never out,' said Bognor to Aubergine Bristol who was fielding nearest to him at first slip.

'Nothing like,' she agreed, hitching up her skirt, 'but you wait till Pendennis has a go. He's just as partisan.'

'Really?'

'Like our next batsman.'

Bognor peered at the swarthy individual now waddling myopically wicketwards from the pavilion. 'Who he?' he enquired.

'Luigi Dotto. The chef from the Grand at Dynmouth.' She executed a couple of brisk bowling movements and clutched at her shoulder. Bognor watched the undulations of her breasts. 'Hence partisan,' she continued. 'He was an anti-Mussolini chap. Aubrey made up a rhyme about him once during the team photos:

> *"There once was an Italian partisan*
> *Who lived on a diet of parmesan*
> *When asked to say 'cheese',*
> *He replied: 'If you please,*
> *I'd really much rather have parma ham!'"* '

Bognor smiled. 'I see,' he said. 'Was he a friend of Scoff's?'

'Very much so.'

Bognor returned to third man. Dotto swung cross-batted at the first ball which found an outside edge and ran slowly to where he stood. He saw it in time, managed to stop it and put in a passable throw. Someone on the boundary clapped. He felt enthused and fell to attempting a similar limerick about the Italian chef who soon began to plunder the bowling in an entirely foreign, not to say Latin fashion. Within another twenty runs and two more safe, though unexciting pieces of fielding he had come up with:

> *'A genial Italian named Dotto*
> *Cried out in a* voce *quite* sotto
> *"Beware of my hook*
> *Which is worse than I look*
> *And more deadly by far when I'm blotto."* '

'That's all very well,' said Aubergine, whirling her arms again, 'except that his hook is his worst shot, and he doesn't drink.'

'What, not at all?'

'No. Never. That's what makes him such a dangerous customer.'

Their conversation was interrupted at this point by Aubrey Pring who chucked the ball in Aubergine's direction and called out, 'You have a go, Ginny.'

Bognor retreated once more. The score had reached sixty-one for two, but Aubergine proved more effective than her boyfriend. She had Dotto caught at the wicket; bowled the new man second ball with one that cut back off the seam; and within a couple more overs took a neat caught and bowled. At the other end the score rattled along more easily, but as the wickets fell so the quality of batsmanship diminished. The middle-order batsmen gave evidence, by girth and complexion, of their calling, but nevertheless the score had advanced to one hundred and twenty-seven for seven wickets when lunch was taken at one o'clock.

The meal, which, unlike the forty minutes allowed for lunch at first-class matches, was spread over an hour and a half, was every bit as lucullan as the circumstances would suggest.

It is traditional to maintain that tables and sideboards labouring under the weight of large quantitites of food 'groan', but the word was altogether too gloomy to convey any emanation from the tables in the Petheram marquee that lunchtime. Naturally there were the roseate lobsters and soft fruit, crisp green lettuces and cucumbers, golden fowl and pinkish brown pâtés which Bognor associated with the traditional buffets, but Gabrielle and her team had produced them only as a concession to the more conservative palates. Not for them the Gâteaux Berichonnes, the eel galantines, the quiches of crab, the tortes of chocolate, the glazed salmon á la Russe with its garnish of truffles and fresh tarragon leaves, the Queen Mab's pudding with its cacophony of candied peel and ginger and currants and bitter almonds, the guinea fowl in tangerine and turmeric, the pistachio-coloured

Sauce verte, the Oeufs saumonées en croûte, the claret jellies and the snowy textured Sorbet à la fine champagne.

Bognor remembered the team teas of his school days: thin sandwiches filled with spread and currant buns. He blinked and turned to his neighbour, Anthony Ebertson, and exclaimed quite simply, 'I say!'

'They put on a good show, wouldn't you say?' agreed the American who had spent a quiet morning patrolling the far boundary. 'I always used to think it was something only Scoff could do, but it does look as if Gabrielle has assumed the mantle with some success.'

Bognor salivated, all thought of the game and the batting to come quite forgotten.

'But where to begin?' he murmured.

'Try the Oeufs saumonées,' said a voice at his elbow. He turned, looking rather blank to find the lop eyes of Amanda Bullingdon staring at his admittedly eccentric attire. 'It's a sort of smoked salmon and scrambled egg mixture stuffed into a crust. Delicious.'

'Did you make it?'

'Sort of. But it just means scrambling a whole lot of eggs and chopping smoked salmon into bits.'

'And stuffing them into crusts?' He smiled facetiously.

'Exactly,' she smiled back, but amused, he was sorry to see, *at* him rather than *by* him. Still, the amusement was not unfriendly. They walked over to the Oeufs saumonées, already much depleted, and both helped themselves. They were difficult to eat elegantly. Bognor avoided egg on his face but got crumbs on his chin, the result of trying to force too much into his mouth at the first attempt. Greed, he conceded to himself, ruefully. Amanda managed hers more elegantly, like a cat.

'That man, ffrench-Thomas,' she said, as they removed themselves to a relatively secluded corner of the tent, while Bognor tried, through a mask of food, to say '*Fright*fully good'. 'That man ffrench-Thomas,' she said, 'was trying to hit Blight-Purley. Terribly dangerous. It could have killed him.'

'Oh, surely it was a mistake,' said Bognor, wanting to

believe himself at all costs. 'Just one of those things. Though you're perfectly right he could have been very badly hurt. Old man like him.'

'Still pretty quick on his feet though.' It was, inevitably, Blight-Purley himself who had shuffled into their orbit without their noticing. 'I'm glad you both agree. That was deliberate all right.'

'Oh, come on,' said Bognor, wondering whether to go and grab another salmon and scrambled egg concoction or try Crab quiche or Gâteau Berichonne. 'Why?'

Blight-Purley put his glass down on a side table and tried to fork up a helping of eel galantine. 'Who knows?' he said quizzically. 'It would hardly be company policy. Delphine and I know each other too well for that, but I promise you ffrench-Thomas is too good a cricketer to do that by mistake.'

'I'm going to get some pie,' said Bognor. 'Would you like some?' He wandered away to find food for two and almost knocked over Gabrielle, locked in apparently antipathetic discussion with Luigi Dotto, the chef from Dynmouth.

Bognor congratulated her enthusiastically on the food. She introduced him to Dotto. 'I have heard of your investigations,' said the chef, without enthusiasm. 'I am delighted to meet you.'

'Me, too,' said Bognor, continuing to the buffet. Returning a few minutes later he noticed that the conversation was still in progress. The pair had been joined by ffrench-Thomas. It seemed to Bognor that the two men were trying to persuade Gabrielle of something. Their attack gave every evidence of being concerted. He frowned.

'Dotto and your would-be assassin seem to be having a bit of a go at Gabrielle,' he said, addressing Blight-Purley but handing over a plate laden with goodies to Amanda Bullingdon, who regarded the abundance with disbelief.

'Assassin's putting it a bit strong,' said the Colonel. 'Warning me off more like. The idea of his being in cahoots with Dotto strikes me as eccentric.' He speared a segment of eel and frowned.

As lunch progressed Bognor began to feel more and more euphoric. He circulated widely, eating and drinking as he went, renewing old acquaintances and making new ones. He seemed to speak to almost everyone there, even greeting Massimo, the sinister waiter from the Dour Dragoon, with an effusiveness which he would not normally have vouchsafed. Massimo was disconcerted by this – had in fact been on the point of ignoring him – and was hard pressed to smile wanly and accept the proffered hand. Ebertson was urbane, Pring polite in his silence over fielding lapses, Gabrielle seemingly edgy, but he put this down to the tensions involved in catering for so large and discerning a party. Dotto was ebulliently tactile, ffrench-Thomas suavely reticent. As they returned to the field after the repast, he was compelled to loosen the tie at his waist. He was drunk enough to be able to kid himself that it was this that was making him giddy and not the quantities of Bitschwiller with which he had lubricated the equally vast amount of banquet he had consumed.

'I'd like you to have a bash, second over,' said Pring as they strolled across the sward. He put his hand on Bognor's shoulder, implying great confidence.

The effect of this was instantly sobering.

'What, me?' he asked, half stifling a burp compounded of mingled apprehension and satiety.

'Who else?' His captain (playing) gave him a parting shot and sauntered off to his fielding position, leaving Bognor to ponder the various follies which had exposed him to this torment. He was so unnerved that he scarcely noticed the over's passage.

At the end of it Pring tossed the ball nonchalantly across. Bognor caught it and stared sadly at the misshapen red leather sphere with its loose stitched seam. The batsmen had not hitherto seemed markedly ept. Their runs had come from the edge, not the centre of the bat. They had been struck often and sometimes painfully on various parts of the body. Nevertheless they were still there. Bognor hitched his trousers, rubbed the ball on his upper thigh, just as he had seen professionals do on television. 'You going over the wicket or round?' enquired the umpire who, Bognor realized with a start, was Hugh ffrench-Thomas. It was quite usual for members of the batting side to umpire when the regular umpires needed a rest. 'Over,' he replied, remembering dimly that this required him to deliver the ball while standing on the left-hand side of the stumps. ffrench-Thomas regarded him superciliously as he jogged lightly in, ball held tightly in his right hand. As he reached the stumps he twirled his arms, let go of the ball and watched it spin slowly away from him. It passed the opposing batsman on the second bounce, well out of his reach. ffrench-Thomas turned to the scorers in the pavilion and stretched his arms out. 'Wide,' he said. Bognor blushed, picked up the ball, thrown back to him by the wicket-keeper and tried again. This time it was within reach of the batsman, who lunged at it in an agricultural manner and hit it over the square leg boundary for four. The third ball, similarly placed, was similarly treated. Pring approached, brows furrowed. 'Try pitching it up a little, old man,' he said. Bognor tried. The ball flew, faster this time, at the head of the batsman, who withdrew to one side, allowing it to pass by. The wicket-keeper, surprised, misfielded, and the batsmen crossed for a single. Bognor took a deep breath. Only three to go. The next one was almost straight and the batsman played it circumspectly straight back along the ground. He fielded it cleanly, turned, trundled in, watched appalled as the ball, which had slipped from his grasp a second too soon, pitched halfway down the wicket. The batsman opened his shoulders, danced down the wicket as if he was doing the polka, and hoisted the ball away over the mid-on boundary. ffrench-Thomas, grinning broadly, raised his arms aloft to indicate six. Fourteen runs, one wide and one bye off the over. It was not good. He waited for the ball to be retrieved from some long grass and cow parsley, waited patiently while Pring, with the air of a man who was suffering badly, spread the fielders to the far corners of the ground. Then he ran in for his last ball only to feel it slip out in precisely the same way as its predecessor. Again it pitched short. Again the polka. Again the hoist. But this time the mighty blow, though higher still, was falling short. Beneath it stood the spruce figure of the American culture vulture, hands cupped in supplication. Everyone watched as the ball began its descent. It looked like a space capsule coming home and any minute Bognor expected to see a little silk parachute billow out and slow its progress. Instead it accelerated until with startling suddenness it landed neatly in Ebertson's outstretched hands. For a second he stood stock still, then leaping skywards he hurled the ball back up with a mighty bellow of 'Howzat!' The appeal was superfluous. The batsman was walking. ffrench-Thomas smiled at Bognor. 'Very cunning piece of cricket,' he said, smirking. It was not a view shared by Aubrey Pring, who did not ask Bognor to bowl again, instead recalling Luton to the attack. The remaining two wickets fell with little more ado, and Pendennis' team were all out for one hundred and fifty-eight.

Batting at number seven it seemed unlikely that he would be called upon for an hour or so, and he decided to find a deckchair and snooze; a diversion which was interfered with by Ebertson.

'Quite a combination, our wicket,' he said, sitting down in the chair next to Bognor's. 'I brought a celebration.' To Bognor's horror he produced an unopened bottle of Bitsch-willer and two glasses.

'Oh, God,' said Bognor, then collected himself. Champagne wasn't really drinking. 'No, that was a fantastic catch. Really fantastic.'

'Fine piece of bowling,' said Ebertson. 'Let's drink to it.'

They drank to it, and watched half-heartedly as Aubrey Pring and Basil Luton marched out to do battle with the Pendennis bowlers.

'Can we talk?' enquired Ebertson, tentatively, after a few moments of uneventful cricket. Bognor realized with a start that his eyes had closed, and he had almost dropped off.

'Of course.' He wondered what Ebertson meant. Clearly by 'talking' he intended something more meaningful than idle chatter about gastronomy or games. He eased himself further back into the yielding striped canvas of his chair and waited.

'I'd like to extend our field of mutual understanding

beyond catching and bowling,' he said, searching Bognor with a forensic stare.

Bognor wrestled briefly with the sentence, failed to find any hidden meanings, and said, after a pause, 'Go on.'

'I'll put my cards on the table,' said the American with the air of a poker player revealing half a hand. 'We didn't kill Petrov.'

'That's rather a negative beginning,' said Bognor incisively. 'Who said Petrov's even dead?'

'Okay, Simon, if that's the way you want it.' Ebertson struggled up out of the chair and made as if to remove the still half-full bottle.

'Relax, relax,' said Bognor, realizing that however improbable it might seem he could be on the verge of the breakthrough which had been so conspicuously absent hitherto. 'All right, I know Petrov is dead.'

'And I'm correct in saying that your people didn't do it either.' He was sitting down again.

'I think you're right,' said Bognor. He was uncertain himself, and said so.

'I'm going to be very frank,' said Ebertson. 'We are very interested in the Scoff set-up, and we would like to acquire it for ourselves. More important we don't want it to go elsewhere. Certainly not to Moscow. So, frankly, our people weren't too sorry about Dmitri, but . . .'

'You didn't do it.' There was a clatter of applause from the spectators. The shiny red ball was speeding inexorably to the mid-off boundary. Basil Luton stood watching it, bat held aloft theatrically.

'No, we didn't do it.'

They both sipped at their drinks. Then Bognor said, 'But if neither of us did it, who did? His own people?'

Ebertson shrugged. 'Doesn't fit. Look, the reason I'm saying all this is that we're interested in the destination of the Scoff system, but we're not being greedy.'

Bognor thought he twigged. 'In other words, you don't mind us having it, but you don't want it going to what some of our people refer to as "an unnamed power"?'

'Right.'

'I see,' said Bognor. 'But look, are you even certain that Scoff set up a proper network?'

'Oh, yes.'

'And what? Gabrielle has inherited it?'

'I would guess so, though there may be some sort of internal power struggle going on. My guess is that some of the leaders are for going on like Scoff as an independent who sold to the highest bidder. Some of the others may want a firm long-term contract.'

'I see.' Bognor gazed out at the idyllic scene. Green grass, white figures far enough away to seem elegant, birdsong. A smell of ordure and animals. In the context the conversation seemed impossible.

'Who else would bid?' he asked, 'assuming your diagnosis is right.'

'That's what I don't understand. My hunch, and it's only a hunch, is that the Russians are out of it.'

'The unnamed power?'

'Precisely.'

'What does that leave us with? Zionists . . . Arabs . . . what do you reckon?'

'I'm not certain I reckon anything. Oh, good catch. Poor Aubrey. He won't be happy about that.' Aubrey Pring had dabbed feebly at a short ball from ffrench-Thomas and been caught by Luigi Dotto behind the wicket. Dotto had produced a spectacular horizontal dive which seemed unlikely in one so corpulent.

'When are you in?' enquired Bognor.

'Eleven,' said Ebertson. 'Aubrey's not entirely happy with my batting.'

'You may not have to go in at all.'

'Oh, yes.' Ebertson sighed. 'We never win. It's part of the ritual. I shall survive approximately three balls.' He poured out more wine. 'Maybe if I drink enough I might last four.' He laughed, a dry chuckle from well back. 'Anyway, all I'm saying, unofficially, mind, is that as far as we're concerned it's no contest. We would be quite happy to see you British take over the network, always provided the usual understandings continue.'

'Quite,' said Bognor. 'By the way, who do you think killed Scoff?'

'You don't think he killed himself?' Ebertson's voice took on a harder note. 'It seemed obvious enough.'

'Up to a point,' said Bognor. 'But there's something fishy about it.'

'Oddly enough,' said Ebertson, 'we didn't consider there was anything particularly "fishy", as you put it, until you yourself appeared on the scene.'

'You mean . . . ' Bognor paused as batsman number three, an athletic PR man with an off-licence chain, had his stumps flattened by one of ffrench-Thomas's quicker balls, 'you mean you realized I was investigating Scoff's death right at the beginning?'

'Oh, sure. I think we all did.'

'Oh,' said Bognor, humiliated. There didn't seem a great deal more to be said, and the sun and the drink continued to exact their toll. They dozed, chatting only desultorily, as the score was pushed along steadily by Basil Luton while wickets fell at the other end. As the fourth went down with the score at seventy Bognor went to get padded up. The fifth batsman was dismissed at ninety-four, and the players adjourned for tea. Coming relatively soon after the earlier meal it was more in the nature of a digestif than the fully fledged cream bun and éclair occasion which Bognor remembered from youth. There was a choice of teas: Russian Caravan, Lapsang Souchong or Earl Grey, and cucumber or tomato sandwiches, sliced very thin and crustless. More drink for those who wanted it. Bognor sipped Earl Grey and nibbled a cucumber sandwich while his playing and non-playing captains briefed him. 'Just stick there,' they said as one. 'No heroics. Just stay in and leave the runs to Basil.' Basil, they told him, was batting beautifully. Indeed he had just passed fifty. 'It's up to you,' said Pring. 'After you there's only Aubergine as a sort of surprise package, and after that it's just rabbits.'

Bognor looked round to see if Ebertson could have overheard this opprobrious description. No. He was talking coolly, elegantly even, in a far corner to Gabrielle. Aubrey was trying to boost Bognor's morale but was only succeeding

in making him feel more inadequate. 'Don't try to hit anything outside the line of the stumps,' he said. 'Just go very
carefully, and we're home and dry.' Amanda Bullingdon
wandered over. 'Best of luck,' she said. So did Aubergine
Bristol. 'I'm not expecting to have to go in,' she said. Bognor
smiled. Had he felt less apprehensive he would have asked
why, in that case, she was wearing pads.

On the way out Basil Luton said, 'I'll do my best to keep
you away from ffrench-Thomas. He's the real menace.
Otherwise nothing to write home about. We'll try to go for a
single at the end of each over. All right?'

Bognor adjusted his cap, which had so far attracted no
remark, and nodded. 'All right,' he said.

Luton faced the bowling, which was ffrench-Thomas's.
From where Bognor stood it indeed looked frighteningly
fast. Off the first four balls Luton took a two, which Bognor
ran efficiently if ungracefully, and a four, which he did not,
of course, have to run at all. On the other two he missed one
and played the other safely but without scoring from it. The
fifth ball he prodded to third man. One run. So far so good.
It meant that Bognor had but one ball to face. He selected a
guard of middle and leg, peered round at the field in the
approved fashion, and settled down as ffrench-Thomas began
to run in. It was a long run, and he ran faster and faster.
Bognor tapped his bat nervously. He was very frightened, but
he was also rather drunk. The ball was a rocket. It screamed
down at him with a sinister whirring noise, swinging as it
went. He scarcely had time to consider whether it was
straight or not but, with a reflex culled from the recesses of
some long-forgotten textbook, he threw his bat gently, at the
same time advancing his left leg towards the ball, which he
could not see at all clearly. There was a sharp clunk as the
willow and leather collided. He opened his eyes just as he
heard a voice – Luton's he realized – exclaim, 'Oh, shot!'
Then he saw that almost without knowing it, he had propelled
the ball with some velocity past the cover fielder. It had gone
for four runs. No point in bothering to run.

The end of the over. A hundred and five for five. S. Bognor
four not out. Luton came down for a conference. 'Is that a

Gordouli cap?' he asked. Then without waiting for an answer he continued, 'Can't think what you're doing at number seven. Forget the singles, we'll get it in boundaries.' Bognor felt elated and drunker still. The next bowler was a trundler, and Luton, evidently inspired by Bognor's cover drive, hit him to all corners of the ground. Four, four, two, six, four, an unexpected nothing, bringing the score to one hundred and twenty-five for five with Luton on eighty not out. Only thirty-four needed and suddenly it seemed that Blight-Purley's team had it almost in the bag. The final ball was turned adroitly off Luton's legs to long leg. 'Take three,' called Luton as he crossed Bognor on the first run. Bognor grimaced. A cricket pitch is twenty-two yards long and in his present state Bognor found anything over that hard to contemplate. At the end of Luton's second run Bognor was barely embarked on his. As he grounded his bat for his second Bognor turned to wave Luton back. He could not manage more. In fact he felt nauseous. He also had a stitch. Luton, however, had set off and was halfway down the wicket. 'No more, no more,' croaked Bognor waving feebly at his partner and watching petrified as he saw the strong arm of the fielder, none other than ffrench-Thomas, poised for the throw. It was too late. The throw was unerring and strong. It reached the Italian wicket-keeper first bounce and Dotto had removed the bails with Luton a clear yard out of his ground. 'Howazzazat?' he cried, and for once Blight-Purley, standing in the crucial umpiring position, was forced to acknowledge the justice of the appeal. His finger went up. Luton looked at the ground, muttered noisily and expletively, and marched back towards the pavilion. As he passed him Bognor said, plaintively, 'I'm awfully sorry, old man.' But his victim merely stabbed at the turf with his bat and said something which Bognor thought sounded suspiciously like 'Piss off!' He winced. After all, it wasn't his fault. He'd told him. It had been Luton's idea to run three, not his. It was that bloody cap that had done it. That and the flukey cover drive.

Aubergine Bristol came sauntering out to take up the struggle. Her bosom looked splendidly ample under the white shirt, stretched tight across her chest; her thighs showed sturdy and masculine under her divided skirts. She waved her bat with aplomb and menace. Bognor came to meet her, fearing a message of rebuke from his captain. Instead she merely said: 'Only just over thirty. Aubrey says not to hurry, but it's up to us. There's no one after.'

Bognor smiled wanly and returned to the batting crease where he was now due to face ffrench-Thomas. When he got there he found Luigi Dotto, the wicket-keeper-cum-chef. He slapped Bognor amiably on the back with his leather gauntlet. 'Hugh and I hope you aren't getting out of your depth,' he said, smiling. 'We don't want you to be hurt.'

'Very solicitous of you,' said Bognor, trying to appear cool.

'We would prefer you not to continue to pester Gabrielle,' he continued, still smiling. His voice, however, was charged with exaggerated Mediterranean menace.

'Oh.' Bognor disliked intimidation, even though it frightened him. 'I have a job to do, I'm afraid.'

'What a pity,' the Italian smirked, and raised a glove in the direction of ffrench-Thomas.

'Come along you chaps,' shouted Blight-Purley, irascibly. 'We haven't got all day.' All day was exactly what they did have, thought Bognor ruefully. He settled down to watch the bowler thunder into action once more. It was an unnecessarily long run, quite as alarming as Dotto's spoken threat. He watched the strides lengthen, raised his bat to meet the challenge and gulped as he saw the Bitschwiller rep hurl the ball into the ground a good three yards short of where he stood. In the words of the cricketing experts it then 'flew'. The earth was rock hard and the ball bounced back at a sharp angle and sped up at him at around a hundred miles an hour. It all happened very suddenly and he was so shocked by the hostility of the assault that he remained stock still as it swung away from him, passing just over his right shoulder. 'Well left!' called Aubergine Bristol enthusiastically. She had obviously taken his drink- and terror-induced immobility for steadiness under enemy fire. Bognor went very cold. Behind him Luigi Dotto, who had caught the ball cleanly, came wandering closer. 'The next one may not miss,' he said softly. 'You still persist in your pestering intention?'

Suddenly Bognor became very angry. 'Sugar off, you deplorable foreign person!' he said, and watched, quite without fear this time as the wicket-keeper shrugged and again waved a glove in the direction of the bowler. It was obviously the signal for another bumper, but Bognor was not going to be intimidated. He marched three paces down the wicket and very deliberately smacked the turf with the back of his bat as if to indicate that the ball's behaviour had nothing to do with ffrench-Thomas' strength or skill but was merely the result of some abnormality in the pitch. Then he returned. He was going to go down fighting. This time he waited until the bowler was halfway through his run up and then straightened and walked three paces backwards rubbing at his eye. ffrench-Thomas was forced to halt. Bognor went on rubbing, then returned to the crease. 'Sorry!' he called up to umpire and bowler, 'something in my eye. Gone now.' Behind him Dotto whispered, 'Next time there *will* be something in the eye.'

The ball, when it came, was even deadlier than the last. Definitely designed to kill, if not to maim. His response was determinedly suicidal. Just as it was delivered Bognor gave a sort of manic hop, raised his bat, and aimed a blow which was halfway between a swing and a karate chop. There was a hideous moment when it seemed the ball must hit him smack between the eyes but an instant before that happened he felt the immensely satisfying thud of his bat striking the leather exactly where the bat is supposed to contact the ball. He half stumbled from the force of the impact and was then aware of really quite enthusiastic applause. The ball had cleared the square leg boundary full toss. His effort of self-defence and defiance had turned into a textbook hook shot – precisely the sort of thing which the very best batsmen are supposed to employ in such circumstances. Aubergine Bristol exclaimed 'Shot!' and ffrench-Thomas stood with his hands on his hips staring angrily and thoughtfully. The next four balls were gentler, and he managed to score two runs from them, such was his confidence. The game regained something approaching composure. The two of them pushed the score along surely until Aubergine edged one to first slip where it was caught. The next two batsmen managed a mere single between them while Bognor watched helplessly from the other end. As Ebertson arrived at the wicket, a further nine runs were still required. Bognor was twenty-one not out and the effects of Bitschwiller and bile were beginning to wear thin. 'This is where we cement our alliance,' said Ebertson, speaking rather fuzzily. Bognor realized with surprise that he was wearing a gumshield. 'Pring says "well done, but take it slow".'

'Right you are,' said Bognor.

ffrench-Thomas had been rested for an over or two. Now he was brought back to finish things off.

Bognor viewed him with less stark terror than before, but he was still nervous. Besides, the nearness of victory was making him apprehensive. The first delivery was quick and straightish. He was caught in hopeless indecision, uncertain whether to play forward or back. To his chagrin he missed altogether and was appalled to hear the collapse of his wicket behind him. Out. Bowled. He stood for a moment surveying the ruins, and then turned to walk, only dimly aware of a shout from behind him. Halfway to the pavilion he was joined by Ebertson. He seemed very excited. 'You're not out. Back. Blight-Purley called a no-ball. He says ffrench-Thomas threw it. Chucked it. It wasn't a legal delivery.

Finally the message got through. Bognor turned to see that altercation was taking place. The players had crowded round the two umpires who were themselves engaged in noisy and acrimonious debate. By the time he had returned, however, the decision had been confirmed. No-ball. He was still in and there were only eight runs now required. Somehow he played out the rest of the over, scoring no runs from it but retaining his wicket. As the field changed over he held a conference with Ebertson again. The American was confident. 'I'd say ffrench-Thomas and Dotto have it in for you and Blight-Purley,' he said. 'I wonder if their dislike extends to me?'

'Let's concentrate on one thing at a time,' said Bognor. 'Let's beat them at cricket, then we can consider the other.'

'Maybe.'

Ebertson's stance was unusual, owing much, of course, to his American antecedents. His legs were slightly splayed, and he carried the bat high off the ground as if he were intending to hit across the line rather than down it in the approved English manner – sabre rather than foil. This was exactly what he did with the first ball bowled at him. It was a medium pace full toss, the sort of delivery one might have expected from a baseball pitcher, and Ebertson swung mightily and half successfully. The ball caught the edge of the bat and screamed away towards third man. It was not what he had intended but it was effective. They ran two. Six still to win. Ebertson was evidently intent on dangerous living for he played an identical shot to the next ball. He missed. The ball was not, however, straight. The mistake was not important. Nevertheless it was obvious to everyone that Ebertson was on borrowed time. The principles of batting may seem eccentric but they were well founded. The American was not applying them. Bognor realized that it was imperative to get Ebertson away from the bowling even though it was not particularly hostile. It would also help to score the necessary runs before the decidedly more dangerous ffrench-Thomas returned. The next ball hit Ebertson's thigh and ran away towards an empty space in the field. 'Run,' shrieked Bognor to the immobilized Ebertson, who was too busy rubbing his leg to consider runs. The leg bye was duly completed. Five to win, three balls of the over remaining. From the first, Bognor achieved an undignified prod past point which brought two; the second he missed; and by great good fortune the third he turned to long leg for a single. The end of the over. Only two runs needed, ffrench-Thomas bowling to Bognor. This over was crucial. He stared long and hard at the ground, wondering what on earth to do. His concentration was such that he scarcely noticed the appalling Dotto mutter, as he passed him, 'This will hurt.' Instead he found himself reciting the words of Sir Henry Newbolt:

> *'There's a breathless hush in the Close tonight –*
> *Ten to make and the match to win –*
> *A bumping pitch and a blinding light,*
> *An hour to play and the last man in.'*

Not entirely accurate, but uncommonly close. The last man *was* in. The fiendish ffrench-Thomas was bowling fast; the pitch seemed bumpy. The crowd, or spectators ('crowd' being too grand a term for the distinguished but not overlarge concourse gathered by the pavilion and tent) was extremely silent, gripped presumably by the tension and drama of the situation. There was at least an hour left, but it was not going to be necessary.

> *'And it's not for the sake of a ribboned coat,*
> *Or the selfish hope of a season's fame,*
> *But his Captain's hand on his shoulder smote –*
> *Play up! Play up! and play the game!'*

Well, he wasn't doing this for Pring. He was doing it, in an odd round-about sort of way, for his country. In some bizarre fashion, no longer very clear to him, the heroics he was performing were connected with the death of Escoffier Smith and Dmitri Petrov. Moreover, the battle between him and Hugh ffrench-Thomas and Luigi Dotto increasingly seemed to have to do with something more than cricket.

He snapped out of his reverie, pulled at the peak of his cap, looked around at the predatory fielders, and settled himself to await the onslaught. Thud, thud, thud – ffrench-Thomas' boots thumped the turf with the sound of a race-horse entering the final furlong. The ball speared to exactly the same spot as the other bouncers, reared before Bognor could decide on an appropriate response, and struck him just above the heart. Dotto had been right. It did hurt. He dropped his bat and massaged the affected spot, screwing his face into an expression of anguish as he did so.

Umpire Blight-Purley came unsteadily across to see if

he was all right, and to offer partial advice. 'Stand up to the bugger,' was what he said. Bognor merely grunted and picked up his bat. The next ball landed a little closer and shot up. This time he played back but the ball cut in, missed the bat and caught Bognor full in the middle of the stomach. Immediately he doubled up, half winded and gasping. Dotto and Blight-Purley both approached, but he waved them away still grimacing. The second blow had removed all trace of inebriation, but it was at least two minutes before he felt well enough to stand and take a third. Again the ritual: the heavy, powerful, ever-quickening run; the flurry of arms; the searing pace of the projectile; its angry, fizzing sound. Bognor watched, the pain promoting a desire for swift and comprehensive revenge. For once ffrench-Thomas' aim was marginally less sure. The length was the same, but instead of being straight, this one pitched well outside the off stump to Bognor's right. With surprising alacrity he flashed at it in a passable imitation of a square cut, his right foot across, arms outstretched, bat almost horizontal. Not for the first time aggression, bravado even, paid off. The ball flew from the bat, fell short of the man fielding at point, evaded his grasp, sped on past and rolled like an angry little meteor across the short-cropped turf and over the thin white boundary line. Four runs. Blight-Purley's XI one hundred and sixty for nine. Bognor twenty-eight not out. Ebertson two not out. Blight-Purley's XI win by one wicket. Bognor experienced a feeling of achievement and euphoria such as he could not recall since he had passed the Civil Service Exam and been accepted by the Board of Trade.

The first to congratulate him was Ebertson: 'Played, dammit!' he exclaimed striking Bognor smartly on the shoulder. 'First time that's happened in living memory.' Blight-Purley echoed this. Likewise Pendennis who had been umpiring at the other end. Other members of the opposing team, though conspicuously not ffrench-Thomas and Dotto, proffered similar applause. Back at the pavilion there was more. It was heady stuff. Pring was standing there, a glass of bubbling Bitschwiller in each hand. 'Well played, you chaps,' he said, giving them both champagne. 'Historic

stuff. I'd no idea you had it in you, Simon. Fantastic.'
'Fantastic!' 'Well played, old boy.' 'That six was the best
thing I've seen in years.' 'How are the injuries?' 'That
second one must have hurt.' It was all most unusual for a
man more accustomed to the world's and his intimates'
brickbats, but Bognor found that he slipped surprisingly
easily into the part of traditional British hero. All that was
required was a self-deprecating half smile, an occasional
shrug, a few 'thank you's', and a measure of appreciation
for the efforts of others. He did not say, 'It was nothing
actually', but that was the impression he managed to convey.

The celebration continued for an hour or so in almost
entirely liquid form. Bognor smoked a cheroot or two and
drank. Aubrey Pring and Aubergine Bristol, it now transpired, were spending the night at Petheram. So was Gabrielle.
Amanda Bullingdon, who had driven down with Gabrielle,
was offered a lift home in Blight-Purley's Jag. Eventually, at
around half-past seven a distinctly intoxicated trio fell into the
car preparatory to the long drive home.

'Good day,' said the Colonel, as he turned the car unsteadily on to the main London road.

'*Very* good day,' echoed his passengers.

'Neither of you two in a particular hurry to get home?'

'No.'

'I thought,' Blight-Purley coughed and crashed the gears
simultaneously, 'we might stop off at Wittering Saint Jude
for a snackerel.'

'What, the Orange Lily?' asked Amanda Bullingdon.
'Cedric Pottinger's place?'

'Yes. Not far off our route. I'm sure we could have an
agreeable light supper there.'

No one could think of any reasonable objection. Bognor,
comfortably sitting in the rear seat, allowed himself to
contemplate the back of Amanda Bullingdon's head, which
seemed in the evening light to have taken on a rather alluring
sheen. They were all in their different ways feeling mellow
with confidence and the satisfaction of work well done.
They were not, as Blight-Purley would have put it 'on the
qui vive'. Which is why none of them noticed the blood-red

Maserati behind them, an ostentatious machine with infinitely more power than the Colonel's aging Jaguar, but which obstinately refused to pass them; which, indeed, never came within thirty or forty yards, but which never quite lost sight of them.

Chapter Six

The Orange Lily was named in honour of the Royal Sussex Regiment who had earned the sobriquet in their days as the 35th Foot. The Earl of Donegal had chosen orange facings for the regimental uniform in deference to his hero, William of Orange. The lilies had come later after they had routed the Royal Roussillon French Grenadiers at Quebec in 1759. The modern pub originally dated from a similar period and, although it boasted a public bar which attracted local residents of the more prosperous kind, it was less of a pub than a restaurant with rooms, in the French manner. The food was very good and very expensive and rooms were always full at weekends. Unless there was racing at Goodwood there were few weekday residents, but the restaurant continued to earn the patronage of the county's numerous stockbrokers and barristers.

'Colonel,' said Cedric Pottinger, as the party debouched into his hostelry. 'How very agreeable!' He was a surprisingly thin man of around fifty with shifty eyes and a mauve-veined nose.

'Cedric,' said the Colonel. 'Good to see you. This is Amanda Bullingdon, whom I think you've met, and this is Simon Bognor, whom I believe you haven't. Simon has just won a vital game of cricket virtually single-handed, and we're celebrating.'

'Congratulations,' said Pottinger. 'That would be at Petherham I suppose.'

They agreed that it would be at Petherham and proceeded to the saloon bar, be-beamed and be-chintzed, where they ordered Pimms all round. They arrived in silver tankards complete with orange and lemon and sprigs of borage. Bognor noticed that Pottinger continued to shimmer about greeting other guests and rubbing his hands. Evidently he was not what in catering circles was called a 'grand bonnet'; more of what Americans referred to as a '*maître d*'. He seemed to Bognor to exhibit an unpleasing attitude of perpetual cringe.

'The chef's Albanian,' remarked Blight-Purley, noticing Bognor's disapproving attitude. 'He can cook too, unlike most Albanians.' The menu bore a few peripheral signs of Albanian influence – a rose-leaf jam offered as a sauce with some of the puddings, potatoes with Macedonian honey, dolmas and a touch of yoghurt here and there. For the most part, however, it was glossy Anglo-French, and suddenly realizing that they had eaten extensively during the day, they all opted for the same: Vichyssoise followed by Vitello tonnato and salad. To drink with it, Sancerre.

'We were lucky no one got hurt,' said Blight-Purley when they had ordered.

'Speak for yourself,' said Bognor, whose bruises were painful.

'No, but nothing broken. There could have been, you know.'

'There did seem to be a rather violent attitude about,' said Amanda Bullingdon. 'I mean more so than usual.'

By common consent, however, they left it there or thereabouts. On their own Bognor and Blight-Purley might possibly have sifted the significance of the unusually hostile fast bowling and ffrench-Thomas' rifling blows in the Colonel's direction. But neither, it seemed, wished to involve the girl. Or conceivably they were sufficiently suspicious, in the omnivorous manner of their profession, to avoid giving her any indication of what exactly it was that they now suspected. Instead they turned to more trivial discussion – travel, politics, sport and, inevitably, food and drink. This proved so engrossing that none of them noticed the distinctive purr of an aging Jaguar from the direction of the car park. The noise occurred at about the moment that they were taking the first mouthfuls of emerald green mint and grapefruit sorbet: a soft, low, throaty hum; a slightly crashed gear change; acceleration into the distance; silence punctuated by the slosh of their sorbets and the muffled indiscretions of their fellow eaters. After they had finished, Pottinger insisted they have an Armagnac for the road, so they went back into the flowery lounge and drank that and coffee with homemade fudge and strange sweet pink confections composed mainly of coconut. It was after ten when they finally went back out into the car park. Bognor stretched and sniffed country air. He felt sleepy and replete.

'I enjoyed that,' said Amanda Bullingdon. He had sat opposite her during the meal and they had flirted mildly, sharing a conspiratorial amusement at the older person's idiosyncrasies, not to mention his contrived gallantry.

Now in the early summer night Bognor decided he really quite fancied her. 'Yes,' he said, feeling her close to him. He wondered if it would be in order for them both to make the journey home in the back of the car. Not that anything improper would occur. He merely relished the idea of proximity.

From a few yards away there came a sound of near senile annoyance. It was Blight-Purley. 'I don't think he can find his car,' giggled Amanda, stifling the laugh in the shoulder of Bognor's jacket. A match flared; revealing the haggard visage of the Colonel peering hopelessly. 'I say,' he called, 'bloody car's gone.'

'How do you mean, "gone"?' shouted Bognor.

'Gone,' he repeated. 'Gone. Vanished, Disappeared.'

'Oh, God,' whispered Bognor to the still giggling Miss Bullingdon. 'You were absolutely right. Come on, we'd better help him find it.' Louder, he shouted, 'It wasn't over there anyway, sir. It was over here, under the chestnut.'

He and the girl walked to the spot. Where they thought the Jaguar had been was now nothing but empty, unoccupied tarmac. 'Funny,' said Bognor, 'I could have sworn it was there. What do you think?'

'Yes,' she said. 'Someone must have moved it. One of the staff. Perhaps it was blocking the way.'

Blight-Purley joined them. 'See what I mean?' he asked.

Amanda repeated her suggestion. 'They couldn't have,' said Bognor. 'They'd have needed the keys. Nobody came in for them.' There was a hush. 'Always supposing' continued Bognor after the moment of quiet, 'that you had the keys on you.' There was no mistaking the meaning of the silence this time.

'Must have left them in the car,' said Blight-Purley eventually. 'If you ask me some sewer's pinched it.' The accuracy of this assessment was increasingly evident.

They returned to the establishment and sought out Pottinger. 'Dear dear,' he said morosely, 'it sounds like it. We'll ring the police, but I doubt they'll be able to do much for you tonight. You'll have to stay. We've plenty of room.' Pottinger and Blight-Purley left for the former's office while Bognor and Amanda Bullingdon stayed in the lounge.

'Who would have done a thing like that?' she asked, looking depressed.

'Joy riders, I should think,' said Bognor. 'Village boys out for a quick thrill. You must admit a set of keys in a nice old Jaguar is a fairly irresistible temptation.'

'I suppose so.'

The two others returned from their telephone call looking lugubrious.

'Police say there's nothing much they can do except keep a look out for it,' said Blight-Purley. 'Nothing for it but to stay here. Pottinger says he can put us up.'

'Oh, God,' said Bognor. 'I'd better ring home.' Pottinger guided him to his office, a severely functional room with notice boards and calendars and plain brown colours. 'Help yourself,' he said, motioning him towards the telephone and creeping obsequiously out.

Monica's mood shifted quickly from concern to irritation, her first questions: 'Where on earth are you?' and 'Are you all right?' giving way almost immediately to statements such as, 'You've been drinking.' He had been looking forward to regaling her with his part in the Blight-Purley XI's un-expected victory, but it was obvious that she wouldn't be interested. Besides, his enthusiasm for retelling it had diminished.

'I'll see you when I see you then,' he concluded crossly. 'Sleep tight.'

'I've no doubt,' said Monica, putting down the receiver. He frowned at the remark and understood it in the hall just before entering the lounge. 'Tight,' he muttered, 'tight as a tick. Sleep drunkenly. Very funny. Ha ha.' An expensive middle-aged couple passed him on their way out and favoured him with a pair of old-fashioned looks.

Back at their table he found that they had been provided with more coffee and Armagnac. Beside the cups and glasses were three keys. 'All the rooms are named after champagnes,' said Amanda, brightly.

'We've put you in Bollinger, Colonel Blight-Purley's taken Krug, and I'm in Pol Roger.'

'What, no Bitschwiller?' he asked facetiously.

'For once, no,' she smiled.

'Oh well,' he sipped at his Armagnac, noticing for the first time that Pottinger had left the bottle on the table, 'it could be worse. I mean there must be less congenial places to be marooned in.'

'And less congenial company,' she smiled back.

'Bloody silly thing to do,' said Blight-Purley grumpily. He seemed deflated by the incident, caught out by such un-characteristic inefficiency. They drank in silence. A few minutes later the Colonel hauled himself upright and said, 'I don't have your stamina any longer, I'm afraid. I'll leave you two children to it, but I wouldn't mind a quick word, Simon.' He jerked his head towards the hallway and winked. It occurred to Bognor that he was slightly unhinged. How-ever, he too rose and followed him out. Outside Blight-Purley turned on him quite fiercely.

'There's no alternative,' he said in a stage whisper, 'but we must be exceedingly careful. I don't like this one bit.'

'Sorry,' said Bognor. 'How do you mean?'

'Has anyone said anything to you today? About you know what, I mean?'

'Yes, as a matter of fact, at least in a manner of speaking.'

'What?'

'Ebertson came over very palsy-walsy,' he said, wondering what had induced him to use such a curious expression the moment he had uttered it, 'and that fat Eyetie slug made some typically unpleasant suggestions about not pestering Gabrielle or I was going to get hurt.'

'Did he?'

'Yes. He and ffrench-Thomas are obviously in cahoots.'

'I don't like it.'

'What are you getting at?'

'What I'm getting at is that it's no accident that the car's gone missing. For some reason someone wants us here tonight.'

'Aren't you being a bit melodramatic?'

Blight-Purley glared. 'Shut your window and lock the door,' he said, 'or we may find we're in real trouble.'

They said good night to each other. Blight-Purley walked heavily upstairs while Bognor returned to the lounge for a final Armagnac.

'What was all that about?' enquired Amanda Bullingdon, folding her legs to show more of them and smiling.

'Oh, nothing. He's just a bit overexcited about the car that's all.'

'I see.' She sipped and looked at him straight in the eyes as if she were a diffident human trying to outstare an insubordinate dog. 'Who were you telephoning?' she asked, after Bognor had dropped his eyes.

'Questions, questions,' he said. 'Why do you ask?'

'Because I'm curious. Wife?'

'No, not wife.'

'But more than casual girlfriend.'

'You could put it like that I suppose, yes.'

'Are you fond of her?'

Bognor considered the question, which was one he had been asking himself with increasing frequency of late. 'Sort of,' he said fatuously, and then before he quite realized what was happening, the two of them were embarked on the sort of intimate conversation which is only really possible late at night after too much drink. It was two hours before they agreed that sleep was called for. Half-heartedly Bognor suggested that the bottle of Armagnac might be finished together in Bollinger or Pol Roger. Demurely she demurred, and leaving the bottle with the other debris, they ascended the creaking stairs to the first – and only other – floor.

Pol Roger was first. They paused at the door, then Miss Bullingdon let herself in and turned. 'Thanks,' she said simply and, leaning forward, kissed him on the cheek.

'Pleasure,' said Bognor, oddly flattered. The door closed on him, leaving him feeling pleased and tired. He walked on slowly, let himself into Bollinger next door, paid scant attention to the floral furnishings and the winebibbing prints on the walls, and quickly stripped off. The room had its own bathroom. He looked quickly away from the ravaged face staring at him from the mirror under the harsh neon light, splashed at himself with cold water, dried perfunctorily, and sank gratefully on to the soft double bed. He lay there for a second reliving his innings when there was a light tap on the door. Immediately he remembered Blight-Purley's words of warning. Without turning on the light he fumbled on the floor for his underpants then walked stealthily to the door, just as there was a second knock accompanied by a whispered 'Simon!' It sounded like Amanda Bullingdon. He froze. 'Who is it?'

'It's me, Mandy.' He opened the door and looked out. She was standing in the corridor, still in her dress but minus her shoes, and grinning. 'I haven't got any toothpaste,' she mouthed. 'Can you lend me some?' Before he could answer she had taken two steps forward and closed the door behind her with the heel of one foot. Almost at the same moment she put her arms around him and began to kiss him, tentatively at first, and then as Bognor's steely puritan intentions and Blight-Purley-inspired suspicions evaporated, with growing urgency. 'Mmm,' she said, withdrawing just far enough for speech, 'I quite like you. In fact I think you're rather nice.' She returned to the business of kissing before he could say anything remotely coherent and only stopped to say, 'It seemed such a waste for *me* to stay in Pol Roger all night while you were all on your own in Bollinger.' Bognor started to speak, but she silenced him with her mouth, then whispered; 'Come on. Bed.' He was beyond resistance.

124

He woke surprisingly early to find himself alone. It took him several moments to get his bearings and recall the events which had led to his present situation. Indeed it was not until he had rolled over and caught sight of the key with its tag saying 'Bollinger' that he remembered what had happened. His head ached. So did the rest of him. One way and another he had taken quite a bashing. He sat up, put a hand to his temple and groaned heavily. His watch said it was seven fifteen. Curious how a really heavy day and night out so frequently led to an early start. He sat up and wondered if anything had been said or done about morning tea or a paper. Would the staff of the Orange Lily be about at this time of the morning? Country hotels had a habit of beginning breakfasts un-usually late. And where was Mandy? Had it happened? Should he feel guilty? He remembered Monica's brusque behaviour on the telephone and decided that guilt was quite uncalled for. Besides it was not as if they were married. They only lived together. Any arrangement was entirely tacit. He reached for the telephone and was relieved to hear an answer-ing voice. 'Could I have a pot of tea in Bollinger?' he asked, speculating as he did on what such a mixture would taste like. 'Tea for two?' asked the voice. 'Tea for one please.' There was a pause, pregnant with something Bognor was unable to identify. Could it be that what he remembered doing with Amanda Bullingdon had actually happened and that the hotel staff were already aware of it? That was too bad. The image of Luigi Dotto crept unsolicited into his mind. He imagined that fat slug lurking at the keyholes of the Grand Hotel, Dynmouth, watching every dalliance, monitoring every phrase of endearment, notebook, or more likely Leica, always at the ready. The image was slow to disappear. He walked to the bathroom and forced himself to turn on the light and look in the mirror. Not a pretty sight. He ran a basin of hot water and began unpeeling the paper skin from the packet of soap. His appearance was worse sober than it had been drunk. Correction. His appearance *seemed* worse now that he was sober but that meant only that his percep-tion of his appearance was now clearer. It was probably that his real appearance was better. Except that he had grown stubble overnight – his face was covered in short black prickles. He sat on the loo, picked at his toenails and tried to sort out the essential difference between things observed when drunk and things observed when sober. All he could manage was the idea that when drunk, things seemed better. He certainly played more effective cricket when drunk; he remembered he made love with more panache when drunk; he looked more wholesome when drunk; and yet it was always maintained that sobriety was necessary for efficiency in any activity one attempted. There was a knock at the door. He put on his underpants, just as he had done a few hours before, and opened it to an altogether less appealing proposition: a stout middle-aged woman with a tray. He took the tray, put it on the bed and poured a cup. It was strong Indian. He had taken one throat-cauterizing mouthful when there was another knock. This time it *was* Mandy Bullingdon. 'You look good,' he said involuntarily. She seemed crisp and washed and starched, as if she had had eight hours' sleep and nothing to eat or drink but wheatgerm and fresh orange.

'I've been for a walk,' she said, 'and I've seen the Colonel, looking like thunder. It's bad news I'm afraid. They've found the car.'

'Oh. Come in, come in. Have a cup of tea.'

She did. 'Good God, you look terrible,' she said when she was properly inside.

'I *feel* terrible,' he conceded.

'Those bruises,' she exclaimed, jabbing at his ribcage. 'They're nothing to do with me are they?'

He peered down at the dull purple patch. 'No, ffrench-Thomas I think. Cricket.'

'Oh, of course, I'd forgotten. Sorry. You ought to have some witch hazel for it.'

'Probably. What did you say about the car?'

'They found it. The police. About five miles away. He was quite right. It *was* joy riders, a couple of local kids and their birds. Unfortunately for them it wasn't much of a joy ride. They ended up in hospital.'

Bognor began to feel a prickle at the base of his spine.

'Are they going to be all right?'

'I think so. The girls were just cut about and shocked. The boys were worse, but they're serious rather than dangerous. I don't understand the language of doctors.'

'It means they're not going to die,' said Bognor. 'I wish I could say the same for myself.'

'That sounds rather melodramatic.'

'I feel melodramatic. What about the car? What happened?'

She frowned. 'It won't go. They don't seem to be sure whether it ever will. It's being checked by the local garage; but the oddest thing is the accident itself.'

'Oh.' Bognor felt the clammy prickling again. It was a sensation which seldom betrayed him. Indeed, he often considered that his best work was done, if not under the influence of alcohol, then under that of some apparently extrasensory perception. 'Don't tell me,' he went on, 'it had been got at.'

She looked at him sharply. 'How did you know?'

He shrugged. 'I felt it,' he said, 'in my bones. Where I work people are always tampering with other people's cars. What was it? Brakes or steering?'

'I think a bit of both,' she said. 'There's a long hill about two miles away on the Horsham road and a corner at the bottom. There's a wall.'

'Into which . . . '

'Exactly.'

They stayed gazing into each other's eyes. Then Bognor said, 'There but for the grace of God go we.'

'I suppose so.' She drank a mouthful of the tea, now tepid, from Bognor's cup.

'About last night . . . ' he began, not sure what he wanted to say, feeling something ought to be said.

'I'd rather not talk about it,' she said.

'But . . . ' He realized he was being hopeless. He lacked the experience. Or had forgotten it.

'I understand,' she said, 'honestly. There's no need to say anything. Just drink your tea.' She handed the cup back. 'I'm much more concerned about the car. We might be dead.'

He felt very wet and inadequate. 'Have you had breakfast?' he asked. She shook her head. 'Feel like some?' She nodded.

'Hang on while I dress.' He was fond of her, he decided gormlessly. Was he about to get himself in a muddle? Probably.

'Maybe nothing was tampered with,' he called out from the bathroom, where he was trying to comb his hair into shape with his fingers. 'It's an old car. Things go wrong with old cars.'

'Not steering *and* brakes at the same time.'

'We don't *know* that – it's just what they said. Besides I don't imagine they were used to driving ritzy limousines. Tractors would be more their line.'

'The Colonel said he'd had it in for a service only last week. It's a very reliable garage, he says. They'd have checked the brakes and the steering.'

'My experience,' said Bognor, emerging from the bathroom, still trying to sort out his thinning locks, 'is that cars come away from services worse off than when they went in.'

'Here, let me,' She produced a comb from her bag and passed it through his hair four or five times. 'That's better,' she said, standing back to consider her handiwork. 'At least it'll have to do. You are a bit hopeless, aren't you?'

'Yes,' said Bognor, wryly. 'Let's have some breakfast.'

Downstairs Blight-Purley was already eating kippers with morose enthusiasm.

'You heard about the car,' he said, looking up momentarily.

'Yes,' Bognor sat down heavily and picked up the menu. 'What do you reckon?'

'I reckon,' said Blight-Purley, inserting the blade of his knife under the spine of the fish and removing the bone with the careless dexterity of a man who has been doing it all his life, 'that someone has turned vicious.'

Bognor decided against porridge or prunes. 'Tomato juice,' he said to the round pink country girl who had come to take their orders, 'and Worcester sauce. I'd like the bottle please. And then scrambled eggs and, er, coffee.'

He returned to the Colonel, now partially obscured by the rim of an enormous willow pattern breakfast cup. 'Aren't you rather jumping to conclusions? I mean the scenario is perfectly plausible. Jaguar in car park. Keys in dashboard. Rough cider in local youth. In they all get. Off they all go. Faster and faster. Vrrooom vrrooom. Long hill. Sharp bend. Lose control. Bang! Splat! Finish!' He made a sharp concluding movement with his right hand and dislodged a knife and spoon which fell noisily to the highly polished wooden floor. 'Sorry,' he said, bending to pick them up. The effort worsened the pains in his head and also brought him into close proximity to the Colonel's serviceable brown brogues. He wrinkled his nose and returning to table level said, 'I think you've trodden in some dog . . .'

'Oh, shit,' said the Colonel.

'Precisely.'

There was a brief, embarrassed silence and then Bognor said, 'I hadn't realized you'd been out.'

'Your deductive processes are in remarkable working order,' said Blight-Purley sardonically. 'Yes, I've been out where I inadvertently trod in a dog turd. I also noticed tyre marks on the rose bed. Little buggers seem to have demolished a couple of rather charming floribunda on their way out.'

'Which bears out my hypothesis,' said Bognor, stirring large quantities of Worcester sauce into his tomato juice.

'What?'

'That they were drunk and incapable.'

'And that they had a dog with them I suppose?' The Colonel laughed hollowly and Bognor went red.

'I'm sorry,' he said. 'What do you think happened? Who did what and to whom as they say?'

Blight-Purley chomped on a slab of toast covered in dark home-made marmalade heavy with rind and mature consideration. Amanda Bullingdon, markedly silent, tapped gently at her mottled brown softly boiled egg with the end of her silver spoon, and squinted slightly in her determination not to miss all that was being said. Bognor addressed himself to the scrambled eggs which were, unlike almost every other institutional scrambled egg he had attempted, buttery, soft, and self-evidently constructed almost exclusively from eggs.

'Someone must have known we were here,' said the Colonel, his voice blurred by toast. 'None of us even knew we were coming here until we'd got in the car, so we must have been followed.'

'That's assuming the car *was* nobbled,' said Bognor.

'That's what I am assuming,' said Blight-Purley with a quelling glare.

'It could have been an inside job,' said Amanda.

'How do you mean?' asked Bognor.

'What makes you think that?' asked Blight-Purley.

They both looked at her with surprise and interest.

'It's obvious,' she said. She wiped her upper lip with a napkin thus removing the odd crumb and a thin splodge of egg yolk. 'The people who work here knew we were here. Pottinger, for instance. He could easily have nipped out and done whatever he had to do.'

'Out of the question,' said Blight-Purley.

'Why?' asked Bognor. 'I think Mandy has a point.'

'I've known Cedric for years, and he doesn't know anything about cars and their innards. Also I think he's straight. And finally, because of his hands.'

'His hands?' they chorused.

'They were spotless throughout the time we were having dinner. They'd have been covered in oil and grease if he'd been fixing the car.'

'He could have got one of the waiters to do it,' said Bognor, doubtfully.

'I believe we were followed,' said the Colonel with emphasis. 'It would have been far too risky for anyone from the Lily to have done it.'

'He could have washed his hands,' offered Bognor.

Blight-Purley ignored him. 'And I have a hunch that ffrench-Thomas would know about cars.'

'Can you prove that?'

'No. Just intuition. I sense he's the sort of chap who knows about car guts.'

'Should be easy enough to find out.'

'Quite.'

'But why?' This was Amanda again.

The other two looked at each other. It was true that they had told her very little.

'Um,' said Bognor, trying to give the impression of a man who had seized the initiative. 'ffrench-Thomas obviously thinks we're on to him.'

'And are you?'

Bognor appealed mutely to the Colonel, who said, 'In a manner of speaking.' He then embarked on a brief but lucid summary of his suspicions and his reasons for harbouring them. At the mention of Scoff's espionage ring she said, 'You don't have to tell me about that. I know most of it already.'

'Oh?' said Bognor. 'Tell.'

'Nothing to tell, much,' she said, 'he never said anything to me directly. But I found some letters once in an old file; and I overheard a telephone conversation. That kind of thing. Wasn't difficult to piece it all together.'

'But you never told me.'

'You never asked. Besides you're Board of Trade. It's hardly your pigeon.'

'What about Gabrielle?'

'You forget,' she raised her eyebrows. 'Gabrielle was the main reason I left.'

'Oh.'

Blight-Purley continued his résumé. Most of it was familiar to Bognor who allowed his concentration to pass from it to the remains of breakfast and his persistent hangover. Only when the peroration was reached did his mind snap back to attention. 'So you see, my dear,' he said, 'that is the situation. We think that Scoff's suicide was connived at by a person or persons as yet unknown, at least unknown to Simon and myself.'

'I'm sure we know them,' said Bognor. 'It's just that we don't know which ones were responsible.'

Again the Colonel glowered.

'Whoever did it wanted Scoff out of the way because they wanted to acquire his espionage ring, or whatever we choose to call it. It could have been one of the ring's members. An ambitious baron, as it were, anxious to usurp the power and position of the throne. The only members about whom we are absolutely certain are Gabrielle herself and Luigi Dotto; but my impression is that ffrench-Thomas is implicated.'

'But,' said Amanda, 'ffrench-Thomas is part of the Bitschwiller organization and surely that would mean . . . '

'If you think about it, it means nothing,' continued the old man. 'As the Bitschwiller rep he does a lot of travelling. He could have been a useful link for Scoff. He could perfectly well have been involved.'

'Without Bitschwillers realizing?' This from Bognor.

'Of course. Delphine is beyond reproach. And nothing can be done in her organization – officially that is – without her knowledge and consent.'

'All right,' said Bognor, 'Scoff's death could have been a palace revolution, but what about Dmitri Petrov?'

'You mean . . . ' said Amanda, 'but I thought. . . . '

'I'm afraid so,' said Blight-Purley. There was a respectful pause while the three of them stared deep into their cups.

'So that rules out the Russians,' said Bognor.

'Not necessarily,' said Blight-Purley. 'The Russians might have induced Scoff's suicide and then removed the man responsible, thus covering their tracks in the best possible fashion.'

'But who's taken Petrov's place in all this?'

'That we don't know.'

'We don't seem to know much,' grumbled Bognor, aware once more of the tortuous ramifications of this case, 'but from what Ebertson said, we can rule out the Americans.'

'That I doubt,' said Blight-Purley, enjoying his role as dispenser of cold water. 'What could be more natural than for the Americans to remove Scoff and then turn round and say, "*Pax!* Nothing to do with us. You British take over and we won't interfere." '

'But what about Petrov?'

'Well?'

'Could the Americans have killed him too?'

Blight-Purley sighed. 'I see no reason why not. As I read it the Americans were frustrated and angry about Scoff's ring and the way he ran it. Having removed him, they were anxious for it to be controlled either by themselves or their nominee. It looks as if they have now decided to back the British interest.'

'But the British aren't interested,' wailed Bognor.

'But they don't know that.' Blight-Purley smiled. 'In their innocence they are assuming that your own presence in all this is an indication of British interest.'

'So you think Ebertson's bluffing?' asked Bognor, ignoring the implicit insult.

'In a sense,' said Blight-Purley, 'though I'm sure you can count on his co-operation from now on.'

'Which,' said Amanda, 'leaves the internal candidates.'

'Precisely.' They were pondering the implications of this when Pottinger shimmered over, face concentrated in a furrow of worry. Bognor thought it contrived but did not say so.

'Police, Colonel. On the telephone.' Blight-Purley rose and staggered off. 'I can't tell you how sorry I am that this should have happened,' continued their host, simpering. 'I blame myself. If the car park had been better lit. . . . If only we could have an attendant. . . . But these things cost money.'

'Oh, don't worry,' said Bognor. 'It's not your fault. It could have happened anywhere.'

'And the publicity,' he went on, not apparently hearing. 'I've had the *Advertiser* on already. It doesn't help.'

'You didn't hear anything yourself,' asked Bognor, 'nothing unusual, I mean?'

'You saw yourself.' He spread his arms out in a gesture of mock-Gallic despair. 'We were busy. In any case there would have been nothing unusual to hear – just a car starting and driving off. That happens all the time.'

'Quite.'

Bognor and Amanda exchanged glances that would often be described as pregnant with meaning. In fact all they meant was that they were now bound together in some form of partnership or conspiracy from which Pottinger was emphatically excluded. Both would have been pushed to define the meaning behind their meaningful looks, but

Pottinger rightly concluded from them that his presence was not required.

'He gives me the creeps,' said Amanda, after he had beaten a retreat in a fog of ritual remarks about hoping they had had a good night and hoping they had had a good breakfast.

'He couldn't care less whether we had a good night or a good breakfast,' said Bognor.

'They never can,' she agreed.

It took time to effect a departure for London. There was no question of using the Jaguar, but Pottinger agreed to drive them the three miles to the nearest railway station. Before that, however, Blight-Purley had to make a formal statement to a police sergeant who arrived self-importantly about half an hour after the completion of breakfast. Bognor himself was called in for brief corroboration. It was still too early to say with any certainty that the brakes or steering had been interfered with, but all four of the now greatly chastened thieves agreed that at the bottom of the hill the car had responded to neither. Keith, who had been driving, was adamant about the speed ; no more than thirty, he said – and the fact that he had put his foot hard down on the brake pedal and turned the steering wheel as far to the left as he could. The car had continued with increasing momentum and in an unerringly straight line until it had hit the wall. The police were inclined to believe this version since the injuries were, in the circumstances, comparatively slight. It looked as if all four had been prepared for the crash and had had time to take some action to diminish its effects. The car being old and expensive had proved at least as resilient as the wall and though seriously damaged had not concertina-ed as a cheaper, younger model might have done. Blight-Purley regarded it as a definite case of sabotage perpetrated by Hugh ffrench-Thomas. He did not, however, voice his suspicions except to Simon and Amanda. There seemed relatively little point, certainly none until any interference had been established by a post mortem on the machine.

'What neither of you have explained totally satisfactorily,' said Amanda, when they were all established in an otherwise unoccupied first-class compartment, 'is exactly why anyone should want to kill us.'

'Nobody wants to kill you, my dear,' said Blight-Purley trying to wipe grime from the window pane with his rolled up *Daily Telegraph*. 'It's me they want to kill.'

'And me,' said Bognor, offended.

'But I would have been in the car as well, and they would have realized it,' she said.

'You would have come into the spilt milk or broken egg category, I'm afraid.' The Colonel smiled his vaguely sinister smile. 'There would have been no use crying over you, and they couldn't have made an omelette without you either.'

'I see.' She frowned. 'But I still don't understand what sort of threat you pose. I mean you don't even know for certain who "they" are.'

'But that,' said Bognor looking smugger than he felt, 'doesn't prevent them from thinking that we know. They know that I'm officially investigating it all for the Board of Trade, and they know that Colonel Blight-Purley is helping me out in an unofficial capacity. As they say.'

'But . . . ' she looked even more perplexed, 'they still wouldn't kill you. Surely?'

'They've killed twice already,' said Bognor, 'for reasons which might seem trivial or even absurd to the normal person. But we aren't dealing with normal people. We aren't dealing with a normal world. We're dealing with people and things which, if they weren't utterly lethal, would be quite staggeringly silly. Espionage and organized crime are like that.'

'A bit like life,' said Blight-Purley sententiously.

The truth of these observations was borne in on him more than an hour later, after he had checked back into the office. It was almost lunchtime and the place was deserted. However, he was sufficiently sated, and aware of it, not to have any need of further food. Instead he eased back his mock leather swivel chair and put his feet on the desk. His thoughts were a mixture. On the one hand there was the memory of his masterful performance on the cricket field; on the other the increasing realization that the hand of death had only just been stayed. Moreover, his demise had not been avoided by any cleverness on his part. His survival was pure fluke. He was a wanted man. Somehow he had got someone rattled. That in itself was a more or less pleasing thought. He felt like Robin Hood must have felt when he saw a 'Wanted' notice signed Sheriff, Nottingham, pinned to a forest oak. Or Billy the Kid. He pulled on his cheroot and tried jutting his jaw. Unfortunately it wasn't the sort of jaw to which jutting came easily. He allowed it to sag back into its usual weary position of acceptance and humility, then consoled himself by trying to recall precisely what it was that had happened to him in bed. He had asked Mandy on the platform at Charing Cross when he would see her again, and she had replied that it was up to him. He had said he would telephone. He looked at the telephone. It was too soon. It would indicate a lack of cool. He sighed and, suddenly, as if in answer to his interest the phone rang. Surprised, he allowed it two or three rings before picking it up. The voice at the other end was muffled as if it was being passed through a thick woollen scarf.

'Mr Bognor?'

'Yes.'

'You enjoyed your stay at the Orange Lily, I hope.'

Bognor's antennae twitched. The fuzzy-voiced enquirer was not, he realized even through his hangover, a simple well wisher. 'Who is this?' he asked.

'Let us just say it is someone who has your best interests at heart.'

'Do you think you could take whatever you've got in your mouth out? I can't hear what you're saying. Who are you?'

'My identity is immaterial. I don't wish you to come to any harm.'

'Very good of you. Is that all? I'm extremely busy, and I'm afraid I really don't have time to fiddle around talking to complete strangers on the telephone.'

'Oh come, Simon, don't be so petulant. I'm trying to help you.'

'I don't need your help.' He wished he could recognize the voice but the disguise was effective.

'I do hope Monica is well,' said the voice.

'I've no idea,' he said crisply. 'I haven't seen her since the day before yesterday.'

'Precisely,' said the voice, breathing a touch heavily in the prescribed manner of anonymous telephone callers. 'She will have been concerned about you.'

Bognor said nothing. He had, in all honesty, forgotten about Monica. Not since early that morning had he given her a passing thought. Then in the unfamiliar, even exotic surroundings of the Orange Lily, he had decided that guilt was uncalled for. Now he wasn't so sure. Last night seemed less pardonable. More of an aberration.

'Of course,' continued the voice. 'I know you're not married or anything but living together does suggest certain, how shall I put it, obligations? I don't imagine Monica would be amused to hear how you spent last night.'

Bognor tried to persuade himself not to be rattled. It was only partially successful. 'What are you getting at?'

'Oh, come on, Simon, we're both men of the world, you and I. You know quite well what I'm getting at. If Monica were to receive certain information about you and Miss Bullingdon there might be trouble. Even in these permissive days. . . .'

Bognor thought. It was perfectly true that Monica would not be chuffed. Far from it. Perhaps that was what he wanted. Perhaps he wanted to end the relationship. However, if that were so he wanted to end it on his own terms and in his own way. He did not want a scene.

'What do you want?' he asked, realizing sadly that despite what he might have thought he was just as easy a blackmail victim as anyone else.

'I'm delighted you're being so reasonable,' continued his opponent. 'The photographs aren't developed yet, of course, but I am quite optimistic about them.'

'Christ!' swore Bognor. 'Pottinger, you rat!'

Through the scarf there issued a sardonic, superior chuckle. 'I'm afraid it wouldn't be in anyone's interest for you to be aware of my identity,' said the anonymous black-mailer. 'This is, of necessity, a rather one-sided transaction.'

'So I gather,' said Bognor bitterly. 'Even supposing that I go along with your implications, what exactly are you suggesting?'

'Not much. One, that you have nothing further to do with Colonel Blight-Purley. We consider that particular liaison to be most undesirable. Two, that you should terminate your blundering inquisition into the deaths of Mr Smith and Mr Petrov. They are no longer amusing. Do you understand?'

'Yes.'

'And do you agree?'

'I shall have to think about it.'

'Ah. Well. I shall know immediately if you do not do as I suggest. And if you are foolish then we shall be in touch with dear Monica. I make myself plain, I hope.'

'Perfectly.'

'Excellent. Good-bye then, for now. I have enjoyed our little talk.' There was a click followed by a renewal of the dialling tone. Bognor remained holding the receiver in his hand for a few moments, then noticed that his cigar had gone out. He replaced the receiver and swore, then smiled. 'So there *is* a spy ring and they *do* deal in blackmail.' It was confirmation of his suspicions though he was as far as ever from discovering the ideal way of having his suspicions confirmed. He was supposed to be the hunter. Now, it seemed, the roles had been reversed.

Chapter Seven

'A watching brief,' repeated Parkinson, dwelling censoriously on the 'r' of 'brief' which he rolled around his mouth as if it was cognac. 'A watching brief.' He stared at his subordinate with unconcealed resentment. 'And for what exactly will you be watching?' he enquired. 'And how brief is brief? And to what are we to attribute this sudden diminution of enthusiasm? Dyspepsia perhaps? Or is it worse than that? Is your liver beginning to give out? Having trouble sleeping at night? Is that what it is? Too much cream and alcohol? Eh? Eh?' He jabbed at Bognor with the rubber end of his pencil. 'Is this an admission of failure?'

'No,' said Bognor, re-crossing his legs. 'It's simply that I think some of those concerned are beginning to rumble my true intentions, and I think we would be well advised to lie low for a little.'

'I see,' said Parkinson, 'lie low for a little. . . .'

'Yes.' In the distance Big Ben struck half past the hour.

'This is rather sudden, Bognor. The last time we spoke you seemed markedly enthusiastic. "Salivating" one might say. What exactly has induced this sudden change in attitude?'

Bognor swallowed. 'There was this cricket match,' he said, and stopped.

'Yes?' prompted his boss.

'Well, there was quite a lot of rather obviously threatening behaviour.'

'Isn't that cricket?'

'Not necessarily. And in this case I'm fairly certain there was an ulterior motive. They as much as said so.'

'Is that all?'

'No, there was a problem with Blight-Purley's car.'

Bognor, long used to signs of incipient choler in his superior, did not fail to observe the gleam in Parkinson's eye.

'*Whose* car?'

'Erskine Blight-Purley's.'

'I thought I gave you specific instructions to avoid that man.'

'It was his cricket team.'

'Oh, for God's sake.'

They sat staring at each other, momentarily immobilized by their mutual despair.

'What happened?' asked Parkinson eventually, his voice heavy with gloom. Bognor told him.

'You seem to be fulfilling your usual catalytic role,' he said when the tale, expurgated, needless to say, so that Amanda Bullingdon's role was given in less than its entirety, was complete.

'How do you mean?'

'Until you got caught up in all this we just had one probable suicide whose death was tinged with the merest hint of a suspicion. No more. Since your arrival we've had one death – definitely murder – a horrendous cricket match with projectiles narrowly missing a number of targets, plus a car crash which seems to have been as obviously and artificially induced as the late Scoff's suicide. I suppose if I hadn't put you on it nothing would have happened and everyone would have been living happily ever after.'

'I wouldn't bank on it,' said Bognor. 'Besides, we know Scoff was getting useful information, and we know that with his death the supply of that information hasn't dried up.'

'Hmmm?' Parkinson did not seem to be concentrating.

'Oh, forget it,' said Bognor.

Parkinson tapped his upper lip with the pencil. 'Very well,' he said, 'a watching brief it is. You're in charge. Just carry on. Keep me informed and stay out of trouble.'

Bognor was greatly relieved. 'I still hope Acapulco will yield something,' he said cheerily.

Parkinson's expression remained unchanged. 'I believe we had an understanding about that place,' he said.

'Yes,' said Bognor. 'If I solve everything there, then well and good. If not you dock my leave.'

'By double.'

'Of course.' Parkinson stretched his mouth in what might, in another man, have passed for a smile. Then he said, 'Meanwhile, while you're keeping your profile appropriately low there is some routine positive vetting I should like you to get on with.' He opened a drawer and shoved two folders across at Bognor. They were ordinary tasks: a research chemist from a large pharmaceutical firm who had been taken on by the germ warfare people at Porton Down, and a bright young philosophy don who was being hired to give a little much needed extra tone to the Cabinet Office. They needed checking out, just to make sure they weren't known rapists, junkies, Maoists or any sort of deviant who might be undesirable in either place. Bognor would have to interview a small number of their friends and associates. It was the sort of boring but essential enquiry which seldom if ever produced anything remotely untoward.

'Fine,' said Bognor. He put the folders under his arm and walked out, gratified by the ease with which he had managed to satisfy Parkinson and, by extension, the demands of the anonymous muffled voice on the telephone.

He did not want the blackmailer, whoever he was, to tell Monica what had happened at the Orange Lily. Far less did he want photographs to be bandied about. Secretly he doubted whether photographs existed, but he was not prepared to take risks. Perhaps, in what he told himself might prove to be the fullness of time, he might jettison Monica, but it was not something about which he was prepared to be precipitate. Unfortunately, the embarrassingly personal nature of the blackmail was such that he found it difficult to confide in anyone, least of all the person in whom he usually confided – and who frequently provided him with the answer which was staring him, unobserved, in the face – Monica herself.

'What's happening with the Scoff–Petrov business?' she

asked him, a few nights after the incident at the Orange Lily.

'Oh,' he said, airily, 'we've decided to give it a bit of a rest until Acapulco. Lull our suspects into a false sense of security.'

'Your opponents are always lulled into a sense of security,' she said waspishly. 'The trouble is that it's never false.'

That was as far as it went. Otherwise their life together pursued its usual affectionate if humdrum course, untouched by anything that Bognor felt or did not feel about Amanda Bullingdon.

Quite what he did feel about her was less than sure. He did telephone her one morning, and she did agree to have lunch with him. During the meal she was pleasant and polite but almost distant. Certainly no one would have guessed that they were lovers. It was as if nothing had ever happened. When, over coffee, he mentioned the blackmail phone call, she blushed.

'Who could it be?' she asked. 'The same people who fixed the car?'

When he mentioned the possibility of photographs she giggled.

'I'd quite like to see them,' she said, and then, noticing his pained expression, changed her mind. 'Oh well, perhaps not.'

The possibility of a repeat performance was not mooted. Bognor did not know how to without seeming indelicate. It was not something you discussed at lunch – at least not something Bognor discussed over lunch. And there was Monica. And the chance of yet more blackmail. For the time being at least he decided to restrict their meetings to lunch. He could kid himself that such encounters were a necessary part of a watching brief.

Fearful of exciting further telephonic threats, he steered clear of his new gastronomic friends, though invitations continued to arrive from all and sundry. He accepted the more impersonal – large wine tastings for example – and eschewed the more intimate on grounds, usually legitimate, of pressure of work. The positive vetting, though boring, was time consuming and did not leave him much time for anything else. He continued to converse, slightly nervously, with those he met at such functions – Ebertson, Pring, Aubergine Bristol among them – but tried to avoid Blight-Purley as much as possible. Before long the old man inevitably spotted this and telephoned to ask for an explanation. Bognor prevaricated but finally explained that he was biding his time on the investigation and was, anyway, under great pressure from Parkinson to have nothing whatever to do with the Colonel. This was more or less true and Blight-Purley seemed to accept it.

What worried him more than anything was the invitation to Acapulco. His anonymous caller had not mentioned the trip, but he was fairly certain that to go there would involve a breach of whatever agreement he was supposed to have reached. On the other hand he wanted to go, partly because he was mildly curious, partly because he had a hunch about it. Besides, Parkinson, despite his initial hostility (perhaps because of it), would undoubtedly smell a rat if he were to drop out of it now.

Accordingly, on the last day of May he was at Heathrow, a jaded, chubby, apprehensive figure in an all too obviously brand new lightweight suit. As always on venturing abroad, he was in a state of constant, if subdued, panic, fretting over the seemingly endless items essential for safe departure and arrival. His suitcase was packed and checked in, but he nevertheless felt obliged to consult his baggage check every five minutes. He kept repeating to himself, 'ticket, passport, travellers' cheques, wallet,' and patting the relevant pockets to make sure they were all in place. This was made the more difficult because every so often he would withdraw one or other just to make absolutely certain. He would then replace it in a different pocket thus rendering the next patting of the pockets even more frantic than the last.

'Having trouble?' Aubergine Bristol and Aubrey Pring stood before him. They both carried glasses of what looked like gin and tonic and hand luggage which Bognor was sure was the work of someone called Gucci or Pucci. He could never remember which.

'Sorry?' he said.

'We thought you had fleas or something,' said Aubergine, smiling. 'You were sort of hitting yourself all over.'

'Oh,' he coloured, 'no. I'd just mislaid my, er . . . diary.'

'Oh.' They seemed unconvinced.

'Any sign of Hugh ffrench-Thomas?'

Bognor changed colour rapidly from puce to off-white. 'Is *he* coming?'

'Of course. He's the Bitschwiller rep. He's more or less in charge. At least he's in charge until Roissy. Why?'

'The cricket,' said Aubergine pretending to kick him. 'I shouldn't have thought you'd be worried by that,' she continued. 'It seemed to me to be a victory for you rather than him.'

'I suppose so.'

There were about fifteen of them as it turned out. Very much the mixture as before. In fact Bognor was beginning to realize that the *monde gastronomique*, or at least that part of it which was concerned in one way or another with its popularization, was an extremely small one. ffrench-Thomas marshalled them with reserved politeness into a small VIP lounge where there were bottles of Bitschwiller. Aubrey and Aubergine knocked back their gin and tonics and filled up with champagne. Conversation became convivial and Bognor wondered, as he peered around over Ebertson's left shoulder, whether the man who had made the anonymous phone call was in the room. Neither Dotto nor Pottinger was among the guests and they were his most likely suspects. He wondered also whether the inducer of the Scoff suicide and the murderer of Dmitri Petrov were among them, and he wondered, too, whether his hunch was going to turn out correct, and that something significant was going to happen in Acapulco.

'Hel*lo*,' said an effusive, mildly effeminate voice. 'Haven't congratulated you properly on your innings.'

'Oh, Mr Pendennis,' said Bognor smiling. 'Whenever we meet we seem to be drinking this.' He held up his glass and watched the bubbles silhouetted against the neon strip lighting. 'Are you joining us in Acapulco? I hadn't realized.'

Pendennis looked pained. 'Surely you remember Château Petheram?'

'Château Petheram? Oh, of course.' How could he ever have forgotten it, he wondered, recalling the disgustingly acid red muck that Pendennis had served up on his first visit. 'You're introducing it to an astonished world in Acapulco, aren't you?'

'Absolutely.'

Bognor could not for the life of him imagine how the man had the effrontery. It was undrinkable. No amount of endorsement from la Veuve, no ludicrous snobisme about it being an English wine, could possibly persuade any normal palate of anything else.

'I hope it travels,' he said.

'It will travel.'

They were interrupted by ffrench-Thomas, still looking as youthful and fit as he had on the cricket field. He was asking them to drink up and board. They did so. It was a more painless exercise than usual. Less of a queue. The search for bombs or guns was more perfunctory, and when they arrived on board they were ushered into the first-class compartment and plied with more alcohol. Bognor disliked flying, but if he had to do it then this was the way in which it should be done. By the time they arrived on French ground he and his colleagues were in a uniformly genial frame of mind.

'You'll enjoy Delphine,' said Blight-Purley, as they ascended a moving staircase built into a transparent plastic tube which led to the main reception areas. He was standing on the step behind Bognor, flushed and buoyant as a school-boy going on holiday.

'I hope so. She sounds rather daunting.'

'Don't be daunted.' He lowered his voice and leant forward so that his lips almost touched Bognor's right ear. 'Made any progress?' he asked, *sotto voce*. For a moment Bognor was tempted to tell him about the anonymous phone call. If he was right, then merely by making this trip he had called the caller's bluff – if bluff it was. Monica might even now be being apprised of his infidelity.

He was on the point of imparting the confidence when a thought struck him – a new one. Perhaps his blackmailer was Blight-Purley himself. He knew what had happened that night. Perhaps he was frightened by Bognor's persistent enquiries. Bognor wondered what the Colonel's voice would sound like through a handkerchief, softly. 'No,' he replied, as they emerged from the perspex and were spewed out into a wide glassy concourse. 'No progress at all.' And then partly because the idea that Blight-Purley might after all be villainously inclined, and partly because it was true, he said, 'I have an idea it's one of those mysteries which may just go away. A lot of people seem to think it might be better left unsolved.'

'Ha.' Blight-Purley's eyes sparkled with irritation and something which appeared almost like lust. 'Don't forget the Jag.'

'Of course not.' Bognor's amnesia seemed worse than usual today, though in this instance it was only temporary. The Jaguar had merely slipped his mind, not escaped it altogether. 'Had it been tampered with? Did they find out who did it?'

'Yes and no. Yes to the first; no to the second.'

'Ah.' They had traversed the hall now, following obediently in ffrench-Thomas' footsteps. He turned left down a corridor and the crocodile turned with him, emerging almost immediately into a large and distinctly merry cocktail party. There seemed to Bognor to be about two hundred men and women in the room – all of them undeniably foreign and probably French. It wasn't that he was in any sense a xenophobe – rather the reverse – but the foreignness was obtrusive and mildly disturbing. They seemed to be enjoying themselves more than any similar English group would have done. And smoking more. Foreign noise; foreign smells; tantalizing foreign canapés being hurried about by uniformed lackeys; in every hand a glass of what Bognor was beginning to think of as *that* drink'. He mentally flexed his nose and ears and eyes, an islander preparing to do battle with the great abroad.

'Come and meet Delphine,' said Blight-Purley, putting a hand on his elbow and propelling him, none too gently, through the throng. Bognor's senses were assailed by unaccustomed vowel sounds accompanied by that aroma of garlic and *gauloise* which he knew was too characteristically French to be true. Nevertheless here it was. Perhaps they were Frenchmen from Central Casting.

Suddenly they were out of the scrum and in an oasis of decorum. Throughout their passage Blight-Purley had been wringing hands and exclaiming in passable Gallic accents such things as 'Maurice . . . *comment – ça va*? Pierre . . . *mon vieux . . . enchanté.* Monique you are looking *irrésistible*,' and so on. Now a small woman clothed entirely in grey and black caught sight of him and exclaimed in tinkling tones: 'Erskine!' She emphasized the last syllable making it sound like 'skein'.

Blight-Purley kissed her on both cheeks, then said, 'Delphine, I'd like you to meet a young friend of mine, Simon Bognor.'

'Of course.' She held out a hand which Bognor shook diffidently, wondering after he had done so whether he should have kissed it. Blight-Purley, looking on, muttered something about, 'Delphine Bitschwiller, our hostess.'

Bognor, relinquishing the hand, looked up at the eyes which he realized, disconcerted, were studying him with an amused, almost supercilious attention. They were steel grey like her hair and her pearls, and they looked as if they didn't miss a trick. 'And how is the Board of Trade?'

'Fine, thank you,' he replied inanely.

The thin-lined face smiled, though the pleasure was not reflected in the eyes. With that sort of person in that sort of position, he had long since learnt, it never is.

'You had an enjoyable flight?' The remark was addressed to both of them, and they proceeded to a minute or two of very small talk until she excused herself and moved on to another guest. Bognor just had time to confirm his first impression which had in turn confirmed what he had already heard. Charming, formidable, shrewd etcetera, etcetera: typical Frenchwoman, typical businesswoman.

The Bitschwiller plane was on charter from Air France. It was a Boeing 747, the original Jumbo. Bitschwiller had their own jet, but it was not large enough to accommodate the cocktail party. Bognor learned from a voluble French restaurateur, who had fought with a Maquis near Lyon and was thus on intimate terms with Blight-Purley, that there had been a move to go by Concorde. Unfortunately it would have taken two to get them there, and even for Bitschwiller and their co-sponsors that represented too great an expense. The final choice meant that though their party was a large one there was still room to wander and stretch. Bognor, like most of his fellow passengers, watched the film (*All the President's Men*) which he had seen already and was rendered incomprehensible by some bad dubbing into French. He also ate and drank excessively and well, and slept fitfully. In between a certain amount of fraternizing went on. La Veuve Bitschwiller and her immediate entourage were in the upstairs section normally reserved for first class. Occasionally an aide would appear and summon one or other of her less privileged guests for an audience. They had just passed Bermuda and Bognor was dozing off for the third time when he was tapped on the shoulder by a minion enquiring if he was Monsieur Bognor.

'*Oui*,' said Bognor, rather crustily in his schoolboy French, '*Bien sure Bognor c'est moi*.' La Veuve, it transpired, wanted the pleasure. He stumbled upstairs rubbing his eyes.

'Oh, Mr Bognor,' she said in English which was almost too perfect. 'I thought I should use the opportunity for a little chat. I have heard so much about your mission. Tell me about it.'

He sat down heavily next to her. 'We're looking at the top end of the food and drink market,' he began, and went through his spiel once more like a sleepwalker. As he did so he was thinking about his real mission: the double deaths; the threats; the spy and blackmail ring.

'So, you would be looking for some way to assist a new English wine for example,' she said. He realized with a jerk that he must have finished his exposition.

'Like Château Petheram,' he said, quick, he thought to himself, as a flash.

She smiled knowingly and said, 'Did you know Escoffier Smith?'

In his head alarm bells began to ring.

'No. That is, I used to go to his restaurant until he died.'

'I think he was the best chef your country has ever produced,' she said quite seriously. 'Of course, we had hoped that he would be with us today but . . . ' She made a little gesture with her hands which appeared to suggest that Scoff's death was one of those tiresome events which happen from time to time and must be accepted with fatalism.

'I'm sure Gabrielle will fill in very adequately,' he ventured.

'Gabrielle is merely a girl.'

'But she knows her stuff. I mean, she learned a lot from Escoffier.'

'She is a girl. She has no – what would you say in England – no "flair". She has no originality. She is a deputy. She is suitable for peeling vegetables.'

'Oh.'

'There is a Mr Petrov who is also dead.'

'Yes.'

Bognor had forgotten that Petrov was, as far as most people were concerned, merely missing, presumed dead. Now, suddenly, he remembered it. 'That is unfortunate.'

'Extremely.'

'He was a gourmet, I should say. For a Russian that is unusual.'

'I suppose so.'

'Death is not something which concerns you at the Board of Trade?'

'How do you mean?'

'During the war I was, you know . . . involved . . . in the Resistance. My husband and my father were both captured by the Germans. That was also unfortunate.' She smiled glacially. 'It is also, as you say, another story. During the war I had a great many dealings with your British Intelligence personnel. Many of them were not . . . probable.'

'Oh, I don't have anything to do with anything like that.'

'No.'

'Have you been in Mexico before?' he asked, rather obviously.

'Quite often. *Entre nous* I prefer Vallarta to Acapulco.

Acapulco has no *chic*. It was an American idea. Do you know Acapulco?'

'Only from films.'

'It is better in films.'

They chattered for a few minutes, then Bognor announced that he must not keep her from her sleep. She did not demur, but, as he was leaving, she said, 'You must not believe everything that Erskine tells you.'

'How do you mean?'

She put her finger to her lips and pursed them, smiling thinly.

Bognor smiled back and went downstairs.

Acapulco *was* very like the films. The drive from the airport in air-conditioned coaches took them past the Acapulco Princess, a vast hotel constructed in the style of an Aztec pyramid. One of its swimming pools had underwater music; Howard Hughes had died in its penthouse. A very small Mexican guide with a whining falsetto voice pointed it out and told them, 'the superlative chefs of the Princess speak only the language of the *haute cuisine*'. The English party tittered. Next to Bognor Amanda Bullingdon yawned widely and said, 'Oh really!'

A few miles further on they turned a corner and saw the resort itself. 'Lulworth with skyscrapers,' said Bognor feeling jaded.

'Oh, come on,' said Amanda. 'It's a beautiful bay. And look at that sea.'

'Very blue,' he admitted. It was, he privately conceded, a very picturesque bay, though marred by the presence of the rusty tramp steamer in the middle of it. A tiny speedboat churned the surface, sending up creamy foam behind and towing something. He looked for the water-skier but couldn't see one.

'Isn't that parachute fun!' said Amanda, pointing. He followed her finger and saw that the boat was pulling a parachute of red, white and blue; from it there dangled a person.

'Very Acapulco,' he said.

The coach stopped at a smart gate-house with a cluster of pink and white jeeps outside. 'All French and German guests alight here,' said the Mexican guide, adenoidally. The French and Germans did as they were told, noisily and with much throwing about of hand luggage. When they had gone the English were the only ones left in the coach.

'We're at the Bristol,' said ffrench-Thomas, standing up. 'There wasn't room at Las Brisas for everyone, and in any case I thought we'd all rather be downtown where the action is.' He laughed hollowly. They were driving along a wide avenue flanked with tall buildings and tourist oriented bars. Bognor noticed one called 'Carlos 'n' Charlie's' and then another called 'Charlie's Chilli 'n' Dance Hall 'n' Grill'.

'Everyone here seems to be called Charlie,' said Amanda.

'And the language is like what the Bushmen of the Kalahari talk. All glottal stops.'

The coach stopped outside a gigantic concrete pile with a revolving glass door and a lime green awning. 'Lunch in the hotel restaurant at one,' ffrench-Thomas kept saying, as they checked in. Bognor filled in his marital status, age, sex, and passport number, and ascended sleepily to his room on the seventeenth floor. Before going to sleep he phoned down for an alarm call and discovered that it was ten past ten local time. He flung himself down on the bed and was almost immediately dreaming fitfully of lobster and guacamole and chilli sauce and then, more disturbingly, of being held down by four Mexicans called Charlie. They wore ponchos and vast straw hats, and they were chanting '*Gringo*' repeatedly while a fifth, a dour scarfaced man with an exaggerated Zapata moustache, poured alternate bottles of tequila and Bitschwiller into a funnel held to his mouth. Finally, just as he was on the point of drowning in alcohol, he woke. The phone was ringing. His watch showed eleven-thirty. He swore.

'Hello, it's Mandy, can I come round?'

'Well. . . . ' He attempted to focus. He wasn't in the mood for sex. Too tired. Besides, even though he was fond of Amanda he wasn't sure he wanted to get involved.

She read his thoughts. 'It's all right, don't panic. I'm not going to rape you. I've just had rather an intriguing phone call. I thought it might interest you.'

'Can't it wait till lunch?'

'It's a bit private, and I have to go up to the restaurant after lunch to help Gabrielle.'

'I thought you and Gabrielle didn't get on.'

'Oh well, you know how it is. Anyway, it's about her.'

'What?'

'I'm coming round.' The receiver went dead and a few seconds later there was a knock on the door. It was her. She looked crumpled and untidy but excited.

'What is it?' he asked tetchily. 'It had better be important. I was asleep.'

'Don't be so bad tempered,' she said. 'It's interesting.'

'Tell me,' said Bognor, rubbing his eyes.

'Well, Gabrielle rang. She's having a dreadful time in the kitchens with all those foreigners. It's ghastly. There's a Taiwan chef working with the Americans, and the Chinese are objecting, and none of the blacks will work with the South African girls who've come to cook bobotie, and she says the kummel tastes of sewage.'

'Don't be ridiculous,' said Bognor. 'Kummel can't taste of sewage.'

'Mexican kummel can.'

'Mexican kummel can't.'

They stood glowering at each other.

'Is that all?' asked Bognor eventually.

She grinned. 'No. She said Aubrey had been round to see her and made a nuisance of himself.'

'How do you mean?'

'She was very hysterical. Something about the Dour Dragoon losing its rosette in *Bitschwiller*.'

'What has Aubrey got to do with that?'

'I don't know. She was hardly coherent. All I really gathered was that Aubrey had been pestering her. And then there was this business about how she didn't want to lose her *Bitschwiller* rosette.'

'Now *you're* being incoherent. I heard the first time. Aubrey came round and pestered her, and she's worried about losing her rosette. Okay. But what I want to know is did Aubrey tell her that he had the removal of the rosette in his power?'

She looked blank. 'I don't know.'

'It's important.'

'Well.' Again she hesitated. 'I think that's what she said. It's certainly what she implied.'

'It's certainly what you inferred.'

'I thought you'd be interested.'

'I'm sorry. Yes, I am interested. Why was Aubrey pestering her?'

'I'm not sure. I began asking her, of course, but then I think she suddenly realized she'd said too much.'

'And you're going to help her this afternoon?'

'There's no one else, and it's a dress rehearsal this evening.'

'How do you mean – no one else?'

'Only local boys. They're no good. She's been here two days already, and she says it's driving her mad. They had an earthquake yesterday.'

Bognor raised eyebrows. 'An earthquake? Here?'

'Only a small one. But it cracked a whole lot of Gabrielle's eggs. I feel really rather sorry for her. One of the Italians keeps making passes.'

'What do you expect? If he's Italian, he's bound to make passes at her.'

'It's not a "he", it's a "she".'

'Listen.' Bognor sat down heavily on the bed and wagged a finger at her. 'Find out everything you reasonably can – only don't be obvious about it.' He thought for a moment. 'Aubrey must have gone straight round there as soon as we arrived. He must have been very keen.'

'On what?'

'That's what you've got to find out.'

'Oh, I see.' She smiled, wrinkling her nose. 'Are we going to have lunch?'

It didn't take him long to decide that Acapulco was not really his sort of place. After a lunch of leathery enchilladas and rubbery prawns with over-priced vinegary Mexican wine, he went for a stroll along the Costera Miguel Aleman and then back along the beach. It was hot – hot enough for him to remove his lightweight jacket and dangle it casually over one shoulder. The buildings were tall and new except for the many restaurants and curio shops which fronted the bay. Vendors of fairground bric-à-brac accosted him with offers of hats and rude dolls. They continued to do so when he sat on the beach and took off his shoes and socks and scuffed his feet in the sand. The waves were noisy and forbidding, and there was a smell. After a while he decided to return to the hotel and use the pool, which meandered all around a centrally placed bar and restaurant. He changed into his pantaloon-style tartan swimming trunks, looked down at his spreading flaccid white stomach with something approaching dismay, and slipped gently into the tepid water. Swimming around in a clockwise direction, he came upon a row of bar stools in the water. They were unoccupied, and he sat down on one and rested his elbows on the side of the pool as if it were a bar counter. A waiter approached and asked something incomprehensible. Bognor nodded knowingly and said, *'Si per favore.'*

The man went away and returned with a coconut shell from which there protruded two candy-striped straws. The waiter bent down and put the coconut by Bognor's elbows, at the same time producing a bill and a biro. Bognor signed it and wrote down his room number then sucked on the straws. The cold liquid tasted of coconut and alcohol. He was unsurprised. This, he supposed, as he caught sight of a dark brown fleshy body waggling past in an orange bikini, was the life. He pulled on the straw and wondered why Aubrey Pring should have gone round to Gabrielle so smartly, and precisely what he had done to upset her. He had never thought Aubrey suspicious before. On the other hand he had always harboured a hunch about Acapulco. Perhaps Aubrey was about to reveal himself.

'How are you liking it?' Anthony J. Ebertson executed a deft half somersault behind him and ended up sitting on the next stool.

'What?'

'Oh, Acapulco, your drink, life in general.'

The American's body, Bognor noticed enviously, was slim and muscular.

'So-so.'

Ebertson ordered a fresh orange juice. 'I hear the future of the Scoff syndicate is still unresolved,' he said.

'Oh?'

'How big a pitch are you making for it?'

'I wouldn't say we were making much of a pitch at all. I think I mentioned before my people's attitude towards it is a bit like yours. Negative.'

'We'd like to see it becoming a little more positive.' He raised his drink in the direction of Bognor's coconut. 'Good health,' he said. 'Gabrielle apparently thinks she can run the show on her own, together with people like ffrench-Thomas and that fellow Dotto, the wicket-keeper.'

'How do you know?'

'We have someone in the kitchen.'

'In the Dour Dragoon kitchen?'

'He's a waiter really. Not altogether reliable but we have something on him. He's part of the family you could say.'

'Not Massimo?'

'Right in one.' Ebertson seemed mildly impressed. 'You know him?'

'We've met.'

'He tells me Aubrey Pring has suddenly started showing an interest.'

'Really?' Bognor affected an indifference he was far from feeling. 'Anything definite?'

'Simply an interest. Pring's there a lot. Talks to Gabrielle in hushed whispers.' Behind them there was the splashing of a swimmer slowly approaching. As it came closer they could hear that the splashing was mixed with elderly asthmatic breath. Turning they saw Blight-Purley rounding the bend. He was propelling himself with a very correct, military side stroke.

'*Pas devant le colonel*,' said Ebertson softly. 'Don't trust him.'

'Oh. Right,' said Bognor as Blight-Purley hoisted himself

unsteadily on to one of the stools. *His* body sagged a little like Bognor's, but he was, after all old enough to be his father.

He ordered a Margarita.

'Bloody hot,' he said conversationally.

The first official – or semi-official – event of the gathering was the next day in mid-morning. Although the *pièce de résistance* was the great dinner, there were many smaller events organized by individual delegations. A demonstration of *wok-work* by a couple of the Chinese; of *cuisine minceur* by an unofficial French delegate; of a hundred and one ways with haddock by the Icelandic White Fish Authority; of how to provide meatless saddle of mutton and baron of beef by the International Vegan brotherhood.

The British were presenting a gloomily pedestrian film called 'A History of British Cooking' and, of course, the famous Château Petheram. This was being presented by the side of one of the Las Brisas swimming pools high up on the hill. Its only competition came from a Korean buffet consisting of 'Food of the noble and beloved President Kim Il Sung, the great leader of the Korean people'. This was in a tatty hotel downtown and, apart from those few representatives of the communist bloc who felt obliged to attend on grounds of political solidarity, it was not popular.

'I'm afraid this could prove embarrassing,' said Blight-Purley, elbowing through the throng of international gastronomes. His face had been burnt to a still pucer colour than usual by the Mexican sun.

'Is there going to be enough to go round?' asked Bognor briefly, glimpsing a view through the scrum.

'The wine's not important,' said Ebertson. Like everybody else he was drinking a tequila-based cocktail. 'It's a pretext.'

'That sounds unduly cynical.'

'He *is* unduly cynical,' said Aubergine Bristol, 'or hadn't you noticed?' The sun had turned her an instant brown. No sign of burning at all. 'Aubrey and I are going to try out one of those parachute things this afternoon. The ones you tow behind boats. Why don't you join us?'

'I'd need a few more Margaritas before I go up in one of those,' said Bognor.

'The point is,' said Blight-Purley, who had not been listening, 'the wine won't pass muster.'

Just as he said it a silence reverberated out from the steps at one side of the pool. Conversation died away under a chorus of shushing noises and the banging of a gavel. A loudspeaker system gave a sudden ear-splitting whine followed by a click. A man in a red coat said, 'My lords, ladies and gentlemen, *messieurs, mesdames* I bid you welcome to the tasting of *le premier vin rouge Britannique* and pray silence for Madame Delphine Bitschwiller of the House of Bitschwiller.' There was applause and outbreaks of chatter in Spanish and Italian from isolated portions of the audience. These were loudly hushed by the Anglo-Saxons and the French. La Veuve spoke in French, and she spoke briefly. Then with a wide but frigid smile she introduced Freddie Pendennis who spoke at greater length and some tedium, inducing still more mutter from the Latins and flashing glances of disapproval from his allies. When he had finished, a band of Mexican wine waiters trooped out from behind him and began to circulate with glasses of the Château Petheram.

'I suppose we have to,' said Bognor, who was enjoying his second Margarita.

'Indubitably,' said Blight-Purley.

The little knot of English, huddled together for security, if not warmth, all went through the sniffing and gargling in unison, like a circus act. There were no spittoons, and the crush was too great for spitting on the ground. Bognor toyed with the idea of doing it into the hibiscus-littered pool, but thought better of it. Similar thoughts clearly passed through the minds of his compatriots, but after hesitation they all swallowed. After doing so there was a moment's contemplation, and then a chorus the tenor of which was 'Gosh, I say.' The wine was good.

'Somewhat akin to what took place at Cana,' said Blight-Purley.

'What?' asked Aubergine Bristol.

'Water into wine,' said Bognor. 'Blasphemous joke. It does seem to travel well though, doesn't it?'

Blight-Purley was holding his glass up to the sun. Then he put his nose in it. Then he poured some into his mouth and gargled. After he had swallowed he held the glass to the sun again and rotated it. He was frowning. 'That's not from Petheram,' he said. 'That's from between Lyon and Avignon. What's more, I can tell you exactly where.'

'But Erskine,' said Ebertson, 'it says it on the bottle. Look: "Vin d'Angleterre". And the note on the back about how it's done. I admit it's improved beyond recognition in the last few weeks, but it has to be Petheram. It can't be anything else.'

'That wine you're drinking,' said Blight-Purley, speaking very distinctly, 'comes from a vineyard a few miles out of the village of Condillac in the Rhône valley. It's called the Château Oreille de Cochon.'

'Pig's Ear Castle,' translated Bognor, partly for the benefit of Ebertson and partly to make sure he'd got it right.

'How on earth do you know that?' asked the American, addressing the query to the Colonel rather than the interpreter.

'It belonged to Delphine's uncle, Yves,' said Blight-Purley, staring into space. 'I last tasted that thirty years go. It's the suggestion of loganberries that's so distinctive.'

'But it's very good whatever it is,' said Bognor.

'Of course it's good,' said Blight-Purley, 'that's the whole point. They can produce a lot of it, but because of the snobbery of the international wine market they were never able to get anything like a proper price for it. Côtes du Rhône just isn't fashionable. It's always been like that. Hence the château's unlikely nomenclature.'

'You mean,' suggested Bognor, now groping, 'you can't make a silk purse from a sow's ear.'

'Precisely.'

'But I don't see. . . . '

Blight-Purley put an arm round Bognor and shifted him away from the others. 'Listen,' he said, 'this is quite serious.

If I'm right, and I'm certain I am, then there's some hanky panky going on.'

'Explain.' Bognor thought he saw what the Colonel was getting at.

'Yves is dead,' said Blight-Purley. 'He had no children. Oreille de Cochon went to Delphine. It's hers. The wine's good but they can't sell it for enough because it comes from the wrong place. It's every bit as fine as all but the best burgundies but no one believes it. Prejudice, pure and simple, but there it is. So the Bitschwillers have never bothered to put it on the market. Some of it they drink themselves, some they adulterate with rubbish, probably Algerian, and pass it off as a French carafe wine of indeterminate provenance. You follow?'

'I'm beginning to.'

'Now Pendennis comes up with this hare-brained scheme to make an English red. Right?'

'Yes.'

'And it's like anaemic vinegar.'

'Yes.'

'So he does a deal with Delphine. She puts her useless wine into his bottles, and they flog it for double what she could get for Oreille de Cochon and a million times what he could get for his undrinkable Château Petheram, so-called.'

'Is that possible?'

Blight-Purley grimaced and regarded the inky red wine with a baleful expression. 'I wouldn't have said so, but that's what they've done.'

'What are you going to do about it?' Watching the crowd Bognor was aware that those not awash with tequila were approaching Pendennis' product with surprised appreciation. They liked it, to judge from the satisfied smiles; their satisfaction, to judge from the way it was being studied, was mildly incredulous.

'I shall raise the matter with Delphine.'

'You won't report it?'

'To whom?'

It was a fair question. Bognor had no idea. 'The authorities,' he said, feebly.

'The *Mexican* authorities, I suppose,' said Blight-Purley baring his teeth in an expression which made it quite plain that as far as he was concerned the idea of *Mexican* authorities was patently ludicrous. 'The gentlemanly and correct course of action is to present Delphine with my evidence.'

'But you have no evidence as such.'

'I have the evidence of my palate. That is perfectly sufficient. Besides Delphine is a lady. She would shrink from deception.'

'But deception,' Bognor was plaintive, 'is what you're accusing her of.'

Blight-Purley was not listening. 'Yves would be un-amused,' he said, turning, and making off into the crowd.

It was an hour before Bognor saw him again. He had by then taken a great deal more alcohol and was leaning on a balustrade staring out to sea. Bognor on his own approached and enquired: 'Well?'

'Well, what?'

'The wine. Is it Oreille de Cochon or Château Petheram?'

'The palate cannot tell a lie.'

'But what does Delphine say?'

'She says it's Château Petheram.'

'And you don't believe her?'

Blight-Purley swung round to face him. The eyes looked more than usually bloodshot. It was probably the drink, though for a second Bognor wondered if it might not have been some lachrymose evidence of a maudlin disillusion.

'No,' he said.

'Did you tell her that too?'

'Yes.'

That would not have gone down well. No one, least of all a Bitschwiller, enjoyed being called a liar. Particularly when they have already just been accused of fraud.

It was difficult to know how to continue conversation after this since, all else apart, the Colonel was clearly (in the nautical phrase Bognor vaguely remembered from some naval relation) three sheets in the wind. They were saved by the intervention of Aubrey Pring and Aubergine Bristol. 'Come on then, you two,' exclaimed Aubrey. 'Come for a whirl in the *bateau*.'

'We're parachuting with José,' said Aubergine.

Bognor and Blight-Purley nodded in a bemused manner. A trip round the bay was certainly not what either man wanted, but one was too drunk and the other too polite to say so. They moved off, clambered aboard one of the hotel's pink and white jeeps, and drove down the hill to the spot where José, a squat hairy individual in a silvery G-string, was waiting with an immensely powerful speedboat and a battalion of equally diminutive helpers. The parachute lay limp on the sand.

'Lady first,' said José, doing an unnecessary amount of waist and elbow clutching to which Aubergine did not seem averse. The three men took off their shoes, rolled up their trousers and waded out to the boat. The helpers gathered around Aubergine and issued instructions as she was strapped in. Then José returned to the boat. 'Now we go,' he said to his passengers.

'Shouldn't she be wearing swimming things?' asked Bognor. Aubergine was in a white trouser suit, though she had now abandoned the jacket.

'She land on sand,' said José, revving the engine. He looked back at the beach and received a thumbs up sign from one of the helpers. He returned it and nudged the engine into gear. The boat shot forward like a jet on the runway, giving Bognor the same jolt in the back and also inducing the same fearful nausea. He shut his eyes for a few seconds and prayed, then raised his head to the sky behind and saw that the parachute had filled with air and was now rising like a gaudy toadstool with the Honourable Aubergine dangling underneath it. They were racing towards the middle of the bay and Bognor began to relax.

'Looks quite easy,' he said.

'Dead easy,' said Aubrey, shading his eyes with his hands to get a clearer view of his girlfriend, who was now barely distinguishable as a human being. 'You come down with a mild clunk, but nothing to worry about. You going next?'

'I'm not very good at heights,' said Bognor.

'We'll send Erskine then. Sober him up.'

Blight-Purley already seemed refreshed by the salt and the wind and the exhilaration of speed. The boat was bouncing along the waters of the bay at a terrific rate.

'You next?' shouted Aubrey.

'Right you are,' said the Colonel, unflinching.

'Are you sure?' asked Bognor, concerned. 'He's still half cut, and he's got a game leg and a probable heart condition. And he's old.'

'I said there's nothing to it. Easy as falling off a log.'

They had swung round now and were heading back inland. The parachute still soared. Aubergine Bristol was still safely attached to it. By a series of manoeuvres Bognor was unable to understand, parachute and pilot moved away from the water until they were hovering over the sandy beach. José cut the engine, and the boat slowed to a placid amble and finally nothing. Behind them the parachute floated gently down until coming to rest a few hundred yards away on the beach where the minions immediately surrounded Aubergine, dusted her down, and sent her back to the boat.

'*Fan*tastic,' she shouted as she strode out to them. 'That *has* to be *the* most amazing experience. I mean the *most* amazing.'

'What's it like?' asked Bognor.

'It's a bit like hash, only healthier.' She laughed. 'Fanbloodytastic. You feel as if you're floating on air.'

'That's what you *were* doing,' said Bognor sourly. He turned to Aubrey. 'You're not going to make the Colonel do it are you? I'm really not sure you should.'

'Oh, don't be so priggish.' Aubrey had already swung himself over the stern of the boat and was standing up to his thighs in the ocean holding his arms out for Blight-Purley. 'You want to try it, don't you?' he was asking him. 'I don't suppose you've parachuted since the war. I don't imagine this is quite the Balkans or occupied France.'

'I should say not,' said Blight-Purley. 'Naturally I want to try it. Try anything once.'

He started to clamber out of the boat, slipped slightly as he straddled the side, but was held firmly by Pring and ended the right way up in the water.

'Come on. I'll help you get strapped in.' Aubrey helped the old boy through the sea to the beach. Bognor watched apprehensively as they waded through the breakers, which were less aggressive than they had been the day before, and reached the apparatus.

'Is easy,' said José, catching his worried state. 'Is so easy a *niño* may do it. Little boy only five year old, he can do it.'

'Colonel Blight-Purley isn't a *niño*. He's probably seventy.'

'Honestly, Simon, don't fuss. It's potty,' said Aubergine.

'I'm not fussing,' said Bognor, heatedly. 'He's rather pissed, and he's rather old and rather infirm, and I don't think he should, that's all.'

'He's a grown man. He can make up his own mind, surely?'

'I wouldn't bank on it.'

It didn't take long for the Colonel to be locked into position. From the shore Aubrey Pring shouted through cupped hands: 'I'll stay here and see the old boy off. Ready when you are!' There was another exchange of thumbs up, the engines roared, the boat surged forward, and the Colonel was borne aloft under his sail of silk.

'There you are!' shouted Aubergine, above the din of the diesels. 'Nothing to it.'

'He's got to get down, too,' said Bognor only half appeased. They craned their necks as the parachute climbed higher and higher until, like Aubergine, he became only a dull black speck.

'Is very high,' shouted José, grinning broadly and turning the wheel so that the boat executed a careening semi-circle. Bognor hung on tightly and watched the wash spread out behind them.

Suddenly there was a shriek from the girl. 'Oh God, no!' she screamed, covering her face with her hands. For a moment Bognor imagined she had hurt herself but then, realizing that she was physically unharmed, he quickly looked back up to the parachute. 'Oh, God,' he said too, only softly. The parachute still floated prettily in the sky but the spiky human form beneath was no longer attached to it.

Blight-Purley was falling with a rapidity which Bognor fatuously realized was 32 feet per second per second. The three of them watched mesmerized as the body plummeted seawards, gathering speed as it did until it hit the waves. The impact made a light smack of sound, like a stone which has been dropped into a well. There was a small explosion of white spray. Then nothing. For a second the three of them stayed watching agog, waiting absurdly for some sign of life, some movement to suggest survival.

'For Christ's sake man, hurry. Get over there now. Before it's too late.' Bognor's voice was raucous, nearly hysterical. It was already too late. He knew that, but there was a need for action, if only as therapy. Aubergine Bristol was very pale under her tan, her face drained of expression. José pointed the bows in the direction of the splash and the vessel leapt across the bay bumping ferociously. As they neared the point where the body (which was what Bognor was already mentally describing it as) had fallen, he slowed and leant over searching the clear turquoise waters for some sign. The boat rocked rhythmically from side to side, and Bognor and Aubergine Bristol also stared hopelessly into the water. From the shore there came the buzz of another engine as Aubrey and some of the Mexicans powered out to assist.

'It's no good,' said Bognor, still staring forlornly. 'No one would survive a drop like that.'

'No,' agreed Aubergine. She sank back into her seat and put her hand to her forehead. 'It's a long way up. You can hardly make people out when you're up there. They're like . . . '

'Ants,' said Bognor without thinking.

The other speedboat arrived. Pring was standing in the bows wearing an expression of tight-lipped, efficient concern.

'What in heaven's name happened?' he called across.

'Your guess is as good as ours,' Bognor hailed back. 'Probably better,' he added under his breath. A nasty suspicion was beginning to form in his mind.

'You go clockwise, we go anti-' Pring shouted. The two boats began a circular trawl of the area, with everyone leaning out, eyes straining.

When they had completed one circle they made another smaller one, then another until they had covered the whole area surrounding the point of entry. 'I wonder how deep it is here?' Bognor asked out loud but of no one in particular.

'Very deep,' said José mournfully, 'very, very deep.'

'And I suppose there are currents?'

'Very bad currents. Very, very dangerous to swim here.'

Pring's boat came alongside. 'I'm terribly sorry, but I don't think that there's any point in going on,' he called. 'Manuel says it's very deep here and there are quite fierce currents.'

'But we can't just leave him.' Aubergine had begun to cry silently, the tears smudging her green mascara and trickling down the laugh lines. 'We should never have let him go. Simon was right.' There was an awkward silence.

'Okay,' agreed Bognor at last. 'Let's go home.'

The parachute had come down now, as well, and they hauled it aboard, a mess of soggy silk, tangled wires and cords.

'Don't fiddle with it,' snapped Bognor as José began to disentangle it. 'The police will want to have a good look.'

'The police?' Aubergine seemed not to understand. 'You don't mean . . . '

'I don't mean anything except that if someone falls to his death from a parachute in Acapulco Bay people need to know why. In England the police would be called to look at the evidence. It doesn't mean that what happened wasn't an accident. There are different sorts of accidents though. There is such a thing as culpable negligence.'

On the beach Aubergine pressed her head against Aubrey's shoulder. Aubrey held her stiffly and caught Bognor's eye with an expression of compassionate contempt. Bognor wondered if there was self-satisfaction there as well.

'Who's going to report it?' he asked.

'I'll see to it,' said Pring, releasing his girlfriend. He walked over to the parachute where it had been flung down on the sand. 'Extraordinary,' he mouthed stroking at the material with the toe of his shoe. 'It was perfectly all right when you were up wasn't it?' he asked Aubergine. She nodded. 'Perfectly.'

'Did he have relations?' asked Bognor.

Pring shrugged. 'I'll have to find out,' he said officiously. 'Don't worry. Just leave it to me. I'll have a word with the Consul. He'll set the ball rolling.'

'I need a drink,' said Aubergine. 'Can we go back to the hotel or something? I don't want to stay here.' They went. As they climbed back into the candy-striped jeep Bognor glanced back to sea and the watery grave of Erskine Blight-Purley, a man of whom, he realized with a sudden pang of sadness, he had actually become rather fond.

'I just don't think it was an accident,' he said. It was an hour and a half later, and he was in his room, lying shattered and disconsolate on the bed. Amanda Bullingdon sat in a standard hotel issue wood and plastic chair and played with her glass. The news had travelled fast, and she had come at once. Not just because she was curious and involved but also because she had found out a little more from Gabrielle. First, however, she wanted to know about Blight-Purley.

'So Aubrey Pring helped strap him in,' she said, recapitulating, 'which means that if it wasn't an accident then Pring was the man who fixed it.'

'It could have been one of the Mexicans. I imagine there would have been some sort of connivance.'

'It's terribly like what happened to his Jaguar.' She inhaled a king-size duty free. 'Could Aubrey have done that too?'

'Anyone in the world almost *could* have done it. But why Aubrey? He can't be involved in espionage. He's hardly a blackmailer.'

'Why not?'

Bognor thought desperately. 'He was at Wadham,' he ventured finally.

'Well, there you are then.'

'Yes. I suppose so. But on the other hand, *why*?'

'Gabrielle is worried.'

'I'd forgotten Gabrielle.' He poured duty-free Hine into

his glass and diluted it with iced water from the thermos at the bedside. 'How is she?'

'Like I said, worried.'

'How was the dress rehearsal?'

She laughed. 'What you'd expect. They over-ran by hours. There were rows all over the place. We'll be lucky to finish by two in the morning the way things are going.'

'And the omelette?'

'The omelettes were smashing. The committee were delighted. The Norwegians were the worst. They're withdrawing their herrings, and the Israelis were jolly lucky to get away with their gefilte fish.'

'Gefilte fish? They're not putting in gefilte fish?'

'They are.'

Bognor's taste buds rebelled. 'Ugh,' he retched, momentarily forgetting death, espionage and the real reason for his presence in the Mexican holiday resort. When he had recovered he said: 'Gabrielle. You were saying.'

'Aubrey did threaten her, and he did threaten her with taking away the *Bitschwiller* rosette, and he made it quite clear that he could.'

Bognor narrowed his eyes and stared into the Hine and water. There was a small insect in it. He put in a finger and squashed it against the side of the glass before removing it. Brandy, he decided, should anaesthetize and destroy any malaria-inducing agent it was carrying. 'Which means only one thing,' he announced.

'That he's the anonymous British correspondent of the *Guide Bitschwiller*.'

'I've always thought some of their verdicts distinctly shaky,' he nodded.

'But you see what it means,' insisted Amanda, whose detective enthusiasm was beginning to get up Bognor's nose.

'Of course,' he responded in a manner calculated to crush.

'It means that Aubrey's been working for la Veuve Bitschwiller all the time.'

'And,' Bognor suddenly became excited himself, 'he

killed poor Erskine because the Bitschwiller bag told him to, after Erskine had gone on the rampage about Château Petheram and Oreille de Cochon.'

He hadn't told her about the Colonel's suspicions of wine substitution. 'God,' she exclaimed, when he had. 'It's all beginning to fit.'

'So Aubrey was threatening Gabrielle and trying to make her hand over the Scoff network to Bitschwillers.'

'She didn't say that.'

'What *did* she say?'

'The usual story. That Aubrey was trying to get her into bed.'

'And would take away the Dragoon's rosette if she didn't.'

'That's what she said.'

'And you think that's likely.'

'It's not impossible.'

'I suppose it happens.' He got up and went to the window where he stared hard at the waters of the bay, rather as if he expected them to part before his gaze and yield up their secret.

'It's still very complicated,' he sighed. 'If it was Pring all along then he would have to have fixed the pills for Scoff, and that could only be done by co-operating with Gabrielle; and if he killed Petrov, then he would have to have been in league with Massimo and the others at the Dour Dragoon. And possibly the Americans. But he obviously isn't any of those things. I think perhaps I'd better have a word with Ebertson.'

Amanda was looking as confused as he felt. He dialled the operator and asked for Ebertson's room. Presently the American's dapper New England voice responded.

'Simon. I just heard about Blight-Purley. You were there, what happened?'

'He fell,' said Bognor laconically, guiltily realizing that it sounded callous. 'Listen,' he went on, 'I need to talk. Can we meet?'

'Come on over. I have a bottle of bourbon.'

'Give me five minutes.'

Ebertson seemed subdued by the news of Blight-Purley's

death. 'He wasn't exactly discreet in what he said to Delphine,' he said when Bognor had given his account of the accident, 'from what I heard. And he had no proof. So he ended up sounding shrill. I just don't see that Delphine would have the old man eliminated because he had some cock and bull story about her doctoring Pendennis' wine with her uncle Yves' pig's ear. It's not enough.'

'But Blight-Purley might have been putting two and two together.'

'And making five. That's Blight-Purley's style all right. Or was.'

'In which case it might have seemed wise to have him . . . eliminated.'

'I don't altogether follow you.'

'He had always thought Delphine Bitschwiller was pure as the riven snow. Whiter than white. He would never have believed that she could be in any way corrupt, but like the rest of us he's aware that a lot of corruption has suddenly appeared in the world of eating and drinking. He's been looking for a villain. Maybe he suddenly decided that the villain or villainess was none other than Delphine. And maybe he was right. In which case the sooner Delphine had him out of the way the better.'

'You could be right,' said Ebertson. He frowned and seemed to be on the point of saying more, then appeared to think better of it.

'We're supposed to be buddies,' said Bognor, rattily. 'If this is your idea of Anglo-American co-operation it's not mine.'

'I said. You could be right.'

'How much do you know?'

'I don't *know* all that much,' he said. 'But if Pring is the anonymous *Guide Bitschwiller* man in the UK then that could explain a thing or two.'

'Such as?'

'The French have been behaving truculently – as usual. Aubrey Pring's been hanging about Gabrielle. There have been one or two ham-fisted attempts at putting the finger on some of our people. They've come from the other side of the channel, but they seem to have originated in the UK. It could all quite easily point back to Pring.'

'That sounds tentative.'

'It *is* tentative, Simon.'

'Do you have anything on Delphine Bitschwiller?'

'I'll be absolutely honest with you, Simon.' He paused and felt in his jacket pockets and produced a meerschaum pipe, which he stuffed full of Sobranie tobacco from a leather gold-initialled pouch. Then he said, 'Nothing. Absolutely nothing. As far as we're concerned Delphine Bitschwiller is a pillar of the French establishment. We have no reason to think that she is anything other than what she seems.'

'I see.' Bognor swigged bourbon and rose to go. 'Thank you,' he said, ironically. 'Most helpful.'

'Don't be like that, Simon,' said Ebertson, puffing. 'Between you and me, and I'm talking in complete confidence now, I'd say you were on to a winner here. I've never cared for Delphine Bitschwiller. She's too good to be true. My guess, and it's only a guess, is that she could quite easily have been supplying information to French Intelligence – and maybe others – and that she's been using the *Guide Bitschwiller* organization to find it. That's only speculation, mind, and it's confidential. But for what it's worth, there it is.'

'Yes.' Bognor shrugged and drained his bourbon. 'I'm going to have a sleep,' he said, 'before this bloody dinner. I might try and have a word with Gabrielle afterwards.'

'Right,' said Ebertson, 'and if there's anything I can do, feel free. . . .'

'Thanks,' said Bognor sarcastically, 'I certainly will.'

He had hoped to escort Amanda Bullingdon to the dinner, but now that she was embroiled in the manufacture of the chocolate omelettes, he was without a partner. There wasn't even the sardonic old man's wit of Blight-Purley. He was off Ebertson. He was right off Pring. He had never been particularly 'on' Pendennis. Aubergine was silly and, anyway, bespoke. As he adjusted his black tie and dabbed Old Spice on his jowls, he felt distinctly sour. He wished Monica and

Parkinson, those two jealous souls who preyed on his con-
science, could see him now.

Not that the dinner wasn't elaborate and lavish. It was
held near the summit of Las Brisas. It was a warm clear night,
and the sky was bright with stars. Down below, the town
was bright with electric light bulbs. The effect was similar:
both sorts of light and an orange moon were reflected by the
Pacific ocean. By the pool a Mexican band with maraccas
and guitars played popular Mexican music. Girls in Mexican
national dress handed round tacos. Guests wore tuxedos
if they were American males and black dinner jackets if they
were European (all except for the odd Italian in tobacco
brown 'smoking'). The women wore evening gowns which
covered most of their lower halves and not much of their
tops. Like the town and the sky and Acapulco Bay, they too
twinkled with bright lights – mostly diamonds. Everyone, in
deference to the host country, drank Margaritas, though
there was Mexican champagne on offer. Everyone knew too
much about Central American wine production to take that
particular risk.

The same toastmaster that had performed at the Château
Petheram affair ushered them in to dinner, where Bognor
found that national boundaries had been crossed and that
he was sitting between a florid Finnish lady and the wife of
the Peruvian vice-consul in Monte Carlo. Neither knew
English. Opposite him was an intense Slovak from the
Czech Embassy in Mexico City. It was clearly going to be a
silent or, at the most, monosyllabic meal. The menu gave
some ideas of its abundance, though when it appeared the
reality proved even more dyspepsia-inducing than the
promise. The Indians alone had come up with Pacha kabab
yakhni, Mattan sukha, Khumbi (also Sukha), Phul gobi,
Turcam molee badam and Navrattan sabzi dum and, as their
contribution to dessert, a cheese fudge, called Sandesh. He
felt more familiar with the French Bouillabaisse and
Quenelles and Coq au Chambertin, though not with the
Burgundian lampreys. The Chinese offered Quick-braised
oyster on toasted bean curd, Prawns on the snow mountain,
Stuffed eight treasure tomatoes, Casserole of lion's head,

Hot-fried shredded carp with celery, and Silver tree-fungi in crystal syrup. All these, of course, were described in their native language but Bognor had no more Mandarin than his neighbours English so he relied on the translations. Those countries less well endowed gastronomically were, naturally, less well represented. The Malays boasted only Satay. The New Zealanders, suspiciously, Hot-pot of South Island lamb.

If the food was frankly an embarrassment of excess, the drink was much the same. Not just claret from Château Lafite and burgundy from Chambertin, but fomented coconut juice from the mountainous interior of Sarawak, juniper-flavoured Kvass from Georgia, a twenty-year-old single malt whisky from the Hebridean island of Eigg, Acapulco Aficionado – a cocktail invented for the occasion by the doyen of the resort's barmen consisting principally of tequila, lime juice and egg whites – Marsala and Muscadet, Tigermilk (or Ranina Radgona Spatlese), and Tokay; even Zoopiyi.

Bognor did not have the stomach for it. Despite such culinary or bibulous punctuation marks as the occasional Trou normand or sorbet, he was soon doing no more than pick at the various dishes set before him. A truffle here, a prawn there, a sip of mineral water even. Others were less inhibited, though before the first hour was out one or two had had to leave the room looking green, and one man, a rubicund white-haired Arab with a mayoral chain of office around his neck, suddenly keeled over into his Langoustine mousse and was carried out by a squad of waiters, pieces of cream and shell fish still adhering to his face.

From time to time Bognor attempted conversation. So did the Czech diplomat and the ladies on either side of him. Such attempts ceased after the fifth course and, indeed, it was noticeable that the general level of conversation slipped as the meal progressed. The chocolate omelettes were served at one-thirty. They were by any standards – even those of their late, lamented inventor – delicious. Bognor dutifully managed a spoonful but noticed, sadly, that most of his fellow guests were beyond even that. He could hardly blame them.

Shortly after two the meal came to a mercifully speechless conclusion as a band began to play what Bognor, who was tempo deaf (rather than tone deaf), took to be a waltz. He waited long enough to see what other replete couples were dancing and then asked the Finn to join him on a circuit. They managed this in shuffling silence. A few minutes later he asked the wife of the Peruvian vice-consul, and they too walked round the floor more or less in time to the music, not bumping into anyone else and holding on to each other in a manner which succeeded in being polite without hinting at any form of intimacy – or even communication. Afterwards, satisfied that his duty was done, he made excuses to his neighbours and went off in search of the kitchens. These, a few yards from the banqueting hall, presented a scene of unspeakable chaos. It suggested to Bognor's food-and drink-sated – and therefore impressionable – mind one of those immense oil paintings to be found in a French museum of a certain sort and entitled *After Borodino*. The atmosphere was heavy with steam and cigarette smoke. There was débris everywhere: bones and raw flesh and egg and oyster shells; blood and chocolate; cabbage leaves and broken brandy bottles. Among this men and women, many in tight check trousers, white jackets or aprons, sometimes a tall chef's hat, wandered about dazed, as if shell-shocked. Others sat on stools or chairs, or slumped over stoves and sinks. Some were asleep, some drinking, some smoking; in one corner a Franco-Japanese group had begun a poker school.

He stood for a moment, shading his eyes with his hands and peering for Gabrielle and Amanda. He found them by a sink where they were lethargically, but conscientiously washing up.

'Delicious omelettes,' he said.

The two women pulled faces. 'Had to cheat,' said Amanda. 'They aren't designed for mass catering.'

'Well, it didn't show. Can I help? Surely there should be someone to do this for you?'

'You must be joking.' Gabrielle's colour tended to conceal ill health or unhappiness until either had got really bad. Tonight she looked haggard and depressed. 'It's a shambles.'

173

'You're surely not washing up everything?'

'No, just the things we brought from London.'

'Gabrielle won't go anywhere without her favourite omelette pan,' laughed Amanda. Bognor lit a cheroot.

'Gabrielle,' he said, 'I hear Aubrey Pring's been pestering you.'

She went on scrubbing at an elderly copper saucepan, but he thought he detected a sudden tension in her, as if his question had put her on her guard. 'Yes,' she admitted.

'Do you want to talk about it?'

'No.'

'I'm not just being prurient or nosy. I have good reasons for asking. I even think it may be dangerous if you don't help me.'

She turned and glared at him, still scrubbing the saucepan fiercely.

'You are a nuisance. You interfere. You stick your nose where it is not wanted. Because of you, people get hurt.'

He winced, not least because there was something in what she said.

'You heard about Colonel Blight-Purley?'

'Amanda told me.'

'Did she tell you that Aubrey was responsible for strapping him into the harness – that he was the last person to talk to him before he went up?'

'No.' She was busying herself neurotically, fiddling with plates and pots in an effort to seem preoccupied. 'In any case I don't see what that has to do with anything.'

'One way or another,' he sucked on the cigar, 'it might have quite a lot. You see, I believe that if you don't agree to go in with Pring and the Bitschwiller organization you could lose more than your rosette.'

She put down a plate and started to dry her hands on a tea towel, staring at him sullenly while she did so. Finally she said, 'You think Aubrey Pring had something to do with Erskine's death?'

'It seems likely.'

'And that if I don't agree to do what he asks, then . . .'

'If you don't sell out Scoff's empire to Pring then . . .

Exactly,' he said. He was, he knew, being uncharacteristically incautious. Nothing he had said was capable of proof – at least not at the moment, and not by him – even allowing for the generally unsatisfactory nature of what passed for proof. Yet to judge by Gabrielle's resigned expression his mixture of knowledge and conjecture was not far off the mark. He decided to say no more than necessary about the cause of the death of Escoffier Smith.

'Okay,' said Gabrielle, undoing her apron and then taking a Gitane from a packet on the draining board. 'Let's talk.'

'Where?'

'Outside. By the pool. And I'd like Amanda to hear everything too.'

Outside, the moon had risen higher and some of the lights in the town had gone out. Cicadas competed with the orchestra, and it was warm. To Bognor it felt as if they were in a low to moderate oven, sitting on a rising loaf.

'Well?' he asked, when they had found a corner hidden from crowds by a mess of bougainvillea.

'How much do you know?'

'Knowing might be putting it a little too strongly,' he said. 'But I believe that Pring is threatening you because the little part-time espionage ring or blackmail ring, or whatever you choose to call it, won't go in with him.'

'I . . . ' she began to protest, but Bognor cut her off. 'At the moment I'm not concerned with what you may or may not have done,' he said. 'I happen to think that you slipped Scoff contraceptive pills, hoping that you would depress him so much that he'd eventually commit suicide, leaving the whole shooting match to you.'

'I didn't think he'd commit suicide. That's not what they said. . . .' She stopped and took another Gitane from her shoulder bag. 'It wasn't meant to turn out like that. Not at all.'

'Just now I'm not concerned with the past. I'm more concerned with what is likely to happen in the immediate future. I don't care who you may have killed or caused to be killed. Not for the moment. I'm much more worried about whether Pring killed Blight-Purley, whether he did so because Delphine Bitschwiller wanted him to, whether he is bullying you. And whether he is bullying you on Bitschwillers behalf. So I only need you to tell me one thing: Does Aubrey Pring want you to enter an exclusive arrangement with Bitschwiller?'

She didn't say anything. The end of the cigarette glowed bright as she inhaled, then he smelt the unmistakable French tobacco smoke as she breathed out and simultaneously nodded her head.

'Providing the same sort of, ah, service that one of your colleagues did when he spied on me at the Orange Lily.'

'You were indiscreet,' she said. 'But that was nothing to do with me. Not my idea at all.'

'You didn't know about it?'

'Not until later.'

'And Petrov, what about him?'

'I thought you were not interested in the past.'

Bognor sighed. 'All right. The past will have to come later. Has Pring given you an ultimatum?'

'Yes.'

'When?'

'I have promised a final decision before we touch down at Roissy on the way home.'

'We don't have much time,' said Bognor. 'What is your answer going to be?'

'I must consult with my . . . colleagues,' she answered, 'but if what you suspect about Colonel Blight-Purley is correct, then I do not believe I have an alternative. It is possible, you know, for someone like Aubrey to destroy me professionally. He would not have to kill me to do that.'

'Especially if he really is the *Guide Bitschwiller* man.'

On the far side of the pool someone stood faintly lit by a mauve spotlight, then dived in and began to crawl gently in their direction.

'But you want to keep your little network to yourself, Gabrielle, is that right?'

'That's right.'

'You're not the only one.'

'You mean Ebertson.' She said the name disparagingly.

Bognor sucked his teeth. 'So he's been involving himself a little more than he cares to admit,' he ventured.

Gabrielle remained silent.

'Which,' continued the Board of Trade's Special Investigator, 'means simply that we have to find some way of sorting out Aubrey Pring.'

'Er, hmmm.' Amanda Bullingdon, who had said nothing throughout this revelatory interlude, cleared her throat ostentatiously and mouthed, 'Cave.' The swimmer was approaching their corner of the pool and was even now clambering up the ladder on to the marble pavement.

He stood there for a minute or two, then wandered, apparently purposelessly in their direction. A few feet away he became recognizable to them, and they, evidently, to him. 'Hello, you lot,' said Aubrey. 'Congratulations on the omelettes, you girls, I can't think how you do it.' He paused and burped noisily. 'Sorry,' he said, as the sound died away, and then turned to go. Just as he was walking away he seemed to think of something and stopped. 'Oh, Simon,' he said, 'you haven't heard from your friend Monica, have you?'

Bognor swore inwardly but answered as evenly as he was able. 'No. Why?'

'Oh, nothing,' said Pring. The damp flop of his footsteps faded away into the Mexican night until they were drowned by the band which had just embarked on a discordant rendering of 'La Bamba'. This time Bognor swore out loud.

Chapter Eight

The return flight to England was grim in almost every conceivable respect. It was delayed; there was what airline officials referred to as 'turbulence' which made Bognor feel even iller than previously; the party was over; the party was hung over; Bognor himself was *very* hung over. He was also more depressed than he could remember. Somewhere in the bowels of the Boeing lay the mortal remains of the late Colonel Erskine Blight-Purley. The Colonel had been fished from the water some twenty-four hours after entering it. Literally. A Mexican fishing smack had netted him not far from the spot where he had dropped in. Subsequent events proved confused and confusing. The authorities had wanted some form of inquest. The captain of the boat had asked for compensation due to the damage inflicted on the netting. The undertaker had been unable to provide oak. There was trouble over identification. The sorting out had fallen to Aubrey Pring and had involved, on Pring's own admission, the greasing of a great many already well-oiled Mexican palms with a ludicrous quantity of vividly coloured Mexican bank notes.

'Only language these chappies understand,' he had said to Bognor as, from force of newly acquired habit, he had pressed pesetas into the hand of the startled emigration official. (PESETAS ARE IN SPAIN.)

'It's the same the whole world over,' Bognor replied, lugubriously. He had bought Monica a large over-priced bottle of scent in the Acapulco duty-free shop. Now, sitting in the jumping jet as it flung them around on the edge of some tropical storm, he wondered again if it would do anything to placate her. He was in no doubt that someone would have fulfilled their part of the blackmailer's bargain and told her of his night at the Orange Lily. It seemed supremely unimportant. Indeed looking across at Amanda Bullingdon dozing in the seat beside him, it seemed inconceivable that they had ever shared anything quite so intimate as bed.

He fiddled with his headphones, trying to find the Mozart. Certainly things had happened in Acapulco. Enough for Parkinson not to dock his leave by double? He doubted it. He had, if he was absolutely honest with himself, no firm solutions to offer, only new crimes to solve. He nodded his head in time to 'Il mio tesoro' and peered out of the window at a cloud. Could it be cumulus? Was Aubrey Pring at the bottom of it all? He wished he knew. Was there such a thing in the world as certainty – or proof? Wasn't there an area of detection in which people dealt with fingerprints and alibis and Bradshaw's train timetables and solid incontrovertible things called facts? 'In this life, we want nothing, but Facts, sir; nothing but Facts!' he recited to himself.

Something else that had happened in Acapulco was that he had contracted a touch of that embarrassing affliction known as Montezuma's Revenge. He unfastened his seat belt, unhooked his headphones, brushed past Amanda and headed down the aisle in the direction of the lavatories. A stewardess blocked his way. She was holding an envelope.

'Monsieur Bognor?'

'Yes.'

'This is for you.'

She handed him the letter and smiled the regulation inhuman smile of airline stewardesses the world over.

'Thank you.' He stuffed it in his pocket and did not take it out until several minutes later when he had returned to his seat. Before opening it he gazed at it. There was no stamp. He had no idea where it came from. He was not expecting any post. Indeed its arrival seemed a violation of air space. Here, thirty thousand feet up, one was surely entitled to some peace. Turning it over he saw that on the flap there was a ritzy 'B', carefully surrounded with what looked like wrought-iron vine leaves. He knew what that meant. The note, in impeccable calligraphy, read:

Dear Mr Bognor,

I am sorry that we had so little chance to talk in Acapulco. I wonder if you would care to stay with us this weekend on your way home. It will be very quiet but there should be an opportunity for you to see how we work. If you are agreeable, you could join us on the journey from Charles de Gaulle and I can arrange for a car to return you to the airport so that you will be in England in time for the office on Monday! Perhaps you would be kind enough to give your reply to one of the cabin staff.

Yours sincerely, Delphine Bitschwiller.

'Ho, hum,' he said, loudly. He had, inevitably, one of those feelings. Pring suspected that he suspected. After observing them at the swimming pool he probably *knew* that Bognor suspected. The remark about Monica had been more than a casual cattiness. He had reported the matter to Delphine. Hence the invitation. But what was Delphine going to do? There were only two possibilities. Either she was going to try to buy him off, or knock him off, just as Blight-Purley and the others had been knocked off. Or conceivably she might try to allay his suspicions. That was the least likely of all. His suspicions were now well past allaying. He took a postcard from the pocket on the seat in front, rummaging awkwardly among the reinforced brown paper vomit bag and the multitudinous maps, then wrote:

That would be very nice indeed. Accept with much pleasure, Simon Bognor.

The same stewardess was walking down the aisle looking officious. Bognor smiled at her. 'I wonder if you'd mind giving this to Madame Bitschwiller?' he asked. She smiled back the same meaningless smile and took the card.

'Plastic bag,' he thought to himself unreasonably. Beside him Amanda stirred. 'What's the time?'

'Mexico time or London time?'

'Oh,' She stretched and smiled a sleepy smile. 'I forgot we were up here.'

'Where did you think we were?'

'Bed,' she said mischievously.

'I'm spending the weekend chez Bitschwiller.'

'God! Why?'

'She asked.'

'But mightn't that be frightfully dangerous?'

He mimicked her. 'Frightfully dangerous. Frightfully *frightfully* dangerous.'

'Many a true word. . . .'

'I'm not jesting. Have you spoken to Gabrielle?'

Since the sudden burst of revelation Gabrielle had avoided Bognor, hardly acknowledging him. She was apprehensive and had admitted to Amanda that she had said too much. Now, apparently, she was saying nothing more, not even to Amanda, with whom she had begun to develop this unlikely understanding.

'No. Well, not seriously.'

'So you've no idea what answer she's going to give Pring?'

'No.'

'You're a lot of help.'

'Sorry.'

Bognor settled glumly back into his seat and tuned back to the Mozart. They were now on to horn concertos. Perhaps it didn't matter whether Gabrielle succumbed to Pring's threats, he thought. Such a capitulation was surely reversible. Besides, it would buy time: time for him to prove Aubrey Pring a murderer. He grimaced. He was becoming increasingly certain that Pring had tampered with the mechanism of the parachute, but there was no way whatever of proving that in a British court of law, much less a Mexican one. 'Oh God!' he said loudly.

Amanda patted his knee. 'Don't worry,' she said, appearing to read his thoughts, 'people who don't know you as well as I do are sometimes quite impressed with your knowledge and perception.'

He removed the headphones. 'Don't be ridiculous,' he said angrily. 'You don't know me *that* well. Besides, who?'

'Gabrielle, for instance.'

'She's not the least impressed.'

'She is, quite. And ffrench-Thomas.'

'He's just a heavy.'

'You underestimate yourself. After all, you represent the Board of Trade. That is part of the government. People are afraid of the British Government, so up to a point, at least, they're afraid of you.'

'Oh, balls,' he said.

VIP treatment was not something to which Bognor was used, and yet at Charles de Gaulle airport this time, VIP treatment was what Bognor got. He seemed scarcely to have time to say good-bye to his friends and colleagues before he was sitting in the back of a well sprung black Citroën. Next to him, a tartan travelling rug over her knees, was la Veuve. In front next to the grey-capped chauffeur was Aubrey Pring.

'I gather you've tumbled our little secret,' he said, half turning to the rear seat, as the limousine creamed away towards the N3 and Château-Thierry.

'I'm sorry,' said Bognor.

Pring smiled with an expression of both duplicity and complicity.

'*La Guide*. That I'm the *Guide* inspector for the UK.'

'Oh, *that*.' Bognor was relieved. For a hideous moment he was afraid there was going to be some confrontation right there in the cruising Citroën. A quick shot, a brief opening of the door, a bloodstained corpse by the roadside. But no. Nothing so obvious. 'Yes,' he confirmed, 'I had rather gathered that was so.'

'It's one of those half open secrets, I suppose,' said Pring, 'but not that many people know. I'd rather you kept it under your *chapeau*. Eh?'

'Of course,' said Bognor, 'I wouldn't dream of embarrassing you.'

'Naturally not.'

'Have you been to Champagne before Mr Bognor?' asked Delphine.

'No, I'm afraid not.'

'Ah. I hope you will find it interesting.'

'I'm sure I shall.' He hoped his constitution was going to stand up to the car ride.

'We should be there in time for lunch,' said Pring.

'Lunch?' Bognor sounded incredulous. Whatever Pring and French time might say, his body told him very definitely that lunch was a long way off.

'Just something light,' said Delphine, 'then we can show you around. But don't worry, we will allow you a little rest after lunch. A nap. Forty winks.' Like a lot of foreigners with excellent English she took an obvious delight in archaic colloquialism.

They lapsed into silence. Bognor dozed. So did the others. The countryside, on those few occasions when he opened an eye and was able to take it in, seemed flatly drab. It was a grey day and drizzle fell in a fog. After about two hours Pring said, 'Vines.' Bognor shaded his eyes and saw a gentle hillside with stunted green shrubs staked out on it. 'The Marne,' added Pring pointing to the river on their left, grey as the day. 'The English dead,' he began and stopped.

The vines continued broken only by villages less glamorous than their name suggested: Try Vassieux, Trossy, Mareuil le Port, Port-à-Binson, Oeuilly, Montvoisin Villesaint. On the outskirts of Epernay the Citroën swung left through Dizy Magenta and Hautvillers and then right on a lane which was scarcely more than a track. 'We are rather out on our own,' said Delphine. 'Many of our competitors are what you would call a little hugger-mugger, all higgledy-piggledy next door to each other in the towns. The Bitschwillers have always been aloof. Proud.' They continued for another winding mile and then Delphine said, 'You will see the house around the next corner.' She was correct. As they turned the corner, Bognor saw through the misty rain a square, stone house with a high pointed green roof and dormer windows. It was surrounded by outbuildings which looked like stables but were presumably dedicated to viticulture in some form. Immediately before the château was a gravelled courtyard. Steps led from this to a raised portico which Bognor adjudged to be something added to the original house within the last two hundred years. 'Most of it is what you would call Georgian,' said Delphine, following his inquisitive look, 'though there have been additions.' A uniformed footman scrunched over the gravel and opened the back door for la Veuve. The chauffeur got out and opened the other door for Bognor. At the top of the steps more servants appeared: maids in white pinafores and starched caps, men in aprons, a butler. 'Mr Bognor, I expect you would like to see your room and wash, before lunch. I suggest we assemble in the drawing room in – shall we say twenty minutes?'

'Fine.' One of the aproned men took his case and led him up the staircase with its twirling balustrade. Bognor noticed the portraits of generations of Bitschwillers: haughty-visaged autocrats with mean eyes. His room was at the end of a long corridor and overlooked first farm buildings and then vineyard, though it was not possible to see further than a few hundred yards on account of the weather. It was a plain room with a couple of nineteenth-century prints on the walls and a four-poster bed with fading hangings in the centre. In one corner was a wash basin with a china pitcher to one side and, greatest luxury of all, a grate with a handful of small logs burning smokily. The servant put down Bognor's cases and departed, mumbling Gallic obsequities.

Bognor rinsed his face and sat down heavily on the counter-pane. Almost unconsciously he reviewed the events of the last few weeks, allowing his mind to race unfettered over the deaths and the deceptions, the threats and the treacheries. It was an inconclusive piece of day-dreaming, except that it ended in the acknowledgement that the ball was firmly in the enemy court. The invitation was clearly the prelude to something, and Bognor was perfectly willing to allow la Veuve and Aubrey Pring to retain their initiative. He had no particular cards to play and he was certain that they for their part were about to reveal their hand.

The drawing room was oddly bare, almost unfurnished, like the bedroom. There was some good, though teutonic furniture; bookshelves which contained, French classics apart, the complete works of Sir Walter Scott in English and, still more remarkably, those of Percy F. Westerman.

'We have always suffered from an *embarras* of Anglophilia,' said his hostess. 'I had an English nanny. Norland. From Eastbourne, I believe.'

'Really.' Bognor accepted the glass of Bitschwiller offered by the minion. It was '69, he noticed. The carpets were sparse and very old. The pictures were few: a couple of family portraits, a water-colour of Champagne countryside. The only other decoration was a large boar's head above the door.

'I thought I'd show you the cellars after lunch,' said Pring. 'Delphine has some business to catch up on, and she also has some organizing for our good selves. She had a plot to invite ourselves over to see the Clicquot people I believe. Isn't that right, Delphine?' Pring was markedly less deferential to his employer than he had seemed before.

Delphine nodded agreement. Bognor did the same. 'Sounds fine,' he said. They had only the one drink before moving into the dining room. The meal was simple but perfect: Oeufs mayonnaise; a lightly grilled entrecôte with frites and haricots verts. The Brie afterwards was a little chalky for his taste, but the Millefeuille made up for it. The main bore as far as he was concerned was that they drank Bitschwiller throughout. Conversation was spare and discreet. They were all tired. Of the three Pring flagged the least. Afterwards there was marc de champagne, good black coffee with the utterly inimitable French aroma and taste, and small Havana cigars brought to France through the good offices of a nephew in the *Corps Diplomatique*.

'And now,' said Delphine, rising to go, 'if you will excuse me, I must make arrangements. I will leave you two boys to take a promenade in the cellars.' She held out a hand for shaking. 'Have a pleasant afternoon,' she said, gazing intently into Bognor's eyes. 'It has been so nice to have met you.'

'I'll see you later,' he said, jovially.

She seemed oddly and momentarily disconcerted. Bognor felt a sudden emptiness in his stomach. Then with an obvious effort she smiled again. 'But of course.' She said. '*A bientôt*.'

'Remarkable person,' vouchsafed Pring, helping himself to another marc when she had left the room. 'They say she has only one lung. Something to do with the Germans, I believe.'

'Goodness,' said Bognor. 'How long have you known her?'

'Oh, quite a long time.' He savoured his cigar. 'How did you enjoy Acapulco?' he asked, conversationally.

'Not all that much,' confessed Bognor. 'I'm afraid the Blight-Purley business rather upset me.'

'Quite,' Pring sipped. 'The dinner was a bit of a farce, too. No style.'

'No, not much.'

'The French manage this sort of thing so much better when they're left to their own devices.'

Bognor considered. 'You've always been a bit of a Francophile.'

'You make it sound like an accusation,' said Pring mildly. Bognor wondered if the mildness was deceptive or real. It was difficult to think of him as being in any way dangerous.

'You have been hiding your light rather.'

'How do you mean?'

'Not letting on that you were the *Guide Bitschwiller* Inspector.'

'Well, it's not the sort of thing that should be broadcast. The Michelin people are anonymous. It's only the sort of egocentric amateurs who advertise themselves in the *Good Food Guide* who are anything else.'

'Did ffrench-Thomas know?'

Pring glanced at him in the old-fashioned way.

'No. Why do you ask?'

'Just curiosity. After all, he is the Bitschwiller rep.'

'That's rather different. He is exactly that. A rep. A lackey.' He took a gold hunter from his waistcoat pocket and clicked his tongue.

'Time for the cellars, I think.'

'Oh. Right.' Bognor looked around the room, feeling absurdly like a man going to execution, catching his last glimpse of the real world. Would he ever see daylight again?

'There's no one there on Saturday afternoons,' said Pring, 'so we'll need a key. Hang on a tick.'

He disappeared, returning shortly with an old-fashioned black key of the style and proportions Bognor associated with dungeon doors.

'Right. Shall I lead?'

186

'Lead on.'

They went out into a hallway, down a corridor and stopped at what could easily have passed muster as a dungeon door. 'Family entrance,' Pring explained, heaving it open. 'The main one's in the yard. Mind your step.' The stairway was steep and there was no rail. The light was provided by dim single bulbs.

'Very dank,' said Bognor shivering slightly.

'It's the chalk,' explained his guide. 'Constant temperature of between ten and eleven centigrade and humidity between seventy and ninety per cent all the year round.' They reached the floor, and Bognor saw that they were standing in a long vault much the same shape and size as the tunnel of a London underground station. Ranged along the walls were countless bottles top downwards in racks. 'Ready for the *remuage*,' said Pring. 'You understand the principle.'

'No.'

'Oh.' He grabbed hold of a couple of bottle bottoms and with quick flicks of the wrist shook and twisted them. 'They do it every day,' he said, 'gets the sediment down to the cork.' He began to lecture, steadily explaining the eccentric process of turning grapes into sparkling clear alcohol. He knew his stuff. Gradually as they paced the damp chill vaults Bognor became absorbed in what he was saying, scarcely noticing the distance they had covered. There were railway lines along some of the tunnels, just like those down coal mines. 'There are a hundred and twenty miles of cellar under Champagne,' intoned Pring, 'and most of it's been here since the Romans. Some of the galleries have never been properly explored. There are no maps.'

'Very easy to get lost,' said Bognor. He had wandered on ahead of Aubrey Pring and was examining racks of bottles dusty with age which extended above his head.

'Ready for drinking,' said the guide. 'This morning's bottles came from here. But that's enough education for now.' His tone had suddenly changed, taking on a new threatening dangerous inflection. 'Turn!' he ordered. 'Hands above head.'

Bognor did as he was told, Montezuma's Revenge mingling

with terror. He'd lost his concentration. 'Idiot,' he said to himself as he saw that in Pring's now extended right hand was a small shiny object. Bognor was no expert on firearms, but even he recognized a pistol.

'As you say, very easy to get lost. There are shafts in places. One quite near here. Several hundred feet deep, water at the bottom. Quite uncharted. Anyone who didn't know his way around could so easily have a nasty tumble, particularly with a little help from a friend. It's happened before.'

'You wouldn't,' protested Bognor, feebly.

'I most certainly would.' Pring grinned. 'I killed Blight-Purley after all, as I understand you suspect. Not Scoff. That was Petrov. I don't suppose Gabrielle told you about her little liaison with him. Gabrielle is less than honest. She will have to be taken in hand. Which, of course, has been the point of the exercise all along.'

'I'm not with you.'

'I wonder,' Pring's manner was conversational, almost amiable. 'The trouble with you,' he went on, 'is that one really can't be sure. My own feeling has been that you know very little, whatever you may suspect. Delphine, alas for you, thinks otherwise. She feels you were too close to the late and unlamented Colonel B.-P. for comfort. It was quite a feat for him to recall the origins of Oreille de Cochon. Extra-ordinary in its way.'

Bognor noticed that Pring was beginning to wave the gun about in a cavalierly casual manner.

'And you killed Petrov?'

'Amazing how things can pan out,' he grinned again. 'We'd wanted him out of the way for ages, and he was making a nuisance of himself bidding for the Scoff network. But those louts ffrench-Thomas and Dotto decided he'd be better off dead as well. It was a very ham-fisted effort, but there you are.'

Drink and jet-lag were beginning to tell. Pring now had one hand in his pocket. With his other, the gun hand, he scratched his ear. Bognor calculated the distance at about fifteen yards. The light was rotten. Behind him it was worse still, and there was a protruding piece of rock about five paces away. A sudden dive and he might just make it.

'What are you going to do with me?'

'Oh, down the shaft. You'll be dead first, so you won't drown. Not like the Colonel. One neat shot through the head and away you go. Nobody will ever be able to find you.'

'But they'll suspect.'

'They won't be able to prove anything. I'll say you wandered off. Next thing I knew there was a scream and a crash and . . . '

Bognor dived.

Behind him there was a shot, but it was very late and very badly aimed. Before Pring could have a second go he was behind the chalk buttress. Another gallery stretched away to his left. It was very dark indeed.

'Don't be silly,' called Pring. 'You haven't an earthly.'

Desperately, Bognor looked around for a weapon. There were only bottles. Bottles! He grabbed one, swung it behind him and chucked it out in Pring's direction. The only response was laughter and footsteps approaching. Bognor picked up another two bottles and made a run for it. Another shot blasted out behind him and caught the chalk above his left shoulder, then another which ripped into a rack of champagne causing another explosion, louder than the first. 'Damn!' shouted Pring, 'You're being ridiculous.'

The explosion had given Bognor an idea. Pring was silhouetted in the entrance to the gallery. Bognor was in relative darkness. Pring presented a target, if only he had a gun. Very quietly he undid the wire around the top of one champagne bottle. Then he gave it a couple of quick shakes, aimed it in the direction of his adversary and eased the cork with his thumb. There was a pop and a shrill exclamation, more of surprise than pain. 'You stupid sod!' Pring exclaimed, laughing slightly madly. Once more he started to advance. Once more Bognor shot a champagne cork. This time there was no response. The gallery was narrowing now. Bognor felt his way along the walls. It was very dark.

Suddenly he moved his foot out and felt it connect with

nothing. He moved it around. Still nothing. Then to back and to one side he felt terra firma. 'It must be the shaft,' he thought to himself. At last a thin, desperate beginning of hope began to permeate his brain. As quickly as possible he eased round the hole in the ground which he reckoned to be a circle of about six feet in diameter.

'There's no way out down there,' Pring's voice sounded sure of itself. 'It's a dead end. You might as well give up now.'

Bognor reckoned there were only a few steps between Pring and the hole. Somehow he must make him accelerate. 'Come and get me,' he injected a note of pleading into his voice. 'My shoulder's gone. That second shot . . . ' he simulated the sound of tears and choking. The acting was hammy but effective.

'Snivelling little creep,' said Pring, 'I should leave you there to die slowly but being, whatever my Francophile leanings, humane and British I shall allow you the luxury of a quick and . . . ' The sentence was lost in the scream which followed the missed footing. He *had* relaxed. He *had* fallen. Bognor, to his enormous discredit, let out a howl of triumph. It was a drawn out, lengthy howl, and it was over when, in the ensuing stillness, he heard from the depths a muffled splash. 'God,' he whispered out loud and, staggering back past the shaft's opening, was suddenly and violently sick.

It took him the best part of an hour to find his way upstairs, and when he did there were yet more surprises. In the hall were two men unmistakably French and, by the cut of their raincoats and the style of their shoes, policemen. They were arguing politely but firmly and volubly with la Veuve. As he emerged noisily and bedraggled into their presence the argument ceased. For a moment he saw a look of supreme irritation cross Delphine Bitschwiller's aristocratic mask of a face. Almost immediately it was replaced with one of worry and concern.

'Mr Bognor,' she cried, 'are you all right?'

'I'm OK,' Bognor gasped theatrically. 'It's your chap Pring. He's fallen down a hole.'

Epilogue

Monica took the credit. Shortly after her lover had left for Acapulco, she received a phone call from a stranger with a muffled voice who told her that Simon had spent a night with a woman called Amanda Bullingdon, at a pub called the Orange Lily.

'*Naturally*, I paid no attention,' she explained patiently when she rang Parkinson. 'You know him as well as I do. It's quite out of the question. But the mere fact that someone has suggested it means that something's up.'

Later, when he had not returned on the scheduled flight, she managed to contact Amanda.

'She denied it,' she told Parkinson, when she made her second call. 'In fact, she seemed rather insulted at the idea. Which is a little insulting for me, don't you think?' Amanda had told her of Bognor's weekend chez Bitschwiller. She had told Parkinson. Parkinson, now, finally alerted and only too well aware of his subordinate's capacity for dangerous muddle, had asked the French authorities to check. They had checked.

'Bloody silly,' they had both said to Bognor when he arrived home. 'A lot of dead people,' said Parkinson, 'but what do we have to show for it?'

'We have unlimited access to the former Scoff network,' riposted Bognor.

'Not interested,' said Parkinson, but he did not dock his leave.

Monica was marginally more charitable. 'Nice to have you back,' she said, 'but you're getting disgustingly fat.'